C000148085

~~MAIN~~STREAM

Praise for ~~MAINSTREAM~~

'In these locked down and unfocused times the short story is a
much needed respite from the current Covid-19 bleakness.
With Mainstream, Inkandescent has gathered together a wonderful
collection of fascinating and eclectic stories. Sad, funny, horrifying
and demystifying, the unique voices within take us on an open
minded journey around the world. Loved it.'
KATHY BURKE

'A riveting collection of stories, deftly articulated. Every voice
entirely captivating: page to page, tale to tale. These are stories told
with real heart from writers emerging from the margins in style.'
ASHLEY HICKSON-LOVENCE,
author of *The 392* and *Your Show*

'A triumphant celebration of exiled voices'
CASH CARRAWAY, author of *Skint Estate*

~~MAIN~~STREAM

AN ANTHOLOGY OF STORIES FROM THE EDGES

edited by Justin David and Nathan Evans

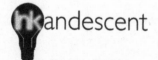

INKANDESCENT

Published by Inkandescent, 2021

Selection and Introduction © 2021 Justin David and Nathan Evans
Individual contributions © 2021 the contributors
Cover Design Copyright © 2021 Joe Mateo

Justin David and Nathan Evans have asserted their right under the Copyright, Designs and Patents Act 1988 to be identified as the editors of this work.

This book is in copyright. Subject to statutory exception and to provisions of relevant collective licensing agreements, no reproduction of any part may take place without written permission of Inkandescent.

A CIP catalogue record for this book
is available from the British Library

Printed in the UK by Clays Ltd, Elcograf S.p.A

This book is sold subject to the conditions that it shall not, by way of trade or otherwise, be lent, re-sold, hired out, or otherwise circulated without the publishers' prior consent in any form of binding or cover other than that win which it is printed and without a similar condition including this condition being imposed on the subsequent purchaser.

ISBN 978-1-912620-08-1 (paperback)
ISBN 978-1-912620-09-8 (ebook)

1 3 5 7 9 10 8 6 4 2
www.inkandescent.co.uk

*for everyone who's ever been kept out
because of who you are or where you are from,
come in ...*

Tell me your stories
Let them exist
Turn off the spotlight for a single minute
I'm angry and I am not sorry

Tell me your stories
Show me your worth
I am the antimatter strangled at birth
I'm angry and I am not sorry

Cos I'm in the dark for most of it
A highly elliptical orbit
I'm angry and I am not sorry

We don't need permission anymore
We don't need permission anymore
Stand back and watch us take the floor
Coming through the front door

Andy Pisanu, Memory Flowers
—PERMISSION 2020

MAINSTREAM

FOREWORD

I wrote my first short story when I was seven years old. It was a brief and tragic tale about a young boy called Tim who received a new bike for his birthday and died in a subsequent crash. Years later, I was struck by the name of my protagonist—Tim. I'd grown up in an Asian household, went to a mixed comprehensive school in Rayners Lane, and as a profoundly Deaf woman of Pakistani heritage, diversity was at the centre of my life. And yet, in the stories I read (and wrote), I had – albeit subconsciously—subscribed to the idea that protagonists should have 'proper' names and exist within a white-British vacuum.

It took years of education, active reading, and cultural analysis for me to unpack these notions and look beyond the white heteronormative blur that books sell to us. Working at Spread the Word, London's leading literary development agency, enabled me to learn about the importance of pushing for change within the publishing industry, and the value in creating more opportunities for writers from different backgrounds to expand our bookshelves. In the past four years, I have seen progress and change. However, as our recent report *Rethinking 'Diversity' in Publishing* shows, there is still a long way to go.

The report—conducted by Dr Anamik Saha and Dr Sandra van Lente, exposed how the book industry's tunnel vision has created a cultural production system that harms writers of colour. It highlighted the lazy tropes and misassumptions about what readers want; and how books are selected and marketed in line with this. Further, it demonstrated that writers of colour are often pressurised into unethical performance gymnastics, believing that they must modify their work to fit into a prepared packaged mould—simplifying, restricting and editing their imaginations.

The same summer that the report was published, Spread the Word formed a new connection with independent publishing press, Inkandescent, who approached us to request support with their call out for submissions for their new anthology: ~~Mainstream~~. They wanted to create an anthology unrestricted by theme and subject that celebrated talented writers and the stories they wanted to write. Just this: the stories that *they* wanted to write. Over time, I became increasingly engaged with this project; enamoured by the enthusiasm that Justin and Nathan brought to the book, and their focus on platforming talented writers from diverse backgrounds.

Emerging writers are published alongside more experienced writers in this collection, creating and fostering a new community. This is a unique feature that anthologies offer: a statement to writers that your stories are safe in this space and you are amongst those who appreciate your differences. Further, the gathering of multiple voices in a collection reinforces plurality and diversity. It tells us that in this big, wide world there are billions of individual protagonists, beyond the Tims, each of them—rightfully—occupying the central role in their own lives, and in their own narratives.

Aliya Gulamani
Spread the Word

INTRODUCTION

The idea for an anthology had been floating around since we set up Inkandescent in 2016. We started by publishing our own work and then the books of a few other underrepresented writers. By 2019 we felt more established and ready to up our game. We consulted 'The Oracle of Publishing' (aka Sam Missingham) about how Inkandescent might bring our books to a wider audience (and become a sustainable business). Sam suggested an anthology of short stories as a calling-card: it had worked for other independents, she said. So that clinched it.

We knew of other anthologies, which had begun a conversation about diversity in publishing: *Common People*—An Anthology of Working-Class Writers edited by Kit de Waal, *The Good Immigrant*—an anthology of BAME writers edited by Nikesh Shukla and *Speak My Language*—an anthology of LGBTQ+ writers edited by Torsten Højer. We wanted our anthology to stand in solidarity with those titles and to represent all those underrepresented groups, which as far as we were aware, had not been placed together in one book before.

Inkandescent was founded 'by outsiders for outsiders', to celebrate original and diverse talent and to publish voices and stories the mainstream neglects—specifically those of the working class and financially disadvantaged, ethnic minorities, the LGBTQ+ community and, crossing the Venn diagram, those with physical disabilities and mental health issues. Because often it's only the work of a small privileged group which gets seen and read. Those less privileged in the population-at-large aren't given the amplification they deserve. Our collection would 'pump up the volume'.

With the help of Daren Kay, our comrade-in-copywriting, we worked through a number of 'concepts', but it was our designer, Joe Mateo, who nailed it: he sent us a digital scrawl of one word—Mainstream—with a line through the 'Main'. A title was born.

We wanted *Mainstream* to feature an equal number of established and emerging writers. Our next step was to invite fifteen of our favourite authors aboard the magic carpet: we were delighted by the enthusiasm with which they accepted. Spread the Word also hopped on to help us find our fifteen surfacing storytellers.

The call out in May 2020 was heralded by the anthem, PERMISSION, written and recorded for us by our long-time musical collaborator, Andrew M Pisanu of Memory Flowers. We had over 150 entries, read diligently by our team: Aliya Gulamani, Alex Hopkins, Angelica Curzi, Keith McDonnell—thank you. From their feedback, we selected a longlist, then it was handbags at dawn between Justin and Nathan for the final selection. Only joking: our choices emerged naturally, amicably. Though there were certainly some brilliant stories to which we were sorry to say goodbye.

Mainstream is our most ambitious project to date and—because of the collective nature of the book—it felt right to crowdfund it. We teamed up with Unbound, reaching our minimum target in October 2020: this meant we could cover the print run, and pay our writers for their contribution. To all those who got behind the campaign, we cannot thank you enough for pledging.

Then the fun bit: editing, production! What a pleasure it's been working with this panoply of talent, and further thanks to Lisa Goodrum for her exacting proofreading.

So, here we are, two years on and our anthology is finally a thing. *Mainstream* really has been a labour of love: we hope you take it to your hearts as much as we have ours.

Justin David & Nathan Evans
Inkandescent

HOME TIME
Kathy Hoyle

When we walked through Gypsy Tony's fields this morning, the horses were swishing their manes in the wind. They always do that when it's cold. Dad says that north wind comes straight from Iceland. I wish I could have jumped onto Bert, or even Nippy and let one of them carry me home to a bowl of soup from Mam's big pot. I'm stuck here with our Kelly instead. The boring beck. There are no other kids here today; most of them stay in their back yards these days. There's all kinds of carry on in the village. Mam says we're not to talk to anyone. I don't really know what we're not supposed to talk about, just that I've to keep me gob shut.

It's Mam's fault I'm stuck here freezing to death. She shoved us into our coats first thing this morning, gave us a carrier bag of jam sandwiches and a bottle of orange juice and told us to bugger off till tea time.

It takes ages to get here. It's way past the park and the slag heaps, but Kelly says it's the best place to catch the taddies. There's no fish in the beck. Kelly says the shit-pipe from the mine runs into it, so no fish live. There's nowt except the tadpoles and loads of green moss. If we catch them and get them into the wooden crate, we can hide them in the coalhouse and then we'll have frogs. First, we've got to catch them.

We've been at it for flipping ages. The bottom of my jeans are soaked—fill the jar, pour the jar, fill again—like little kids in playschool. I've only found three tadpoles all day. I can't wait till I'm older. Then I'll get to say where we play, instead of Kelly. Sometimes she thinks she's me mam. She thinks she knows everything 'cos she's twelve now and I'm only eight.

'We've been out ages.'

I'm not supposed to whine 'cos Kelly will clip me, but I can't help it.

I dunno why we can't stay in on cold days. Me mam says kids should still play, even with what's going on with the bobbies and the pickets 'n' stuff. She says at least fresh air's free 'cos that's all we can afford nowadays. Me nanna says she's full of shite and that they're buckled now Dad's got a new job. Mam says I have to keep me gob shut about that. Everyone else goes to the welfare club for soup and sandwiches but we still go to Fine Fare for our shopping.

I wipe my nose with the sleeve of my anorak then stuff my hands into my pockets. I hop from welly to welly watching Kelly pulling green streaks of moss from the jam jar. She shakes the jar then tips it and smacks the bottom with her palm. A wriggling tadpole falls into the crate. She's caught loads. I pick up a stick from the bankside and crouch beside her, swirling the creatures and the moss around. I spell-cast. The potion should be drunk by my enemies, like that Robert Gooding from third year who spat on my back and called me scab bitch or Charlotte Dawson's mam, who never lets her come for tea at mine and looks at me like something the dog shit out.

Kelly digs me with her elbow. I drop the stick and stand up, brushing the hair out of my face.

'Mam said don't come home till tea time. Did you not hear?' Kelly checks the pink watch she got for her birthday, 'It's only half three.'

'Howay, Kelly,' I say, 'Mam always says tea time. I'm freezing. We can play Sindys. You can have the car this time.'

Kelly stands up and wipes her hands down her jeans, leaving streaks of moss on her legs. Mam'll kill her. She only just got them jeans from the catalogue. She smiles. I hardly ever let Kelly play with my Sindy car.

'We'll put these back first,' she says, nodding towards the crate, 'they'll probablys need their mams, or they'll die.'

'Leave them. They'll be alright. If the mams are owt like ours, they'll be glad to get rid.'

Kelly tuts.

'Don't be daft. She only wants us out so she can get on. She's got to see to nanna and go down the welfare club to give the strikers their dinners.'

'She hasn't been down the club for ages.'

Kelly's cheeks go red.

'Shut up, she does her bit.'

'I'm only saying what Nanna said.'

Kelly picks up the crate and flings the whole lot into the beck. I thought she might bring a few back in the jar but she's gone in a right moody now.

'Howay,' Kelly says, yanking my hood, 'we'll walk slow. And don't blame me if she goes off it.'

We walk along the stone path at the side of Tony's field, stopping to pat the horses on the way. We feed Nippy crusts from the jam sandwiches in our carrier bag, even though we know he'll take a finger off given half the chance. Kelly gives him a cuff on the nose before walking off. My welly digs into the heel of my foot and I pull it off, taking me sock with it. Kelly stamps her feet against the wind while I prod at a blister on the back of my heel.

'Hurry up,' she shouts. My belly flips. I don't want her to go without me. I still don't know all the way home on my own.

I wince as I put my sock and welly on. I try to be dead quick and end up losing my balance, falling on my backside. I swear, under my breath. Last time I swore, Mam nearly took the side of my head off. I've trained myself to say the F words and the S words only on the inside of my mouth. Kelly huffs her way back to me. She pulls me up and yanks the sides of my coat together then zips me in. She takes a tissue from under the cuff of her coat.

'Wipe yer bloody snoz,' she says, curling her lip.

I hold my hand out for the tissue, but she wipes it instead and gives me a sharp punch on the top of my arm before we set off again.

Finally, we get to our back gate. My legs are aching and my blister is stinging like mad. I need the plasters from the biscuit tin in the top cupboard. I'll ask Kelly to get them. Last time, I knocked Dad's whiskey down by accident. Mam slapped the back of my legs with a slipper and said, 'how the fuck's he gonna sleep now?'

Mam and Dad have been weird since the strikes. Nanna says that bastard Thatcher's got a lot to answer for. I asked if I could come and live with her until the strikes are finished and me mam and dad stopped shouting. She gave me a cuddle but she never said yes. I think it's 'cos her legs are bad. She probably wouldn't be able to look after a little kid. Me mam has to take her dinners round.

Mind you, she moved pretty quick when the bobbies were taking Eileen's husband, Jimmy last week. Her and Eileen were shouting 'bastards' and hitting them with rolling pins. Eileen had to stay at me nanna's after. I made three pots of tea—I'm dead careful with the teapot—but Eileen still didn't stop crying. In the end I got fed up and watched the racing with Grandad. Me and Grandad shouted at the telly for a treble up but never won owt. He says he's the unluckiest bastard on earth.

Kelly says it's Dad's fault for getting a new job and shitting on his mates. I asked Dad about it the other night. I woke up after Kelly had made me watch Thriller again. Dad was on the landing. Me and him crept downstairs into the kitchen. I sat on his lap for a bit. We don't normally do that 'cos Kelly laughs at me and calls me a baby, but she was in bed, so it was safe.

'Can you not sleep, bairn?' he asked.

'Nah, Michael Jackson's gonna get me.'

'Nowt bad's gonna get you, pet,' he said, stroking my hair.

I asked him then.

'Dad, are you bad?'

'What do you mean?'

'Well, Robert Gooding says you're a bastard ... and a scab.'

Dad gripped me by both arms, hurting a bit.

'Listen to me, Pet. I do what's best for you all. Even if that means doing something other people don't like. I've never crossed a picket line. EVER!'

I jumped a bit when he shouted.

'I got a new job that's all. Just, the timing was shit and ...'

He let out a long breath, 'I'm not bad.'

I cuddled into him. He smelt of soap and whiskey and I believed him.

I push open the gate and limp up the path towards the smell of minced beef pie. My mam's dead good at baking. Me and Kelly tumble through the back door into the outhouse. 'Me first,' says Kelly, elbowing me out of the way to get to the downstairs toilet—'the posh lavvy' me mam calls it. I pull my wellies off and throw them at the shoe rack then take my coat off and reach up to hang it over the top of Dad's anorak on the coat pegs.

I push open the door to the kitchen. Uncle Gary is sitting on a chair at the kitchen table ... again. His legs are stretched out in front of him, and he's holding up the paper. There's a black and white picture of Jimmy and the policemen on the front. You can see Eileen pulling the policeman's arm, snot and tears all over her face. Nanna's rolling pin is in the top corner of the picture.

Gary puts the paper down just as I'm trying to get a better look. He's got his work boots on and his donkey jacket. It's been two months now since any dads went to work. But he still wears his stupid jacket and his stupid boots.

'Alright, kidda,' he says, like he's my friend.

I used to think he was my real uncle till Kelly told me he wasn't. I used to like him, when he came round with Auntie Linda and Debbie. I loved Debbie. She's older like Kelly, but kind. She always played hairdressers with me and let me do plaits in her hair. They never come round now. Just Gary. He calls me mam pet and love. I think only dads should call mams pet and love.

Mam has her back to me. She's fiddling with something in front of her, but I can't quite see. She turns and scowls.

'Why're you two back? I said tea time.'

'We were freezing,' I say, and walk over to the steaming pie on the counter. Mam taps my hand as I reach out to it. The buttons on her blouse are all done up wrong. I can see the white lacey bit on her bra poking through the gap. She catches me looking and turns away quickly.

I feel something squirm in my belly. I don't feel hungry anymore.

'I need a plaster, Mam,' I say but she's fussing with the pie. Cutting a big slice off and wrapping it in tin foil.

'I'll best be off, love,' says Uncle Gary. Mam hands him the foil package.

'Will you bring Debbie next time?' I ask.

'Aye, maybe.'

'I'll see you out, Gaz,' she says. It's Gaz now.

He stands up and leans towards me. I notice a pink smear of lipstick on his chin. It's the same shade as Mam's.

'Tarra bairn,' he says.

I turn away as he goes to kiss my cheek.

'Bring Debbie next time,' I say.

Kelly comes through the door.

'Get in! Pie for tea.' She goes to the pie and sniffs it.

Mam smiles at Kelly, a pretend smile, all stretched and thin-lipped.

'Hold on. I'll just see Gary out.'

Mam and Gary go through to the front passage, closing the door behind them. I can hear them giggling.

I feel a sharp push in my back.

'Howay then, Sindys,' Kelly says.

'Will you get me a plaster first?' I ask and Kelly rolls her eyes. She climbs up on the worktop, opens the cupboard and pulls out the biscuit tin with the plasters in.

'Pick one then,' she says. I choose a Mr. Bump plaster. I stick it to the back of my heel. No accidents this time.

Me and Kelly go to our bedroom. We pull out the Sindy box from under my bed and Kelly starts making the house. I take the pink car out and wheel it over to her.

Sindy is naked, showing off her bare boobs and long slim legs. I put a small flowered skirt on her. I pick up a boy doll. He's naked too. He has a smooth surface where I know a penis should be. I have boy cousins. I put him in blue trousers and a brown waistcoat.

I squidge their faces against one another.

'Oooh, Gary, I love you,' I sing song, in my 'American' voice.

19

'Oh, Denise, I love you too,' the boy doll replies.

I make them kiss.

Kelly grabs my hands and pushes them and the dolls down hard into the carpet.

'Ow!' I say, trying to pull away.

She glares at me and won't let go.

'Don't you dare tell Dad,' she hisses.

'What?' I'm scared of Kelly when she's like this.

'You don't tell Dad that Gary comes round. Right?'

I nod. Sindy's plastic hands are digging into my palms like sharp pins.

'And don't be telling Nanna either.'

Stupid baby tears come.

Kelly lets go and I breath out.

I throw the dolls down and look at the bright red marks on my palms.

'Sorry,' Kelly says in her kind voice, 'It's just, Dad and Gary will fall out, and Mam'll be in big trouble.'

I wonder if that might be good. Maybe Dad will have a fight with Gary. Punch him, like Robert Gooding punched me, in the belly, so hard that I puked into my own mouth and had to spit the mush onto the grass. Maybe the bobbies will take Gary away, like they took Jimmy, then Auntie Linda can come to ours and cry like Eileen, and mam will make her a cup of tea and they'll be friends again. Maybe Dad will stop drinking whiskey and shouting at Mam. And maybe Mam will stop sending me outside in the cold, or to Nanna's or to anywhere that's not home. Maybe I shouldn't keep my gob shut after all.

GIANT
Lui Sit

The year I turned nine I rode to school for the first time on my own. The quickest way was through the dirt path in the forest that began at the end of our street, but Mum had warned me never to ride down there by myself.

'It's completely hidden from view Simon,' she said. 'If anything happened to you, no-one would know so make sure you take the main road.'

But one day I turned towards the dirt path, not away, and from then on, that's the way I went.

The first few times I was so relieved to make it safely to school that I didn't look at anything apart from the path ahead, but soon, I took in the surroundings more. The tree branches arching above formed a dense canopy, allowing only shallow streams of light to filter through. The woods smelled of damp earth and the sound of birds calling to each other overhead, reminded me that I was alone and no-one knew where I was.

On that day, I was close to the turning at the end of the path which led back out to the main road. As I approached, I turned my head to the left and nodded goodbye to the trees, a gesture I'd repeated each time to keep me safe on the journey which had now become superstition. And that's when I saw it, a strange mound to the left of the track in a small clearing where no trees grew. It looked as if a giant anthill had erupted from the ground overnight, so I stopped and wheeled my bike over. Up close, I could see the mound was not made of earth but a slick, dark

21

ceramic, except that it wasn't ceramic because it was pulsing, like there was a heartbeat or a pair of lungs inside.

I dropped my bike, inching closer. The air around started to smell of burning and all of a sudden, the urge to touch it was overwhelming. Nothing around me was moving, no insects, no birds and even the rustle of the wind in the thin undergrowth had stopped. I reached out my hand and heard Mum's voice screaming, *No*, but my hand met the surface and then, instead of being in the forest on my way to school, I was standing on the face of a giant, his breath hot against me and my hand clutching his nose which was damp and dimpled with pit marks. His eyelids started to open, revealing two bright green pupils, scanning upwards like a pair of spotlights. I pulled my hand away and as I did, the face started to dissolve, the ceramic surface turning into grains of fine, black sand which swirled into the ground, a vortex beneath sucking everything down.

I stumbled backwards, watching the giant's eyes turn from green to charcoal before disappearing altogether. The ground was flat and earthen, as if it had never been disturbed and whatever that was, the giant, the anthill, the moist, dark mound was gone. I felt the wind return and heard the noise of birds squawking overhead. Flexing my hand, I hoisted my bike upright and pedalled fast for school.

That night, Mum closed the book on her lap.

'What did you think of the ending?' she asked.

I shrugged, my hands picking at the duvet.

'Not a fan?' Ok, well you choose the story tomorrow.' She kissed my forehead and smoothed back my hair before standing up.

'Mum?'

She looked back, her brown fringe swinging into her glasses.

'Do you believe in magic?'

Her eyes clouded over.

'Well,' she started, 'I know you do, don't you? Everyone says you have a gifted imagination.'

She paused before continuing.

'Did something happen?'

When I didn't reply her lips creased into a smile that didn't reach her eyes.

'It's ok Simon. You know you can tell me.'

So I did. I watched a tightness pan across her cheeks when I got to the bit about the dark mound and how it had turned into a giant's face, but it didn't stop me from telling her everything, right up to the point where the sand had drained back into the ground and even though that was all there was to tell, I wanted to say more.

'Simon. Stop.' She touched my face, her palm sweaty.

'Do you believe me Mum?'

She sighed and wedged the copy of *The Little Prince* under her arm. We'd just read a story about an alien who talked to a flower. She had to believe me.

'Go to sleep, we can talk more about it tomorrow.' She switched off the light and closed the door, turning the room dark. I pulled the duvet high up over my shoulders, burying myself beneath its weight. I didn't know what else to do but close my eyes and try to go to sleep.

I'm at the bottom of a waterfall. Water is cascading down around me, streaming past either side of my body into the swirling, green pool below. I look down to see my bare feet standing on cold, flat rock. Despite all the water, I'm not wet, my blue flannel pyjamas are dry and warm. I reach out to touch the water but it rejects my hand as if it were a magnet, repelling with equal force. Raising my arm above my head, the flow of water moves with it, as if I'm lifting a curtain. I raise my other hand and the same thing happens. I laugh and wave both hands in the air, the water moving in equal rhythm. This is brilliant! Bringing both arms high above my head causes the water to part, revealing a cave behind the waterfall where a face stares out at me. He's solid again, his whole head etched from the length and breadth of the cave rock. His black granite features seem to have grown outwards from the rock, just as he'd grown out of the forest floor. Gagging, I try to drop my arms but they remained pinned in mid-air. The giant smiles, the dark rock grinding into formation but there is no friendliness in his green stare.

'Simon?'

'Mum?'

I look around but I can't see where the voice is coming from. There's just water, ebony rock and the face ahead.

'Mum?' I shout, my arms tingling from pins and needles.

The giant's smile widens showing a mouth full of grimy, jagged teeth. Except one. One tooth is pale and wriggling because it isn't a tooth, it's a person, wedged between the lower canine and incisor. A person wearing glasses in a long nightgown with brown hair falling down onto her shoulders and into her eyes.

'Mum! My scream bombs through my head just as the giant snaps his mouth shut and my arms flop down, closing the curtain of water. My legs give way and I topple headlong into the swirling pool below.

'Mum!' I was sitting bolt upright in bed, my pyjamas drenched with sweat. I flung the duvet off and ran out of my room onto the landing where I could see Mum's bedroom door shut tight. I pushed down onto the door handle and stepped inside. On her bed, I could see the cushions neatly arranged, propped up against the headboard and the smooth, flat quilt with no body beneath. It looked like no-one had been in it at all that night. Where was she?

I nearly slipped scrambling downstairs, the wooden staircase treacherous against my bare feet. Reaching the hallway, I fumbled for the light switch but nothing happened. I flicked again, but darkness remained. Racing through the house, I tried the kitchen next and then the front room, but no lights worked.

The stillness of the hour started to press on me and I could feel my panic bursting to get out. I needed to pee too. Entering the bathroom, the battery-powered cabinet light was on, the mirrored doors open wide, highlighting the toiletries and medicines inside. As I emptied my bladder, I scanned the cabinet shelves, wondering what Mum had been looking for and if she was unwell. The thought made me shiver in my damp pyjamas as I returned to the kitchen, pulling open the drawer where Mum kept the matches and torch.

'Please work,' I thought as my hand grasped the torch handle. Pressing down, the space flooded with light, the kitchen clock illuminated at 11:45pm confirming that Mum had left me alone, late at night.

My legs bolted towards the front door which I was tall enough to reach and unlock from the inside. Stepping out, the night chill hit me. The streetlamps were on showing how still and quiet the street was apart from a few neighbourhood cats trotting across the road. Our garage shed door was wide open, the car gone.

I padded across the dew-soaked lawn towards Mrs Wilton's house next door. She said that old people didn't need as much sleep as the young which made me think she mustn't sleep at all as she looked ancient. She often looked after me when Mum was working and I knew that out of all the neighbours, she would be the least angry at being woken up. I only had to knock twice for her to appear in the doorway in a faded green robe, her hair in curlers.

'Simon,' she croaked, 'What are you doing here?' Her lined face seem to have grown a few more etches since I last saw her.

'Mum's gone.'

'Mum's gone?' she parroted, confusion creasing her sleep-worn face.

'I woke up and she's not here. The car's gone too.'

'Heavens,' she clucked and scooped me in, crushing my face against the folds of her musty robe. 'Come in. Whatever was she thinking?'

She hustled me into the kitchen, turning on the lights before going to fill the kettle. The warmth in the house started to seep through and I felt a swell of exhaustion break over me as I slumped down into a chair by the dining table.

'Are you hungry my love? Piece of toast?' Mrs Wilton was looking at me like I was an abandoned cat she'd found on the street. She often looked at me like that. I nodded.

'Yes please.'

As she opened the bread bin I wandered to her front room window. The heavy damask curtains were drawn open, showing the street outside that I'd just come in from.

As I stared, the air outside started to shimmer, as if a heatwave had descended onto the street. Undulating and wavering, this air started to form a shape all too familiar.

No. Not again.

The giant's face was formed now. I could see his wide features. The hooded eyelids and sharp rise of cheekbone against the broad, angular jaw. The flat nose broadened further as his nostrils flared, inhaling deeply all the air that I had stopped breathing. The head turned to face me and started to move towards the window.

A noise roared out of me as sweat trickled from my scalp onto my face. My chest felt like it was hosting a family of hyperactive mice, heaving and twitching like there was something living inside. I rubbed my eyes with my fists but the giant's face was still there when I looked again. My mouth pooled with saliva as the giant's lips opened and I saw that all his teeth were gone, the gums fleshy and horribly pink and its tongue looked like a patchwork of swollen slugs.

I squinted my eyes to slits but it didn't stop the massive jaw from craning wider and wider. I pressed myself right up against the window, wanting it to protect me and also let me see everything. My hot breath misted over the glass, smudging when I wiped it with my hand. Suddenly, the air stilled as the giant's mouth stopped opening, frozen into a wide gape as if it wanted to swallow Mrs Wilton's house. The thought sent a bolt of fury through me.

'Go away,' I shouted. 'Stop following me.'

I looked around for something, anything that I could hurtle through the window, smashing the glass to send away that ugly face. My hand found the neck of Mrs Wilton's antique brass table lamp. I lifted it above my head, its velvet green tassels dangling in my face and the heavy weight of it making me stumble but before I could throw it, I saw him.

A small boy, young, with tufts of dark hair sticking out from his head climbing out of that infernal mouth. He was dressed in pyjamas with bare feet. He turned in my direction and it was me, my legs wide apart, my hands holding a table lamp with green tassels which I brandished above my head like a trophy, and the shock of seeing me made the lamp slip from my grasp, the glass bulb exploding onto the ground, shattering shards of glass everywhere.

'Simon.'

Turning, I saw Mrs Wilton, a plate of toast in one hand and a glass of water in the other. Standing next to her was Mum, in blue jeans and her old brown jumper, her handbag slung over her shoulder. She held out her hand, guiding me around the broken glass into the warm kitchen, Mrs Wilton following behind.

'Sit down.'

Mum pulled out a dining chair and patted the seat, as if it were normal to be in our neighbour's kitchen at midnight.

I gulped, my mouth filling up with saliva.

'Mum,' I retched, choking down the spit. 'He's out there.'

I pointed outside but she and Mrs Wilton just kept staring at me.

'Me too,' I gasped, 'I'm out there too.'

Mum reached into her handbag and pulled out a small packet, the label reading Parron's 24-Hour Pharmacy. Seeing that familiar logo in dark red drenched me in a wave of cold sweat.

'No Mum. I don't want to.'

She popped two yellow capsules out from the aluminium seal and nodded at Mrs Wilton who handed her the glass of water.

'Come on Simon. We've talked about this.'

She held the pills out to me but I turned my head away at Mrs Wilton who smiled sadly. Mum grabbed my jaw with her free hand and pried my mouth open.

'Swallow,' she urged, 'we only have a short window before it's too late.'

She shoved the pills into my mouth and some age-old reflex took over as I swallowed them down dry. Pulling me into a hug, I could feel her heartbeat thundering just as urgently as mine.

'I'm sorry,' she murmured. I looked up at her and saw how tired she was.

'But he's out there,' I repeated, peeling my lips apart. The saliva was gone, replaced by a desert. She stroked my hair and tilted my head back so she could see my eyes.

'I believe you,' she whispered. 'I believe you.'

IN THE SHELL MUSEUM
Padrika Tarrant

Limpet; nautilus; Devil's toe. The shell museum is where we wait for the end of the world, like broken glass that dulls in the tide. We have the great huge sea in our lungs. We have sand in every crease and pore. We blink and blink but our eyes are crusted with it and we can barely see.

You still have one of your flip flops, sodden and mouldering. The pink and blue are faded white. Your other foot's bare and crinkled. We stand in puddles all the time; we keep warm as best we can, but our clothes are ruined and there isn't much to live on in the shell museum. When the attendant isn't looking, we steal squares of fudge and t-shirts which say *I have been to Great Yarmouth*. We wear them in layers; the salt always weeps through.

Lion's paw; moonshell; pink coral. The shell museum is huddled around us; your fingers are embalmed, and your nails are ever so long. You clutch your peg-doll; her face has worn away now, but we say she looks just like Mama. Your hair is a tangle that nothing could tease through, not even razor shell, or the pretty combs sold by the promenade. They used to sell spades, sunglasses, little buckets embossed with starfish too. I expect they still do.

Magpie shell; sand dollar; periwinkle. The shell museum is riddled with artefacts, laid out in finicky little boxes like jewellery, waiting to be seen. If visitors come by, they turn the lights on for them. But they don't come and all there is to squint by is the threadbare slant of air from the window.

I hold your hand, seeing as I am the eldest, and we cling together as if to keep one another safe. It is a long time since either of us were safe. I sing quietly when we are alone, nursery rhymes from before. Or else we gaze at the exhibits, tracing the labels of this or that shell, peering at the tiny writing: Genus (with a capital letter) and species (with a small one). You like the seahorses best. You don't understand that they are dead.

One time, another child did come in out of the rain. She was so wet; she stopped right in front of us with her lips moving as if she was remembering poetry. She stared right through me for a minute or more, and I thought, I really thought, that she could see me. She walked away.

Measled cowrie; slipper snail; zebra ark. The shell museum is our home. We crept here very long ago. No-one would ever notice us, if it weren't for the creak of the ocean when one holds us to their ear.

EASY PEELERS
Lisa Goldman

Eat Up, Mrs Knowles says. Eat it all up now.
   No.
   Don't you know how lucky you are?

♀

Mama juggles the Easy Peelers—two, then three, four, then five—orange suns jumping round my head. I'm choking with laughter at something Mama says. We're in what Mrs Knowles calls the Dark Times when the sun was always shining. Before the Big Green King. When Mama juggled for crowds in clown face. Juggled plates and oranges, burning sticks. Swallowed fire.
   I don't like clown face, Mama.
   I put it on, Innochka, so I can save my real smiles for you.
   I'm lying in the festival field, Earth's drum humming through my body. Mama and her new boyfriend Raoul practise juggling. Raoul's a lousy catch. He drops an Easy Peeler. Its thick shiny skin tears easily.
   Clumsy! I laugh at him.
   Must of hit a stone, Raoul says.
   But it isn't, it's a shard of china, a chip from an old plate. Pierced puckered skin leaks bittersweet juice. Raoul digs fat fingers inside the wound and pops the fruit from its orange jumpsuit.
   See, he says to Mama, I told you Easy Peelers are too soft.
   Raoul splits the flesh with his giant hand. Three injured bits for him. Two nice bits for me. Raoul feeds Mama the perfect three.

30

I watch juice dribble down her chin. I'm glad she peeled off clown face—the orange tastes better from her skin.

Greedy, Raoul says to me.

Mama smiles.

⚲

One day at school, Yaz—who everyone wants as a friend—calls me an Easy Peeler when Mrs Knowles is watching. I'm hot and frozen to the spot. Yaz's eyes flick over me.

Back home I ask Mama what Yaz meant by Easy Peeler.

We don't use those words about people, Mama says.

Why not, Mama?

Because no one can help being poor.

After that, I hear it all the time, chat about Easy Peelers.

Too many of them—they've bred out of control.

Didn't buy at the right time. Couldn't buy, to be fair. Now they're out of the game.

Just staring.

Squatted two flats on our block last week.

With Easy Peelers living there, things'll go bad fast!

Why do we even need them there just staring at us?

⚲

I'm collecting with school for the Big Green Clean Up.

The old man smells of wee and his thin coat is torn, but he thrusts a shiny coin into my palm. This is for *you* not the fucking Clean Up. Buy yourself some food, you poor little Peeler.

Peeler again. My fingers turn the golden coin. I could buy Mama an orange and watch the juice dribble down her chin. Oranges are hard to get these days, nowhere down the market, but I've seen some plump and dimpled in a shop we never stop at. If I buy Mama an orange, she'll smile, say something sweet in Russian.

I call her Mum or Mummy now in front of strangers. The only time

I hear her speaking Russian is in her sleep.

The gold coin is hot and heavy.

Yaz says Clean Up money is to fight the Green King's enemies. What if the old man is an enemy? If I keep his money, does that make me an enemy too?

No. The old man stank but his eyes were kind. Perhaps he was just testing my loyalty to the King.

I weigh up this loyalty now against buying Mama an orange.

When Raoul was still alive, I'd catch him staring at my Big Green Clean Up badge. I worried that he might think I loved the King more than him, which wasn't true. Though I did see more of the King, what with his face being everywhere. And after scary May Day when Raoul got shot in the Square and my coat couldn't stop the blood and Mama lost her job and stayed in bed just sobbing, I started talking to the King.

Please Green King, let Mama's voice come back. Let me find enough money to buy her an orange so I can lick the juice that dribbles down her chin. If you make this happen, King, I'll sacrifice everything for your Big Green Clean Up.

Making sacrifices is a big theme at school.

Inna, what did that Easy Peeler say to you? He's sent you into one of your little dreams. Mrs Knowles is as close now as the old man was when he gave me the coin. I look up at my teacher's round, smiling face.

Miss, I ask. What's more important do you think? Making Mummy happy or making the Green King happy?

Mrs Knowles' eyes flash and the world goes dark.

Why would you think those two things different, Inna?

My tummy flip-flops with fear.

What has Mummy said about our King? You know you can tell me everything. Mrs Knowles' voice sounds pulpy and sweet.

I spit it out like an unexpected pip: Mummy doesn't talk since the May Day Massacre.

You mean the London Riots?

I just want to make her happy, Miss.

Mrs Knowles ruffles my hair. But what on earth does all this have to do with our beloved King?

I've got a gold coin, Miss, and I don't know what to do. Should I donate it to the Clean Up or buy an orange for Mum?

Now it's all out in the open and whatever the answer, already I feel better.

Mrs Knowles' eyes are moist as her finger twirls my hair, the same colour and style as her own, though Yaz said Mrs Knowles gets hers out of a bottle.

Don't you think Mummy would be proud if you sacrificed your gold coin to the Clean Up? Mrs Knowles' lower lip trembles. If I was your Mummy, I'd be very proud indeed.

I stare up at my teacher. All is clear.

I push my sweaty coin into the donation tin. My heart swells like our special Crow Song.

I beam across at the other girls and boys busy stopping strangers. I am the greenest, cleanest of them all in the Big Green Clean Up— closest to our King. He's watching me sacrifice everything and there will be more sacrifices now, so many more. I can't wait!

When I step into the path of the next passer-by and ask *Do you want our streets to be safe?* I feel as if I own the streets, as if the King's arms are wrapped around me like a thick, warm coat.

◦

Back in class, Mrs Knowles tells everyone what I did.

It's not where you start in life, she says.

Yaz agrees. You wouldn't get an Easy Peeler doing that. See, Inna's not a Peeler, she's just thin. Some people are naturally thin.

At break, Yaz asks me to teach her to juggle. She's got three apples from the tree in her garden. I wish we could eat them.

You have to keep dropping them, I explain. My mum taught me. That's what learning to juggle is about.

Yaz looks anxious. Then they'll bruise. I gotta barter them.

Life is nicer with Yaz as my friend, but secretly I wish for another life where I bought Mama an orange instead of putting my coin in the tin.

Mama sits proud and alone in the orange bucket chair just staring.

Mrs Knowles towers over her.

Inna, tell Mummy how much money you collected for the Big Green Clean Up.

The highest wasn't it, Miss, the top, the best. I got this special ribbon and the extra is that I keep a signed photo of our King all weekend. Look at his eyes Mama, I mean Mum. They follow you around the room.

Mama stares ahead. She is looking out the window at the crows on the tree. Three crows means good luck but today there's only one.

I can tell you what Mama would say if she could, Miss. I know her better than anyone, don't I Mama, I mean Mum?

Mrs Knowles looks weary. All I need is your signature, Miss Vorobyov, giving permission for Inna to appear at the Big Green Freedom Festival. The producers love her personality.

I want to do it, *please*, Mama.

Inna, show Mummy your routine.

It's hard to remember the Crow Song moves with Mama just staring out the window like that but I do my best to keep the tune.

We love the pure green English land.
We are England's eyes and ears.
We are here to hold your hand.
We are here to end your fears.
Pulling out the old brown weeds.
Crow, Crow, Crow.
Let the English garden grow.

See how happy she is for me, Mrs Knowles? Aren't you Mama?

Mrs Knowles notices my leg jiggling.

Inna, do you need to go to the toilet?

Yes, but it's OK.

Mrs Knowles always sees things first. S'why I'm scared to leave her with Mama.

Sign it Mama, please sign it Mama, please, please, sign it Mama. I don't want to go to Russia. Russia's full of radiation.

Mrs Knowles smiles kindly. Don't upset yourself, Inna. You'll be safe with me. Your 'Mama' made her choice. We all believe in freedom, don't we?

Crow taps on the window. I feel the hot wee juice run down my leg as I run to Mama and cling to her and make her damp but she doesn't notice.

Please don't go to Russia, Mama.

Mama turns to face Mrs Knowles and in that glance I am passed from one mother to another.

𝖞

Mrs Knowles gives me a bike for my twelfth birthday. I call it Raoul but she doesn't know why. Sometimes when we ride it's like we're flying, me and Raoul. Faster than the bullets flew that Raoul caught to save my life, caught them in his giant chest. Did it for Mama—I don't know if he even liked me. Maybe Mama wished he hadn't, maybe she wished I'd taken the bullet, lying with my head blown apart instead of Raoul's heart. She said Raoul did it instinctively because he was a good man. The only good man she ever met. She looked at me with anger when she said that and then she didn't speak again, even when they took her to the Big Clean Up van.

I wish I'd been older. I would have said goodbye.

Raoul always looked after Mama. I don't think Raoul would have become an Easy Peeler, however hungry he got. They would have juggled things.

𝖞

Yaz says they're called Easy Peelers because skin hangs off their bones like the wrong size clothes. Because of the space between skin and flesh. They're the reason the army's been drafted in. And the crows. Because crows have X-ray eyes. There's thirty on the school tree.

Mrs Knowles is leader of the Neighbourhood Taskforce. She stops Easy Peelers on the street. She stops the ones who broke into number three.

Isn't it better than them living on the street, Mummy?

No, says Mrs Knowles. I have to breathe their air every day and they brought it on themselves with their lack of hygiene, their addictions. They're passing it on, the hunger, they're passing it on.

Everywhere, people chat about Easy Peelers.

It was the way he stared at me. Can't even focus. Too hungry.

Not hungry – too far gone. She's half-dead already.

They can't come back from it. They've fallen from the tree.

So what did that one say to you?

He said Eat Me

⚘

I perform my song and dance routine. England's plugged into the sun. We're making the world better. Because we're the best and things are bad. They sprayed something to clean the air and everyone died in Africa. In England we survived. Apart from Easy Peelers like Mama.

They got peeled in the end, the Easy Peelers, before they lost any more juice. The harvests failed so people ate them—some called it the Summer of Shame. But no-one knew what else to do. Except the rich who caused it all—they ran away with the Big Green King. To another place, another planet, another day.

I don't think you can look up to humans really. If I was forced to eat one I s'pose I would, but not if I knew them.

⚘

Eat Up, says Mrs Knowles. Eat it all up now.

No.

Don't you know how lucky you are?

My plate is chipped. I can't stop staring.

You want to end up like Mama?

No.

THE SPINNEY
Gaylene Gould

On that first day of the last year of primary school, Elaine walks Toki across the wide playing fields. Their hands are stuffed into their respective pockets. Toki keeps hers out of reach of her mother's. Elaine prevents hers from running through her daughter's soft curls.

Elaine nods toward the tight knot of tree tops poking above the school roof and says, perhaps for the last time, 'One of those trees back there is alive because of your mum.'

Toki's eye roll is evident in her reply. 'I know Mum. You and Angie Kane watered your tree long after everyone else stopped watering theirs. Now I'm in my last year, do you think I'll get to plant a tree in the spinney?'

The shards of green in her daughter's hazel eyes can still surprise Elaine. Her stomach tightens. Thankfully, the spinney is now off limits to the school children.

'I doubt it Toks. Tree planting was the kind of school project you were allowed to do when I was a kid. They can't SAT a tree now, can they?'

'Oh,' Toki says, kicking a stone with her bright trainers that took an hour to choose in the shop. 'I won't get to see the witch then.'

Elaine lets the pause lengthen. Thirty years on, the story of the witch survived and Elaine still hasn't told her daughter that it's her fault the witch even appeared all those years ago. Now Toki has come of age, Elaine knows that it's time to tell her the truth. Just as she opens her drying mouth, a boy bounces past them. It's the way he slows down, that gacky smell of hair product.

'Alright Toks,' he says.

'Alright Jamie.'

It's the way the blush sweeps her daughter's cheek and how the boy tears off without acknowledging her adult presence that makes Elaine ask sharply, 'Who's that?'

'Oh that's just Jamie. He's in my class.'

The panic rises swiftly in Elaine. She wants to remind her daughter how careful she has to be now that her legs have grown coltishly long and the new fleshy buds have appeared on her chest. She wants to stress how the patch of pale pink blood that appeared in her panties, a whole year before time, has irrevocably changed Toki's life. She wants to say she must never enter those woods but Toki breaks free to join her 'Backing Singers', as Elaine calls the band of friends waiting by the school's front doors.

'See you later Mum,' Toki throws up a hand and skips away. Elaine feels as if Toki is taking a piece of her own flesh with her. She wants to throw herself over her daughter like a fire blanket but Toki is already cocooned in the nest of cooing girls. Elaine reassures herself with the fact that Toki is not the child Elaine had once been. Toki, with her long twisting curls which grow Beyoncé blonde in the summer, is the one the others trail. For a moment, Elaine feels a familiar hollow ache return. She is suddenly as she was at Toki's age, standing stooped-shouldered, with an untameable afro, the back of her skirt riding high on her ample behind, watching the shiny colourful group of light-skinned girls walk away from her. Elaine is left with the dark line of tree tops beckoning above the roof. She turns, with a flick of her long silky weave, and imagines she catches the muggy scent of blackened soil and the ancient musk of tree bark.

Angie Kane had smelt of stale socks, ones that had been worn for days without being washed. She walked past Elaine's hedge every day and Elaine found herself straining at the kitchen window to catch the top of Angie's sparrow-like head. Elaine couldn't be seen to rush out to meet

Angie. It had to look as though she just happened to leave the house at the same time. That way, there would be no evidence of her actually befriending her.

'Alright Angie.'

'Alright Elaine.'

'Angie's smile creased her narrow, freckled face. It was as if she was the size of a normal girl but then had been sucked away somehow. 'Malnourished', Elaine's mum, a nurse, had diagnosed after catching sight of Angie. Elaine was shocked because she thought only pleading-eyed African children on those adverts were malnourished and Angie was white and this was England.

'Did you see the colour of Mrs Prendegast's face when Paulie Bryant called her a silly bitch yesterday?' Angie opened her tiny beak-mouth and let out a surprisingly deep, guttural laugh, which turned the heads of the other children crossing the playing fields. Elaine ducked her own head into her coat collar.

'Paulie Bryant's got a big fat arse. He wants to be careful that someone don't put their foot in it one day,' Angie added, and Elaine laughed.

As if summoned, Paulie Bryant swept by on his BMX bike and slapped Angie on the top of her head, the force causing her to stumble.

'Shit stains Angie!' he shouted at her.

Angie quickly righted herself. 'Wouldn't want to see the size of your shit stains, fat arse!'.

Now everyone was looking at them which made Elaine want to disappear. Instead she asked, 'You ok?'

Angie acted cartoon dizzy for a minute, sticking out her tongue and wobbling, before sashaying toward the school doors.

The children were never usually allowed in the spinney behind the school. They had a playground and playing fields lined with willow trees that swept the ground and made for perfect pretend houses. But that day was different. That day, Mr Randall, their bearded mammoth of a teacher, led them outside to the baby trees, sporting nappies made out of plastic bags.

'Listen,' Mr Randall's Yorkshire boom silenced the excited chatter.

'Get yourself in pairs. Someone you like because together you're going to take one of these saplings and it will be your job to plant, water and tend your tree together.'

Shoes scuffled as friends paired with friends. Elaine made sure not to show relief when Angie finally found her way over.

'Our tree will grow bigger than any of theirs,' Angie said.

They entered the spinney behind the school in snake formation and climbed the small incline that led into the wood. The ground crackled drily beneath their feet until they were plunged into a shady tangle of trees. There, the ground let up a mossy smell. The cool air smelt thick and tangy. The children quietened like they were in a holy place.

They planted the saplings on a patch of neglected scrub in the middle of the spinney. Mr Randall helped them wet the ground and then each pair scored out a bottle-deep hole with a trowel. Elaine watched Angie on all fours, digging her already grubby hands into the mud. Elaine couldn't imagine what her own mum would say if she were to come home dirty like that, so instead, she stood and held the naked sapling and waited for Angie to finish. When Angie finally dug out their tree's resting place, she looked up at Elaine and smiled. Her cheeks were flushed and her hair speckled with dirt. The girls ceremoniously lowered the tree into the hole and Elaine squatted down too to pull the rich cool earth about the roots.

Every lunchtime after that, Angie and Elaine would fill an old white basin with water and gently carry it out to the spinney to douse the ground around their tree. At first, they were joined by other eager pairs of children, each boasting how their tree was taller and prettier than the others. But as the summer progressed and the children began to realise, with some resentment, that nature's infuriating clock meant trees grew by the year and not the day, the pairs began to drop off. Elaine wished she could drop off too. She and Angie weren't real friends after all. Penny Dougall and Sharon Lane were her friends now. But like clock-work every lunchtime, Angie showed up with the white basin and that eager expression.

Elaine agonised over how to tell Angie that she didn't want to water the tree anymore. She wanted to play normal girl games like hopscotch and skipping and Mum's and Dad's with Penny and Sharon because, at last, she had been invited to play. She didn't know how to say this to Angie, the girl who would never be invited.

When the two girls rounded the back of the school together on the hottest day of that year, Elaine did not know that this would be the last time. The shushing, cooling leaves quietly applauded their arrival. Angie was wearing a red dress, the straps of which kept slipping off her shoulders, like someone bigger had worn it before her.

'Isn't she a beauty?' Angie said when they stood beside their tree. Angie and the tree were the same height. They could be sisters, thought Elaine, except the tree looked healthier than Angie. She laughed at that thought.

'What you laughing at?' Angie asked, squatting to test the ground around the roots, like a doctor with a stethoscope.

'Nothing,' Elaine said shortly. She had been practising being mean to Angie so that when she finally plucked up the courage to quit, Angie would be relieved. But Angie never seemed to notice. She simply cleared away the few fallen leaves, like she was tending a gravestone. Caught by a pang of tenderness, Elaine bent down to join Angie, who was squatting, knees akimbo. That's how Elaine found herself staring at the patch of blood on the gusset of Angie's greying panties.

'Even when we go up to the Big School we'll come back here to water her won't we?' Angie was saying.

The heat around Elaine's head intensified and a claggy earthy smell seemed to rise up from that place between Angie's legs.

'Maybe not every day but, like, twice a week. We can walk back here together. I'm sure Mr Randall will lend us the basin ...'

The leaves rattled above them with a cooling burst of relief. As the goosebumps spread down her arms, Elaine knew that this earth-stopping occurrence was her out.

'Angie.'

Angie looked at Elaine with such softness, like the way men and women look at each other in movies, that all Elaine could do was point a tentative finger to the spot between the girl's legs.

Elaine told Penny and Sharon first. She had to. Friendships were sealed through the sharing of secrets like these. After that, news spread like a forest fire and despite the teacher's attempts, there was no way to stem the teasing of Angie. Paulie stole a bottle of ketchup from the dining room and dramatically squirted tomato sauce on Angie in the playground. Angie and Elaine never spoke again but every lunchtime, Elaine found herself seeking out Angie's diminutive figure as she carried the basin of water slowly towards the spinney.

Three weeks after that first day of the last school year, Elaine finds herself rushing across the playing fields urged on by the panicked tone of Toki's teacher on the phone. A high wind shifts the branches of her lungs as she faces down the treetops and can hear, on the wind and across the years, Angie's long and wild scream. She remembers how she stood that day on the playing field, with the rest of the children, and watched Angie's bucking body being escorted from the spinney. She remembers the ambulance waiting, blue lights flashing. That was the day Angie went to water their sapling and she had seen a large black figure hovering in the roof of the trees. The sight of the witch had driven her crazy. It was the smell of Angie's blood that had drawn the witch from the cave, the girls said later. And Elaine fell quiet because she knew it was her fault, that if she hadn't left Angie alone the witch wouldn't have come.

Elaine breaks into a run and with each breathless step reminds herself that she is no longer ten years old, and that there is no such thing as witches, especially those that come to take your bleeding daughter as retribution.

When Elaine catches sight of Toki in Mr Randall's old classroom, she lets go the whimper that has been gathering in her chest. Everything is so small. The tables and chairs, the display boards at elbow height. This is a room for saplings. Toki's shoulders are heaving with each shallow sob and when she sees Elaine, she flies into her mother's arms.

At first, Toki doesn't want to go, until Elaine explains that if they go together, the spinney will no longer hold a spell over them.

'You won't get mad?' Toki slips her hand into her mother's as they walk across the playground toward the back of the school.

'No, I won't get mad. Tell me.'

The trees are quiet when they enter the timeless wood. Elaine feels for a moment as if she and Toki, and she and Angie, are walking hand-in-hand into the spinney.

'No-one ever goes back there because of the witch but Jamie don't believe in witches. He said we should go and prove once and for all and then tell everyone it's a lie. It was dead dark back there and then he ...,' Toki's grip tightens.

Jamie. The boy with the slicked hair. Paulie who squirted Angie with the ketchup and then tried to smear the red liquid into her dress, under her dress. Paulie who would stare at Angie like there was a magnetic repulsion. Paulie who, Elaine remembers now, was there that day that Angie was carried screaming from the wood, who followed her out, his face pale. A memory blooms in her. How could Elaine have forgotten that part of the story? The part overheard later in the girls' toilets, the part where Paulie Bryant follows Angie into the woods, pulls down his pants and yellow stuff comes out of his penis. The part where the witch shows up and scares them both away. How had she forgotten that?

'*I* heard her first,' Toki is saying. 'She was above me, like a big cat climbing in the trees. And when I looked up she was there. It was like moths had eaten her face.' She relishes that line. 'I screamed and Jamie ran away.'

Elaine kneels down slowly, her knees in the grubby dirt like Angie's had once been and wraps herself around her child and the witch that hides inside her.

'Did he—, I mean she hurt you?'

Elaine feels the slight shake of her daughter's head against her shoulder. Later, when it's quiet, when they are curled up close together, she would help her daughter find the words to describe what Jamie had tried to do to her that day.

It's only a small pocket of trees, Elaine now sees, not at all as vast or as dense as she remembers. She tries to recall the steps she and Angie took all those years before but she struggles to remember as the trees are grown now. They are no longer babies.

'I lied to you,' Elaine finally admits to Toki as they pick their way through the undergrowth, 'I didn't water that tree. It was Angie who did it. I got bored and left her alone in the woods on her own. I wasn't a very good friend to her.'

'Oh,' Toki says. Elaine feels as if she is holding onto her daughter's hand rather than her daughter holding onto hers.

'Was Angie ok?' Toki finally asks. 'After seeing the witch?'

When Angie came back to school, the teasing stopped. Angie seemed older than all of them. A few girls once tried to sidle up to Angie in the playground but she smiled the kind of smile that made them turn and back away.

The last time Elaine remembers talking to Angie was a few years after that. They were at the Big School by then and she found herself and Angie walking toward each other in a corridor. They were alone like they had been in the spinney. Angie wore a nose ring and a rock star-ish haircut. Elaine's heart sped up as she levelled with Angie and she mumbled a nonchalant 'hello'. Angie replied by blowing a wet raspberry in her ear. A thin branch slaps Elaine in the forehead now and she laughs aloud causing the roosting rooks above them to make a ruckus.

'Angie did fine,' Elaine says, her hands feeling suddenly light. 'In fact, you remind me of her a bit.'

Toki leaps in the air and lands by a slender tree with silver bark flecked with rough diamonds and places both palms on the narrow trunk.

'This is Angie's tree.' Her leaf green eyes shine.

The tree she has chosen is young and straining with life. Elaine places her dark hands, like the leaves of an aged oak, next to Toki's soft, tremulous ones and breathes in the alive smell.

THE INITIATION
Bidisha

Zakhifa held the knife by the blade and narrowed her gaze onto the chunk of wood that served as a target. When she was as good as her sister, Decca, they would hunt together.

'She's not one of us,' said a familiar voice from inside the hut behind her. The voice belonged to Mo, her friend Enlil's father. 'She washed up from nowhere.'

Zakhifa felt a stab, quick in the gut. The tension seemed to go out of the knife and she put it aside. She crept to the hut's entrance and peered in. She could see her mother Avani binding long blades to their shafts and knotting the leather ties tight.

'Why are you fretting, Mo?' said Avani. 'Don't turn your gums black, gossiping.'

'Every child is an island child. Born on Massor. She'll never be.'

'Everyone knows Zakhifa's not from here,' said Avani, winding ever tighter. 'You never cared about it before.'

'She was a child before. She'll be a woman soon. Think of the initiation. We must consider what she's bringing into the community.'

'Hard labour,' Avani's voice rang, 'the girl can do anything. She hasn't been ill a day in her life.'

She pushed out her bosom and Mo shrank visibly.

'You, on the other hand,' said Avani, 'I know you won't mind hearing it from me 'cause you are truly like a brother. Coughing through the winter, wilting in the sun. Even a dying dog doesn't whine so loud.'

She swung away and sorted the knives into sets of three. Mo glowered behind her.

'You bore Decca as nature meant. But her 'sister' comes from the island before,' he said. 'War destroyed that place. All that washes up from there is death and damaged things.'

'*She's* not damaged, she's blossoming.'

'Even poisonous flowers blossom. That's how they spread their blight.'

Zakhifa crouched outside, barely breathing. Mo spoke as though he hadn't known her all her life, as though she, Decca and Enlil were not best friends.

There was no mystery to her origins: Avani had found her fourteen summers ago when she was searching a net at the coast, sorting through the relics that washed in during the last storm. Avani heard a cry and followed it to a box wedged in the reeds. The boxes usually came busted and empty. The lid on this one fell back and inside lay Zakhifa, a few days old. Avani took the baby to the women's circle and asked to keep her. They said 'yes'. Within a year Avani had Decca with her man, Ruam and the family was complete.

It was the next morning. The sun shone onto the sisters through the weaving of the hut roof. Zakhifa had spent yesterday walking the coast, neglecting her jobs, Mo's words chasing her. When she awoke, she told Decca everything.

'Zakhi,' said Decca, 'Mo's a fool. He's trying to look important. Poor Enlil, stuck with that preacher for a father.'

'We were lucky with *our* father,' Zakhifa said, and Decca nodded.

Ruam had been kind. He died five summers ago exploring the craggy coast that surrounded the volcano, Chamaca. The sea always churned there in savagely sucking spirals; many boat people had tested themselves against it and failed.

'*I'm* the real Massin islander,' said Zakhifa. 'Mo's the untrustworthy one. What's he doing speaking in private, away from the circle?'

'He knows he'd be shouted down. People listen to mama, not him.'

'Girls, I need you!' called Avani.

Decca and Zakhifa rose, rolled up their mats and got ready for their chores. Decca was teaching the younger children how to fish, sailing in the shallows to settle nets and baskets, while Zakhifa was accompanying Avani to the market.

'Stone fruit, pulp fruit, pith fruit, juice fruit! Herbs for the hairy, berries for the bald!'

Lur the witch rubbed her palms together.

'I'll take a tail of yellow-and-whites, please,' said Avani, pointing to a bunch of long vegetables with floppy green leaves. 'Actually, make it two, the girls eat like anything these days.'

'Truly so. The youthly appetite is a thing to envy.'

Zakhifa stood a little way behind her mother, quiet while the older women talked. After the market, they had to return a repaired blade to its owner. Avani was carrying it across her shoulder.

'That's a fine thing,' Lur said, staring in admiration. 'Zakhifa, do you know when a blade's good and ready?'

'When a strike with a fingernail causes it to sing,' Zakhifa answered promptly.

'Oho—nice and easy! Now, what else've I got for you? Something to ease you through initiation?'

'That's cheating, Lur,' Avani reproved her.

'Cheating? It's only natural to evade suffering, damn fool stupid to run to it.'

Lur gave Zakhifa a wink.

The blade-owner's land was in the belly of the island, where the ground dipped like a shallow dish. To get there, Avani and Zakhifa had a long dry march through yellow and green crops.

'Mama, I heard what Mo said, yesterday. He said I don't belong here.'

'He says lots of things, that man. Ignore him.'

The crops waved high around them and Avani cracked a line for Zakhifa to follow, parting the stems without breaking them. Zakhifa took hold of a strand and pulled it. It chafed, tough as rope.

'Don't do that, they're valuable,' said Avani. 'I haven't been here in some time. It was different then. More barren.'

'What's the land-tender's name?' asked Zakhifa.

'Sior. He's got a daughter called Yriana. Her mother died giving birth to Yriana's brother, and the brother died too, as a baby. From water sickness. After that, the others shunned them. Some said Sior did it, because he couldn't forgive the child for living.'

The crops absorbed their voices.

'Do you believe that, mama?'

'No. Sior would never do that.'

Avani parted the last strand. Young Yriana was waiting for them in front of her dark shack, its roof ragged, sides patchily plaited. Hunched and wary, Yriana's hair fell in thin scratches across her face. Ignoring her glowering expression, Avani smiled. 'Yriana, good day. We have something for your father.'

'He's been waiting.' Yriana's voice was thin and ringing, like a plucked wire. Zakhifa waved.

'I'm Zakhifa.'

'I know who you are,' said Yriana.

Zakhifa felt a prickle of unease, but followed Yriana's dragging heels to the shaded work space behind the shack. Yriana's father was lashing stalks into hard parcels. A stack of finished bundles lay on the ground.

'Avani. It's good to see you. Have you come from home?'

He straightened up, his strong body made creaky by overwork.

'From the market.' Avani held out the scythe. 'We fixed the handle for you, and sharpened the blade. If it's not right, we'll see what we can do.'

Sior lifted it out of her hand and put it on the table without looking at it. He said, 'It's perfect. Let me give you something for it, Avani.'

He went inside and Avani followed. Zakhifa turned to Yriana and found the girl standing just a little too close.

'I know all about you,' said Yriana. 'You're different, like me.'

She turned abruptly and walked into the meadow of golden stems. They parted for her.

'Why do you live so far away from everyone?' said Zakhifa, going after her.

'We have to be in the middle of our lands,' Yriana shrugged. 'When my brother died, our crops failed. All of them. We were starving, but

Father couldn't work. He had no strength, no appetite. He slept most of the time and, when he wasn't, I used to catch him, standing, staring at nothing. One day I decided I wouldn't live like that. I went to a circle meeting and stood up and told them I was going to work the lands, alone. They laughed in my face. I worked night and day until the crops flourished. And they still won't let me in.'

'Mama told me it's a great transformation,' said Zakhifa.

Yriana's expression didn't change, but there was a glint in her surly eyes.

'When your father Ruam drowned at Chamaca, Avani was blamed for it. I saw them accusing her.'

'I ...don't think that's true,' said Zakhifa.

'I saw it. They said Avani wanted another man: Father.'

Zakhifa shook her head in disgust. She turned to leave but the stalks closed around her, thick and rustling. They came to a circle of flattened crops. In the middle was a long screen raised on sticks and in the shadow underneath were a bench and table. For the first time, Yriana smiled.

'This is my study. I think here.' The stalks surrounded them like a tall circular wall. Yriana leant against the table. 'I think about how to escape.'

'Why would you do that?'

Yriana assessed her. 'This isn't some sort of wonderful place, Zakhifa. No matter what everyone says.'

'Where would you go?'

'They say there's no other place but this. But *you're* here.'

'From an island that no longer exists.'

'But there must be *other* places.'

Zakhifa looked down at the cluttered work table. There was a small circle of glass on it. She picked it up, running her fingers over the surface.

'I found this, at the coast. It's from the previous island—your island. I didn't show it to anyone, because I knew they'd take it from me. If you hold it a certain way and let the light pass through, a spot on the table starts to burn,' said Yriana.

Zakhifa nodded. The process was familiar to her.

'I see how it works,' she said. 'It's a small object, but it concentrates the great force of the sun, somehow. It takes it and converts it, turns it into flame.'

'Some people are afraid of fire, because of the volcano. They fear Chamaca. But I think it's beautiful.'

Yriana prised a wide blade off the table, chopped a handful of stalks from the edge of the circle, lined them up and struck, cutting them in a clean clip. 'They cut you. At the initiation. They cut you,' she said. 'Did you know that?'

'What?'

'You won't be the same again. I'll never let them do it to me—not that they want to.' Yriana laughed bitterly. 'They don't want people who're different. They think we're a taint.'

'The islanders would never do that,' said Zakhifa. But her body hurt with fear.

'How do you know what they'd do? You're not from here.'

On the way back, Avani was sparkling and light on her feet after her time with Sior, although she made no mention of him, or of the blade she'd mended for him with such care. Zakhifa walked with her for a while before they parted ways. Avani had to go talk to the other women and Enlil had invited Zakhifa to meet him on the grazing land. Enlil was a herder and they often met there, to talk and joke the night away.

She climbed the grassy slope. The sun was setting and she could see across the island to the silhouetted volcano. She found Enlil fast asleep with his herder's blankets around him. Zakhifa shook him awake.

'Sorry ...' He rubbed his face.

'I fall asleep all the time up here,' she said easily, sitting next to him. 'What else is there to do?'

Zakhifa grabbed a handful of long grass and tore it out of the ground. As Enlil watched, she threw it in mid-air. It flickered into soft flames and floated down in a bundle of weak fire. Enlil laughed encouragingly, as always, but Zakhifa sighed.

'Everyone thinks I've brought some enormous talent with me from the previous island.'

'Destruction,' Enlil nodded. 'I heard my parents talking. They think you did something on the previous island and all its power went into you, and now you've come to swallow us up too.'

Zakhifa stared, then laughed outright.

'What do they think I'm going to do once I've swallowed it up, including all my friends and mama and everything I love?'

'Well, they haven't got that far ...'

Zakhifa's teeth were chattering as the temperature dropped. She took the corner of Enlil's blanket and covered her knees with it, but it wasn't enough.

'En, can you wait while I go home to get a cloak? I feel cold.'

'Light a bigger fire.'

'It'll alarm the animals. Just wait for me.'

'Don't leave,' he said, his voice suddenly sharp.

A scream cut into the night.

'Decca!' Zakhifa said. She stood up, pure instinct.

Enlil also got up. He looked frightened.

'That's Decca! That's my sister!' said Zakhifa again. She began bounding down the hill.

'You shouldn't go,' said Enlil, stumbling behind her.

Something in his voice made her stop short.

'Why not?'

'It's Decca's initiation.'

Zakhifa stared at him a moment, then shot down the last of the slope shouting her sister's name.

Enlil followed far behind, out of breath. 'I'm sorry!' he yelled pitifully.

'You knew!' she screamed. 'How could you?'

There was no-one in the family huts. Everyone was in the big shelter used for common activities. Two men—woodsmen, judging by their obvious strength—were standing guard, arms crossed. Zakhifa ran at them and they grabbed her and slung her back.

'Don't interfere, Zakhifa' said one of the men, 'your sister is Becoming.'

'She's in pain!'

She pushed past them. They did not dare come in. Inside was a table covered with a cloth, animal fat lanterns, bowls of spiced oil boiling over short fires and long, thin blades on a delicate rack. On the table lay a body, its legs bare, its torso and face covered. A dozen women were holding the body down, cutting into it in silent, charged happiness. Decca. Dishes on the ground overflowed with thick red blood—her sister's blood.

'Stop!' she roared. 'Stop!'

She felt enormous with rage.

'Zakhi ...' said one of the women. It was Avani.

'What are you doing? Mama ...'

'We're doing what we've always done,' said another woman. Zakhifa recognised her as Ekha, one of her teachers.

'How can you do this?' she said.

'It's normal,' said another woman—Hirat, a butcher and tanner, her palms permanently dyed with animal blood. 'Your age is an age of energy and vigour. It must be siphoned and shared.'

'Get out of my way,' said Zakhifa in a low voice.

'Nobody questioned anything until *you* came along.'

Zakhifa stared from one woman to another. She had known them all her life, learned from them and worked alongside them, yet here they stood, united with each other against her. They stared at her like strangers. Through a gap between their bodies, Zakhifa saw a bone needle and a coarse black thread snaking on the table, next to Decca's skinny hand.

'Decca,' said Zakhifa urgently.

'Let her look. What's she going to do? It's done,' said Ekha.

The women moved away and began to clean up, kneeling carefully and picking up the bowls full of blood. Decca's eyes were closed.

'What you've done is wrong,' said Zakhifa.

'We do it out of love,' said Hirat.

'Love for *what*?' spat Zakhifa.

'Love for Decca. She is our daughter and we love her. We want to be like her. We want her to be like us. Decca is not your sister.'

'I'll fight you to protect her.'

'You see? All this aggression. This is why we drain it off. Initiations create peace and balance,' said Ekha.

'Zakhi, we try to put all the tasks and powers in equal proportion for everyone,' said Avani, 'it's only fair to skim the extra power from the young, where it only agonises them, and distribute it among the others.'

'What do you mean?'

Zakhifa realised that each woman was now standing holding a bowl full to the brim with thick red blood. Each one carefully lifted the bowl to her lips and drank deeply. As one, they drank again until all the blood in all the bowls was gone.

Gagging, terrified and disgusted, Zakhifa lunged forward and picked Decca up. She was light and cold. The women neither blocked her nor moved aside.

'I'm leaving,' said Zakhifa.

'*You* might be. She's not,' said Hirat.

'Mama?' Zakhifa turned to her mother.

'If you leave with Decca, Decca will die,' Avani explained. 'You don't know how to take care of her.'

Zakhifa's shoulders sagged.

'Why didn't you do it to me instead?' she said, her voice thick with pain.

'Nobody would drink *your* blood,' said Hirat, 'We rear everything here ourselves. We like to know where it comes from.'

Trying not to wail, determined not to beg, Zakhifa stared at the ground and bit the inside of her cheek. Avani took Decca from her and carried her out—the guards moved respectfully aside. The other women stayed, watching Zakhifa with unfriendly eyes. As her mood thickened, the air itself seemed to darken.

'What *is* that?' muttered Hirat, turning around.

'Those damn oil lanterns ... They're smoking,' said Ekha, coughing.

They waved the smoke away and tried to move the lanterns without burning themselves on the oil. Zakhifa's blood began to boil with anger and sorrow, revulsion and betrayal, grief and loss. Everything ran together in one ugly smear. It was hot inside the circle, and then it was more than hot, it was burning. Bright yellow flames licked the inside of the roof and slipped down the walls. Then the entire hut ripped into blazing fire. Zakhifa felt euphoric, surrounded by great waves of power. She imagined Yriana's blade slicing down, and the fire reached out for the women.

Zakhifa staggered to the entrance. She needed water. It was too hot and she couldn't think. She shouted hoarsely but the guards were nowhere to be seen. She ran out of the shelter—and straight into Lur's firm grip.

'Well, well,' said Lur, pulling into the undergrowth. 'I was just rinsing a dish in the stream, enjoying the moon, when that gangly friend of yours clattered past, gibbering, and I forced it out of him.'

'And now you'll force me to meet justice—as if *I'm* the miscreant—when all those women so prized in our circle can do something so vile …'

'No, child. I came to help. Where can we go that's safe?'

'Nowhere,' said Zakhifa bitterly. 'Unless … Yriana … we can find Yriana. She's the only one I can trust.'

Lur supported Zakhifa as they hurried to the field of golden stalks. The plants parted for them, guiding them to the centre, where Yriana waited. Her table and bench were gone. Instead, kicking and snorting in the heart of the circle, was a monster.

It was one of the work animals Yriana used. The creature possessed two broad, hinged wings of oily skin, strapped around with a tight harness of black braided ropes. A metal bit cut into its mouth. The animal trapped inside looked panicked, its eyes glowing deep blue.

'I've seen these creatures, but I've never seen them tamed before. A contraption like that won't work,' Zakhifa croaked.

'It does work,' said Yriana, with dark pride. She reached under her tunic and brought out the glass disc, strung on a strip of leather. 'I flash it, it catches the light and frightens them into submission. Moonlight works just as well.'

She took the disc and put it around Zakhifa's neck.

There was rustling, and a small dim light coming closer. It was a lantern on the end of a pole, held by the guards from the shelter. They were fighting through the resisting stalks.

'Quickly,' said Lur. She and Yriana helped Zakhifa onto the animal. She clung to its back, tucking her legs behind the stiff black wings.

'Where do I go?' whispered Zakhifa. She was trembling.

'To the *next* place,' said Yriana.

She slapped the animal's rump. Its wings creaked and sliced, it reared up and Zakhifa was heaved into the air in great arcs, until Yriana, Lur and the men were far beneath her. Zakhifa's glass disc pendant swung, catching the light. The lines of the risen sun struck the disc and shot into the circle. The grass began to smoke and singe and there, by the men's feet, flames sprang up. Yriana and Lur drew together.

The animal strained higher. Zakhifa's body sagged, but life came back to her as they drew away from the island. Close by, growing ever nearer, were the jagged black teeth of the volcano, Chamaca. Slabs of rock broke from the outside of the volcano and crashed downwards. The insides of the volcano were boiled red rock that fell over itself with a slashing sound. Zakhifa laughed as tears rolled down: Chamaca was her heart breaking. It would erupt and consume the island in a ravenous red gulp.

The animal's wings beat, gaining strength as they carried Zakhifa away.

HAPPY ENDING
Golnoosh Nour

This is my first trip outside of Iran. I'm happy once we're off the plane; the air hosts were so hostile they literally threw the food at us. It is midnight and we are finally at the terminal of Jeddah airport. For the first time in my life, I am in an Arabic chador, which makes me feel that I look like a demented bat, and yet I can feel people's glances. These glances, heavy as a baton, follow me all the way to passport control; I presume because I am the only 16-year-old on the flight. An insane-looking guy is shouting into a mic, warning us not to carry drugs, and then we wait in a queue for three hours. By we, I mean, me, my parents and one thousand smelly oldies. But truth be told, I am very excited, not just because I can finally see the House of God, but because I like travelling and seeing new places.

Everybody says this irreligious city hates us Iranians more than all the other cities in Saudi Arabia. After five hours of queuing for immigration, an old man faints. When it's my turn, the passport officers look at me as though they want to purchase me, my mother telling me, 'Correct your *hejab*! Your hair is showing.'

I don't think the officer minds my *hejab* as he is pronouncing my name as though he were singing a pop song, 'Fa-e-zeh!' whilst shaking his head, flashing a row of crooked yellow teeth that make me feel nauseated.

After that we board a bus to the holy city of Medina. I try to remember stuff from school about Prophet Muhammad's victories here; sadly, my mind is blank. The bus driver is driving so fast I think I might vomit any second. The thought of being smashed to bits in a bus in the middle of a desert makes me feel even worse. Passengers whisper that the bus driver is a 'Paki' and that's why he drives like a *'heyvoon'*. I'll never figure out why *heyvoon* is an insult; animals are cute, far cuter than most people.

The only thing our tour leader, Mr. Eslami, does is to *salavaat* in the mic. *'Allahumma salli ala Muhammad wa Ali Muhammad.'* Saying hello to the prophet Muhammad and his family. I wonder if the prophet is watching us. So, I keep accompanying Mr. Eslami sending *salavaats* until I am half-conscious in the tremors of our bus and the monotonous chatter of the passengers, my head on my mother's shoulder. But when it is night time the dark makes me feel awake again; the passengers are no longer talking; I can hear some of them snore like giants. I widen my half-open eyes and encounter the most beautiful scene I've ever seen in my life, the glittery sky of the desert.

I fall into the deepest slumber ever. I dream about my school friend, Leila, who snickered when I informed her I was going to Mecca with my parents. She said I should avoid those 'crocodile-eating Arabs' and stay in Tehran, turning our house into a party den, with her and her secret boyfriend, Arash. The truth is Arash creeps me out more than all these chador-wrapped passengers, but I tolerate his existence, because sometimes when Leila and I are alone, we cuddle, our bodies rubbing subtly against one another and I don't want these moments to end.

When my father taps my feet and wakes me up, I am dreaming of Leila telling me she killed Arash and I need to help her bury him. And I'm looking for the least suspicious place in a godforsaken garden for Arash's burial. I vividly see Leila's lips shine, plumped up thanks to her new lip gloss, the one that got her expelled from school for a day.

We arrive at Medina after two hazy days on the bus. As soon as we arrive in our 3-star hotel, I return to my deathlike slumber.

'You have slept enough! Everybody is performing *ghusl* now!' my dad exclaims. I notice he is wet and naked, with only a white robe around his waist, concealing his private parts. I sit on the bed, and look at my mother who is standing beside my father, staring at me. She is in a white chador, so white it is blinding me. They look like ghosts. 'Get up! Time for *ghusl!*' she tells me as though I do not already know my task. 'We have to be in the hotel lobby for prayers and then the mosque in fifteen minutes!'

My *ghusl* revives me. I happily wrap my white chador around my wet body.

'You look like an angel!' my father says. And we head to the lobby where we meet all our fellow pilgrims. We pray collectively until I find myself yawning. My mother is secretly punching me through her chador. An old man announces, 'It has always been my wish to say azan in Medina before I die!'

Mr. Eslami responds, 'Please do.'

He is singing his azan but seems so old that I think he might pass away in the midst of it; I worry his wish might not come true. Everybody apart from me is weeping. My mother manages to frown at me whilst crying. I try to shed at least one tear and succeed in doing two whilst staring at the sparkling grey tiles. When I feel the weight of someone's glance, I look up to catch a young woman staring at me; she and I are the only people who are not weeping. I almost smile at her but manage to suffocate it, I don't want other people to think I am laughing at the old man's moving azan.

'Aren't you hungry?' my mother asks me worriedly after the old man is done. I wonder what she'd tell me if I inform her of my feelings towards Leila. Does this woman know anything about me really? Apart from how my stomach works? She is already gathering a good amount of *jahaz* for me; television, floral china, silver spoons, for my life with my future husband. I just hope he won't be as creepy as Arash, otherwise my murderous dreams might come true. My father sometimes yells at her that he doesn't have the money to purchase things we do not need right away. But my mother always mumbles that the most suitable suitor will arrive as soon as I am an eighteen-year-old university student. The thought of being a university student both scares and excites me.

Before I know it, I am in the hotel's so-called restaurant, a tight canteen. Every pilgrim has to sit behind the same ginormous table. I quickly spot the young woman with whom I made eye contact. She is not in a chador. She looks like she is in her early twenties, with her young husband, and I presume his parents. She's just wearing a *manteau* and a headscarf like we normally do in Iran.

Suddenly, our tour leader points at her, everybody including myself turn our heads not to miss out on this most thrilling scene. And these are Mr. Eslami's exact words to her: 'The Arabs will abuse you.'

Imagining her response, I stop breathing. I am ashamed that I am praying for a fight, the bloodier the better, her screeching at him, plunging her long nails into his hairy neck, with other passengers getting involved. I hear my mother muttering, 'Oh my God!'

However, the rebellious woman kills the suspense by completely blanking Mr. Eslami, as though our tour leader were nothing but an annoying dog barking under a tree. She isn't even looking at him and carries on chewing the greasy rice. This brutal dismissal makes me like her even more, I want to become like her. Later on, I listen to her complaining to her husband; 'this place is dirty'. Her husband hisses at her, but she adds, 'it actually stinks!' I am not certain why, but her complaining words are a soothing melody to my ears.

I know now Medina is interesting to me mostly because of her. I look at her when we sit behind the table in the canteen. She doesn't confront me about my stares. Sometimes she looks back, and smiles. I smile back. There is something about her that reminds me of Leila. They both seem like they want to tell me an exciting secret.

It is day five and, if I'm honest, I am sick of being in Medina and praying in its beautiful mosques at five in the morning. All I can hear is people fighting over fruit portions, 'Somebody stole my dates!' a woman is shrieking whilst looking at me. I want to beat her to death. But I know if I step close to her, I'll probably die from the stench of her sweat.

Another woman obviously has a cold and is coughing, literally in my throat, I run to the bathroom and puke in the toilet.

Back in the hotel room, I cry, saying I want to be back in Iran. That I do not want to be in Saudi Arabia. My dad is shouting that he is in debt for making this international trip happen; that I should be grateful. I do not back down, I cry louder, he lowers his voice and says he'll take me shopping. He takes us to a shop in the Medina Mall, the seller runs to my father and points at me, asking, 'how much?'

I do not look at him. I dismiss him, like that woman who dismissed Mr. Eslami. I can tell my dad is shaken. I hear him say in surprisingly fluent English, 'We don't do dis. We don't sell our girls.'

And then, without waiting for the seller's response, my parents and I escape.

After spending seven days in Medina, we are finally on our way to the sacred Mecca, our final destination.

When I was younger, I used to dream about being in the House of God, that magical black cube, Ka'ba. However, on the bus from Medina to Mecca, I vomit on my mother whilst repeating that special prayer for the hundredth time. Mr. Eslami is shouting the prayer in the bus and everybody else is supposed to repeat it with him until we reach Mecca. A young man is banging his head on the window. To my gratitude, my mother does not make a scene about being vomited on, and instead swiftly changes her pukey chador, quietly burying it in a black plastic bag. My sick smells like the food in our Medina hotel. I'm impressed by how skilfully my mother changes without showing one bit of her body. It's like magic. I'm certain this is God showing his tricks.

After approximately eight hours on this bus, we finally arrive at Mecca. Although it is night time, we have to do the rituals right away as we are *mohrem* by now. We circle around the House of God seven times, you are not allowed to look back, even though people are pushing you hard. My dad shouts, 'don't push!' at other *mohrems*. My mum shouts back at him, 'Don't do that, you'll stop being a *mohrem* if you shout.'

After this we have to do our Safa and Marwa seven times. Despite my exhaustion and sickliness, I'm pleased that I vividly remember the history of the two hills from our religious studies classes at school. And I am thrilled walking the distance between them for the first time, visualising Hazrat-e Hajar with her baby Ismail, looking for water. And the water from Zamzam well does taste pure and divine. But it also reminds me of the bottled mineral water called Zamzam in Iran. After this, we have to cut our nails and hair.

Because we are Shia Muslims we have to circle another seven times around Ka'ba after our Safa Marwa; for the first time in my life I wish I had been Sunni so I could get some rest. I circle as close as possible to Ka'ba. My father tells me to stay away; I can't bring myself to tell him I intend to walk small circles in order to finish faster.

When we finally reach our neat hotel room, I can't believe all the rituals ended, and I'm happy this is just Umrah, not *Hajj* which is much more cumbersome. And truth be told, I don't think I'll be able to do that in twenty years or so.

Now we have seven days to actually explore Mecca, the city of God. But I feel I need more time to recover from my exhaustion.

As soon as we reach our new hotel, our tour leaders warn us about the black cleaners, telling us they're from Africa and have a history of raping women and children in the shiny elevators.

However, most waiters are Iranians who aren't actual waiters, but do this for free for the sake of God. They are actually rich Iranians from the bazar, one of them gives me extra portions.

I'm happy to see that we have a spacious room in our hotel: a double bed for my parents and a single bed for me. The sheets are super clean – even by my mother's standards.

The tour leaders also tell us to let the men in the cabs first, otherwise the cab drivers might kidnap the women.

On our second day in Mecca, my parents wake me up at five in the morning, so we can go to the Grand Mosque and pray collectively. My body is stiff, and I am certain that if I opened my eyes, they would bleed. I beg them to leave me and, to my gratitude and surprise, they do, telling me today is an exception, and I will have to accompany them tomorrow. When I'm still in bed, half-asleep, I think and dream about Leila. I imagine her beside me on the bed, holding me, caressing me, and I touch my nipples, convincing myself it's Leila caressing them, they get so hard I don't know what to do with them. Leila has told me how she touches herself when her parents are away. I put my hand inside my cotton knickers, I play with my body until I feel dizzy. When it happens, I fall asleep again, dreaming about one of the black cleaners in the hotel caressing my breasts. I enjoy it so much I cry.

Tomorrow arrives sooner than expected. But I feel energetic and ready to visit the House of God again. Once we reach the Grand Mosque, the most sacred mosque in the world, we realise it is packed and we have to push other worshippers a little bit. They do not seem happy about this. We can see Ka'ba and how it is encircled by the stunning Grand Mosque. I like the glory of the Grand Mosque which makes Ka'ba look more like a monstrous black cube. I feel slightly guilty about not feeling as spiritual as I should. Suddenly I miss school. I miss Leila, her soft hands, her spine visible through her grey *manteau*. I miss us sitting on our bench during the geometry class, subtly touching each other's trembling hands, the geometry teacher talking about the most tedious geometric questions, we pretending to be thinking about the solution, but actually thinking about unthinkable things that have nothing to do with geometry.

Unlike many other geeky students, Leila and I rarely worry about exams, because we cheat like our life depends on it. Sometimes I wonder if we cheat for the sake of grades, or for the sake of cheating itself, because that thrill is the most rewarding part, in my opinion. Leila and I usually carry the maths and science solutions and formulas on toilet paper which secretly emerges out of our long grey sleeves during the exams. We know how to look clueless and innocent too, so the stupid teachers are never suspicious. Sometimes we even swap our exam papers as we have similar handwriting. After surviving each exam we hold each other and laugh like mad people. And I wrap my hands around Leila's spine. I feel so alive that I know I shall never die.

I feel guilty for not being able to concentrate on my *namaz*. I am standing beside my mother and a thousand other women, and my father is standing in front of us with thousands of other men. I close my eyes and imagine Leila's spine, how slight it feels in my arms those rare times that we embraced in her bed. Thank goodness her mother has a job, and is not sniffing around the house like mine 24/7, scrubbing away the invisible dust, and watching Turkish TV shows about marriage in which all the actresses look nothing like us and all look the same: balloon boobs, fake-tanned skin, dyed blonde hair, balloon lips. Whenever Leila catches a glimpse of them she hisses, 'these whores are made of plastic.'

And I always feel like replying, 'don't worry, you are more beautiful than them.' But I just laugh—quietly, so my mum won't hear a thing.

In the evening, after we wake up from our afternoon nap, we decide to do what every Iranian is supposed to do in Umrah: shopping. Although, we have to be careful with money as we don't have much, especially after this expensive trip. I can't wait to explore the shopping malls of Mecca that many rave about. My mother told us only before this trip that one of our neighbours who just returned from Umrah, purchased an amazing refrigerator for her daughter's *jahaz*. She then added that such a fine refrigerator would shut the daughter's future husband's family right up.

I don't mind my mother's normally annoying marriage anecdotes as I have noticed she and my father have exempted me from going to the mosque at five in the morning every day. I just sleep on my comfortable bed until nine when they are back and we all go for breakfast. I feel truly blessed for having such open-minded parents. I can see other teenagers and even children in Mecca being dragged to mosques and collective prayers every morning. I see the pain on their strained faces, and this makes me love my parents more than ever. I just noticed I have no idea how many days it has been since we have left Iran.

When we finally get to the most luxurious shopping mall in Mecca, Centerpoint, I realise all the amazing things I heard about it are true. It is ginormous. There are actual fashion brands such as Chanel and Dior that I have only heard about from my classmates. Everything shines in this multi-storeyed mall, including the escalators that are half-golden, half-black, and everything else looks silvery white. My parents buy me the cheapest tops and trousers and a gold-plated necklace with a heart pendant. I don't tell them that I'm saving one of the tops for Leila. The maroon one. Because Leila only wears dark colours, and this is a contributing factor to her fatal coolness.

My dad informs us that this is the rich part of Mecca. As we are waving for a cab outside the mall, I see so many teenagers and even kids driving. Occasionally, some of the boys hold their heads out of the car windows, shouting excitedly at me as though they were in a circus and I, the main performer – despite the fact that I'm lost in my Arabic chador, holding two heavy shopping bags. Their behaviour makes me so embarrassed in front of my parents that I feel like melting into the hot ground, but my dad gives me a shy half-hug, telling me, this is normal behaviour in Arab countries.

I wake up at eight am, too hungry to care about being raped by cleaners, I decide to go downstairs. There are quite a few other pilgrims around; I keep my eyes fixed on the floor, almost acting blind so they will not approach me asking me the most personal questions, sizing up whether I am marriage material for their son. I have heard stories about them doing this to my cousins. And not to be mean, but my cousins are not even pretty. My heart thumps hard when I bump into the young woman who is still chadorless. In Mecca! She says hello to me, widening her already wide eyes. But my heart is beating so hard I can barely respond. I hate the thought that she probably just sees me as a cute child and doesn't take me seriously. She possibly pities me just as I'm pitying people younger than me. I'm not sure if I want to caress her or look like her when I'm a fully-grown woman. Perhaps both. Whatever my feelings are towards her, I'm sure Leila wouldn't approve of them, so I'd rather stay loyal to my only friend. Oh, how I've missed her.

It's been a few days since it's occurred to me that my parents have been playing a game with me. That we've actually moved to Saudi Arabia for my father's job, and this is their way of dragging me here, to tell me it's just a two-week fancy Umrah. And the real journey hasn't even begun yet. I have nightmares of being kidnapped in the back of a cab, or being lost in one of the sparkly shopping malls, not being able to find my way out or even ask for help. Finding the compulsory Arabic language they teach us at school completely useless, as I am unable to utter even one word.

But the happy ending is actually happening: my parents just in-formed me this is our last day in Mecca and we're leaving shortly. We are genuinely going back to Iran. I see our tickets in my father's hands.

Even my mother admits she's missing Iran, but she would like to do another Umrah soon, staring hard at me, taking the strangest sort of pleasure at my annoyance. I'm not saying anything; but I'm not thanking my father for taking us travelling like I thought I would.

When I am coming out of our hotel, carrying my heavy suitcase, the tour mullah who's supposed to help us says under his breath, *'Fa Tabarak Allah ahsan ul Khaliqeen.'* And he does not even offer to take my suitcase. I am irritated at his creepy praise, but my mum is telling me he said it because I am both pretty and chaste. I do not even respond, having learned from the beautiful disdain of the young woman.

When we reach the Jeddah airport the only thing that wakes me up is the officers winking at me, or perhaps I'm having a nightmare again as it's two in the morning.

When the plane finally lands in Iran, I feel so free that I could already be in Leila's bed, pressing her warm body to my heart.

THE BEACH
Hedy Hume

The first place I remember in my life is Abergowydd. The shoreline by the town itself is no place for picnicking, with all the fishing vessels and yachts—but some ways south over the hills, accessible only by a seldom-trod footpath, is a tiny peninsula of shoreline. At its point are huge, jagged chunks of basalt reaching out toward the distant Irish coast.

The sheer distance from town dissuades litterers from making the trek, as my father rejoiced on every trip. The shore is rocky on the north side of the peninsula, sandy on the south, and in between is a gradual transition from one to the other, stones embedded here and there in the sand like teeth.

If you stand on the rocky side, and walk slowly to the other, looking down all the while, you will watch the stones take millions of years to wear down and disintegrate into yellow dust. I was only a few months old on my first visit, the first of many family holidays to that place, and my memory of that time is so much dust; immaterial, timeless, and irrevocable by the conscious mind held captive to the drudgery of daily life.

I return to the beach at Abergowydd, and the sea breeze on my face and the fine briny smell carried by it rebuilds the blurry half-memory like a photographer's darkroom, like a massage for the hippocampi of my brain. Hippokampos—the fish-horse of ancient myth. The dust reassembles into stone, into the bedrock of my life before my self. For the briefest instant everything material is forgotten, and I am a free-floating consciousness surrounded only by the rhythm of the tides and the laughter of gulls.

On my second visit to Abergowydd, I was seven. I had endured almost three years of school, and read far more books than I was expected to. My teacher would tell us about dolphins, that they were sea creatures, and I would add that dolphins are mammals, unlike sharks, and that there are many different kinds of dolphin. My teachers complained that I was 'disrupting the other children's learning'. We were not supposed to discover these things for ourselves; we were supposed to be told what The Facts were.

I had some magpie-like tendencies at that age, and a very basic understanding of geology, so when we reached Abergowydd at low tide, I loudly declared that I was off to find 'crystals'. Mum groaned, because she had wanted to lie down in the sun, but she followed me, because it was the eighties and she would never let me out of her sight on holiday. Dad relaxed on the sand. Mum asked him to watch my sister in her carrier, but he ignored her, and so one-year-old Trisha joined us on my expedition.

We trotted half the width of the peninsula, and when we reached the hinterland of sand and stones I began my search. Forensically, I examined each individual rock in my path, gradually moving forward until I had left the sand behind.

After five minutes, all forensic methods were abandoned as I started galloping over the hillocks of small stones, this way and that, and still the precious crystals that I was certain could be found on this random stretch of shore eluded me. I gained speed and lost even more direction, and even Mum's calls to 'settle down' and 'pack it in' had no effect on me.

Ignoring her warnings and the sound of the waves, with my eyes fixed on the ground beneath me, I have no idea that I am inching closer and closer to the water as I absent-mindedly clamber onto the feet of the basalt rocks— until I am struck by a wave that drenches me from my t-shirt to my underwear.

I scream in surprise and dash back towards the safety of dry land, while Trisha screams in solidarity, and Mum laughs. 'It's freezing!' I yell in outrage. 'Freezin'!' echoes Trisha, and that was her first word.

We went to Abergowydd again the next summer, arriving alongside a week-long storm. Mum started grumbling about the rain as our car came down the hill into town, and the grumbling escalated along with the weather.

'Why didn't you check the weather?' she demanded of my father over breakfast, in a whisper so the pensioners at the next table didn't hear, while rain hammered on the windows and the wind pushed bins down the road.

'It said sunny skies all weekend,' he replied.

'Sunny skies in the Midlands! We're in *Wales*. You have to actually look at the screen! You just don't *care!*'

Dad grunted, continued eating his boiled egg, and filled an answer in his crossword. He just didn't care.

Most of that holiday I spent indoors, playing I-Spy with Trisha and reading. I soon finished *Treasure Island* and that week's issue of the *Beano*, and was reduced to those tourist trap pamphlets you find in every hotel and B&B. Mum ended up buying three cinema tickets to keep us all sane, while Dad stayed in the hotel room with his puzzle magazine. The only films I had seen before then were Dad's boring westerns on video cassette, and I only saw half of each before I was sent to bed.

The little picture house is crowded, and damp, and smells of rotting, over-priced popcorn; but none of this matters to me. Along with everyone else under the age of ten, I am transfixed by The Little Mermaid. *The screen is huge and we are engulfed in a wave of bright colours and joyful music. Ariel is the most beautiful vision I have seen in my life. I love her and want to be her. I want to be—wait for it—part of her world.*

There were significant obstacles standing in the way of this goal: not only was I not a natural redhead, but I was also a boy—or rather, I had been led to believe that I was a boy by the obstetrician, my parents and a society obsessed with creating borders around human experience and forcing people into the spaces between. Some will call it 'scientific' to divide the world based on their own undeveloped ignorance and prejudice, but any actual scientist will tell you that a hypothesis is tested by experimentation and evidence—the evidence is not twisted to fit preexisting belief.

I never heard the word transgender, or even transsexual, spoken aloud while I was young; after all, this was the time of Section 28. But every teacher, picture book and television programme drilled into my developing mind what a 'normal' man or woman should be. Anything so outside of that norm as a woman with a deep voice was to be treated with mockery or suspicion.

And yet despite all that, I wanted to be a mermaid. When I said so after leaving the Abergowydd cinema, my family laughed.

In October, at the dinner table, Nana asks me what I will be for Halloween. 'Ariel,' I reply excitedly. There are loud, angry words. 'I want to be a mermaid!' I insist through tears. I am thrown bodily into my bedroom and I am locked inside. I hear my parents talking that night through the gap under the door. I hear my father call me a fairy. I am confused; I had said quite clearly that I wanted to be a mermaid.

We returned to Abergowydd every year or so, and the weather was always better than the trip in '89. I went swimming every day we spent at the beach; it was a good way to stay apart from the others.

I ended up being very good at swimming and in secondary school I started getting certificates. Dad started calling me 'the little merman'; half a compliment, half a snide joke that was more venomous than even he realised.

At thirteen, my body started growing hair in unwelcome places. My skin became oily and ridden with acne. In the only sex education lesson I received, I was told that I should be happy about these things, because I was becoming a man. I did not have the words or the understanding to express why the idea of becoming a man tied my stomach in knots and made me lie awake staring at the ceiling. It was not the kind of information that could be found in my local library; I had no idea where to look on the internet, and I knew my parents checked the browser history. The closest I could reach was my old dream of being a mermaid.

So I convinced a friend to help dye my hair red. My parents were angrier than I had ever seen them when I came home; but even after a week grounded without TV or internet, my hair was still red. Dad threatened to shave it all off, but I stayed firm, and Mum talked him down, and my hair was still red. This was a small victory, but it was the first victory of my life.

My parents had said they wouldn't take me on holiday 'looking like that', yet when summer came around we were off to Abergowydd as usual. Those were sweltering days, and the sea was coolly comforting—a brilliant blue.

I go diving without my goggles. I sink down, down, and settle onto the seabed, tiny fishes darting about away from me. I watch a crab slowly march into the deep while sun-dappled waves dance distantly overhead.

The crab vanishes into a silty gloom that my feeble human eyes cannot penetrate, but I keep looking. It is not exactly an abyss I stare into. I am welcomed. I am an amphibian of the Devonian period who came ashore to lay my eggs, and now I return to the deep where I belong. Then I realise that I need to breathe.

I don't know how long I was underwater that afternoon, but it was long enough for Dad to stir from his sun lounger, swim out to rescue me, and bar me from swimming for the rest of the holiday.

This incident was never mentioned afterwards, but it put an end to family beach getaways. The words 'swimming' was never spoken aloud at home, nor was 'suicide'. I did not return to Abergowydd for five years.

My A-levels passed by in a blur, desperate as I was to get them out of the way and escape from life in a hopeless town and a home where I waded through the ghosts of unspoken conversations. My heart was set on a marine biology course at an olde worlde university on Wales' northern coast.

This was my best hope, and my parents did their best to dash it. 'What you need is a *job*,' said Mum, so very confident. I knew that being condemned to meaningless work in that meaningless town with meaningless people would only drive me back to the deep, so I begged and pleaded, and promised to pay back the loan they would need to cover my tuition fees. Finally, they gave in. After Mum and Dad had said their awkward goodbyes and driven away England-ward, I felt a weight fall from my shoulders—or maybe what I was discarding was a long-held disguise.

I was a raw gemstone plucked fresh from the earth, and the world battered and cut me trying to render a shape pleasing to them—but now I held the chisel. The self is not, and is not meant to be, a stagnant pool drained until it is empty. The self is a wide, wide ocean, always in flux, ever altered by tides and currents, filled with sparkling reefs and deep trenches of truth, wonders lying out of sight—and we are the moon that weaves those tides like thread upon a loom.

I did not actively look for the LGBT student group. Self-loathing—and the loathing for others that had been taught to me—still had its hold, and warned me that there was no-one truly like myself; or if there were, they would disgust me. But I was drawn to their stall at the freshers' fair anyway, just as a lost dolphin using echolocation finds the way back to its pod.

We had pub nights and coffee-shop afternoons. We had film screenings, and long walks on the beach and in the hinterlands of Ceredigion. We talked and talked and talked and I listened and learned, and at the age of almost nineteen, surrounded by such wonderful friends, I called myself a woman, and by a better name than the one that was forced upon me at birth. Can you guess what?

I return to Abergowydd on my twentieth birthday, piled into a borrowed van with a pack of friends. We come down the hill onto the beach in the late afternoon and set up the barbecue on the sandy side, and as we eat our Quorn sausages, we are bathed in red light from the farewell of day, cast over—and then gradually behind—the great basalt cliff. My hair is red too; a defiant shade, but it harmonises with the peaceful and promising tones of sunset.

We stretch out on the sand, and I tell the story of how I taught my baby sister her first word. It gets a big laugh, probably because everyone is now quite drunk. Snow gets out their guitar, and we all sing badly the pop hits of the mid-nineties. Then Mia remembers that we have forgotten one very important song.

Happy birthday, dear Ariel, happy birthday to you.

We were woken in the early morning by the screaming of a seagull in our faces and the screaming of a hangover in our heads. Faint threads of dawn-light stretched over the hill towards town, and since I alone could not get back to sleep, I gave my legs a stretch.

I find myself knee deep in the waves. It is cold; the sea thinks it is still night-time, but of course it is always night-time under the sea. The shadow of the basalt cliff towers over me. It reminds me of my father and of pain, both in the past and waiting in the murky future. For a long minute, I think about swimming out into the Irish Sea, and diving down to the bottom of the ocean where all pain could be left behind.

Then I turn around, and rejoin my friends, to whom I owe everything. We eat our breakfast, and gather up our litter, and we live.

GOING UP, GOING DOWN
Nathan Evans

#MeAt20 has circumnavigated the planet as swiftly as Covid-19 to bring Guy to my screen, just as I first remember him. But my memory (as much of me) is not what it used to be.

I can clearly see the clock—cross-haired at the end of Beaumont Street—as I sat in the backseat, ready to shoot or be shot. Though it can't have been like that: Beaumont must have been double yellow-lined and we parked in some side-street waiting, necks craning for those gilded hands to minute towards eleven.

Of course, we were early—Dad has always been a devotee of contingency—the three of us steaming the windscreen, wipers metronoming and fluffy dice swinging. Or maybe, by then, Mum had exchanged it for a fluffy Forever Friend; the one she'd given me was mortarboarded. This meant they were proud: first in the family to go to university and I *only went and got into Oxford,* didn't I.

'Prawn cocktail ... Graham won't want them.'

Mum—distributing snacks from the pre-pack on her lap—wasn't wrong: flesh had not passed my lips since I'd heard Morrissey declare 'Meat Is Murder'.

'Cheese and onion?'

It wasn't The Smiths playing, I'm certain, as Dad would've been listening to their archenemy Radio One: music and Mum's interruptions were ruining my reading of the Complete-Shakespearean tome I'd won in school prizegiving. *Hamlet* was my favourite; still is. *Ay, madam, it is common*; as, I thought, were crisps.

'No thanks!'

'Someone just got out that car!'

Dad drew our attention to a motor similarly piled with possessions but rather newer than our own, and to a guy running through the rain. I didn't know it then, but it was him.

'He's going in!'

'Go on, Graham!'

'It's not time!'

Mother's perm shook. Was it permed by that point? Probably not: we'd left the eighties behind a few years back and hair had straightened out.

'If you're not going, I am!'

The thought of her talking for me—of her saying the wrong thing—was enough to send me running.

Approaching those college portals, I was Dorothy approaching The Emerald City. There was no knocker, just a buzzer but a door incised inside the main one did swing open. And—handsome as a young Hugh Grant in *Maurice* (which, to Mum's disgust, I'd stayed up to watch)—the guy was there, his voice so loud, so clear it might have rung the bell up in the clock tower.

'After you.'

'Thank you.'

My voice came without its own amplification system. I stepped in, the door clicked shut and he was gone. *Freshers coming up please report to the Porter's Lodge,* instructed the sign. Which—where I come from—translates as *new arrivals report to reception.*

The porter had a funny uniform, though not in emerald green; I summoned my most confident articulation and gave my name, scanning the grander-sounding ones on the pigeonholes surrounding us as he dived down his list and eventually surfaced.

'There it is.'

The door opened and—key in one hand, the other balancing a box brimming with mugs, kettle, cutlery and some 'fancy teas' Mum had got on offer in Sainsbury's—I stepped in. Magnolia, modern, the room was something of a disappointment. Hoping to avoid loans and get by on my grant alone, I'd taken the cheapest option. But still, I'd been envisaging something more … grandiloquent.

'I'd have nets up those windows.'

Mother had materialised at my shoulder and was looking down her nose at the *quadrangle* below.

'It's my room. I'll do what I want with it.'

I'd overstepped: she dropped the case she'd carried up three flights down on my feet.

'Best get the rest before it gets wet.'

At the gate, I gave Dad a hug. He ducked into the driver's seat as quickly as he could. Was it rain making Mum's mascara run? Her hug lasted long enough for me to clock the guy again—fringe dripping, eyes blinking, waving off his parents in their Volkswagen.

'Come on, Susan!'

Outside the gate, more cars were beeping: Dad's always been reluctant to take up space someone else could be taking. I told Mum I'd *call soon* and then they were gone. For the first time, I was free of them.

Something maudlin from Morrissey's latest album was probably playing and, in the background, walls would've been freshly-plastered with his image as I looked mine over in the mirror. A shiny suit (fifty quid in Willenhall market) jarred with my headstrong hair (alas, no longer). I attempted to *cap* it, checked my invite. 'Shit.' Unlike my father, I'm always late.

I was attempting to adjust my *gown* when Professor Gordon's door swung open. 'Ah, Master Sadler. We were wondering when you were going to join.'

He'd already been joined by two other students, caps under arm. The guy was one of them. I felt myself blush for not knowing the clothing etiquette (and because—when he looked at me—I may as well have been naked). I brushed off my mortarboard, took the hands I was offered. Charlotte and—of course—Guy. Unlike mine, their palms were dry.

'Are you settling in okay?' The professor handed me a sherry.

'Yes, thank you.' I sipped politely.

'Where are you from?' asked Lottie (as she preferred to be known).

'The West Midlands.' I found her interest unnerving.

'I was trying to work out the accent.' Her pronunciation was the received one.

Guy's too, 'Which school?'

'Just a comprehensive. You?'

Guy went to Eton, Lottie to Bryanston. She'd been travelling since leaving. 'India was lifechanging.'

I'd spent my summer working. 'Just with my Dad. He's a builder.'

Guy had interned a whole year with his father. 'At the Duke of York theatre.'

I realised I shouldn't have had the second sherry as we toddled to the *refectory* (the dining room, obviously). By the time starters started arriving, I was starving. Back home, dinner was at dinnertime. And tea was six not seven. No idea which silverware I should've been using, I copied what Lottie was doing.

'I can't believe your father is Teddy Terry!'

Since discovering Guy's dad was one of those actors who popped up in period dramas, she'd lost interest in me and was talking over my head to Guy, who'd been seated on my other side. Either side of them stretched *subfusc*ed students (basically, wearing suits and gowns) three-pronged to a *high table* of *dons*, framed forebears hanging over them. White-gloved waiters worked the room with wine; my pores were pouring: Mum always said *red with meat and white with fish* but what about vegetarian?

White was what we'd had at home. Christmas and special occasions. But the wine I sat sipping was nothing like *Blue Nun*. I wasn't sure I liked it. Or the beer I stood sipping later in the bar. And the more I drank, the harder it became to keep my soul window-paned each time Guy's eyes came in my direction. But they weren't really coming for me, why would they? Anyone could see his eyes were only for Lottie, whose interest was—by that point—quite naked between us. And everyone around us was so bright, so brilliant that I didn't feel I could join the conversation. And knowing no-one would miss me, I took a last sip and out I slipped—from old quad to new one, new room, new bed—lyrics already forming on my lips. *And if you're so clever, why do you sleep alone tonight?* Morrissey. Before he unbuttoned that sequinned young skin and a belligerent old badger stepped from within. *Love is natural and real, but not for such as you and I, my love.* CD spinning, I lay listening. *Oh mother, I can feel the soil falling over my head.* Cuddling the teddy my mother had given me like the best Brideshead cliché.

When I woke in the morning, clutching my cranium, it took some moments to ascertain that the pounding was on the door of my room. Hearing it open, I retrieved some semblance of clothing from the floor and—rounding the corner from my sleeping area—found a woman there.

'Just emptying the bin.'

She must have been about the same age as Mum, wearing a uniform.

'I'm Brenda.'

And was that a West Midlands accent?

'Your scout.'

Scout was what they called their cleaners.

'Graham,' was all I could muster.

'Don't worry, I won't be touching your CDs or anything.' Bypassing the music-system I'd been given when I turned eighteen, she seamlessly lifted liner from bin and lowered in a fresh one. 'My son goes bonkers if I get near his.'

And she was gone, her fleeting familiarity leaving an unexpected pang. The digits of the music system told me it was after ten: Mum would be heading home from her own cleaning round.

The phone was at the bottom of the *staircase* my room was on, so it must have been shared by about twenty students.

'Hello?'

I fed in a first coin. 'Hi, Mum.' An umbilical string stretched taut across county lines and I was connected again.

'What you doing calling this time? Cost a blooming arm and leg, it will!' She wasn't wrong—the phone was eating through change—but I could tell she was made up to hear from her son. 'Didn't think you'd call *so* soon.'

It would've been too much of a climb-down for someone who, as a teenager, had so fiercely cultivated their independence to admit I was missing my mother, so we talked about what I'd eaten, had I made any friends ...?

'Got to go, Mum.'

Someone was waiting—I could see their feet tapping on the first landing. But she's always known how to read me, even when I think I'm giving nothing away.

'Never mind. You'll meet people soon.'

Certain Mother hadn't meant *this*, I hurried to Brasenose College, fingering the flyer in my pocket. *Too nervous to visit us at Fresher's Fair? Come here.* Xeroxed and *pigeon-posted*, the anonymous missive could've been addressed to me directly because that's what had happened, exactly.

I'd signed for the *Union*—pricey, but the first few debates were free—and *Oxford University Dramatic Society*. I was debating whether I dared enter their *Cuppers* competition for Freshers when I found myself rabbited in the headlamps of a *Gay Soc* stallholder—for what seemed hours—before hop-skipping to the safety of the *Music Society*.

I skipped again, past the *Russell Room*. Even if I hadn't learnt the name by heart—terrified I might have to pull that pink paper from my pocket—I would've known I was in the right place, sign-posted as it was from the Lodge, bold as bollocks. I loitered under cloisters, sublimating fear into Shakespeare—*now might I do it pat*—while attempting to look casual. Casual was the look I'd gone for that evening—Morrissey *Your Arsenal* tee, blackest jeans, DMs (obligatory)—nothing too overtly gay. No-one was going in so I sauntered back past, trying to see in. But the shutters were down. Then two guys breezed by and—casual as anything—bowled in. Without allowing myself another *muddy-mettled* moment, I followed them.

In a far from full room, the air was full-fruited with sibilance. Mother's voice rose above them: *people like us aren't like that.* I should never have come, hid behind hair-curtains as I bee-lined for the bar.

'Didn't expect to see you here.'

I was draining my plastic chalice when Guy entered stage left, handsome.

'I could say the same.'

I could feel myself turning the colour of my wine. (I'd tried red that evening).

'Graham—Julian.' Guy had a gentleman with him.

'Charmed.' The gentleman offered a flaccid hand.

Guy offered, 'Another?' As he headed for the bar, I looked after him like a lifeboat off Newfoundland.

'Can't say I think much of the talent.' Julian was surveying the scene. 'So how do you know Guy then?' An eyebrow arched for the ceiling.

'Uh ... Um ...' Struggling as I was with basic phonics, who would have guessed I was there to study English? 'He's in my tutor group. How do you know him?'

'Intimately.' Julian moued, maleficently.

Guy returned with a rubber ring. 'So how long have you been out then?'

'I'm not.' I gulped more wine. 'My parents wouldn't understand.'

'I thought that. But mine were fine.'

'Darling, please! Teddy Terry is even camper than me!' Julian slapped Guy playfully.

I looked away, visions of towering phalluses conjured by even this tiny intimacy. 'It's funny: I thought you and Lottie ...' I could see Guy found that funny. 'She was all over you the other evening.'

'She just wants me for her Cuppers team. Pinter two-hander. You doing something?'

I tried to steer between the *Scylla* of relief and *Charybdis* of jealousy. 'Maybe.'

Maybe had become *definitely* by the time I made it back to my room. But I'd barely begun battle with my Oxford *Opus One* when a knock forced me to down pen. And music: probably Mozza's caterwauling was disturbing one of the neighbours whose double-barrels I was still getting to grips with. I donned my habitual self-effacement, opened the door and found Guy's face framed there.

'I hope I'm not disturbing your studies?'

I'd left GaySoc on the pretext of getting down to my debut essay. Indeed, that had been my intention: I was desperate to make a good first impression and couldn't comprehend the already cavalier affectations of some peers. I'd worked bloody hard to get there, to get the results and—as a result—couldn't believe that I alone could be enough. Which is perhaps why I've always struggled in conversation: I have to find that perfect thing to say, which almost always eludes me. And that was really why I'd made my excuses: I couldn't compete with sharp-tongued Julian. The object of his affectation (and my affection) was looking even more dashing, door-framed, pink college scarf matching cheeks cherubimed by the October evening.

'Do you want to come in?'

'I've not been in one of these rooms yet.'

Guy lit it up: I could barely bring myself to look. 'Where's yours then?'

'Over on the old quad.' That meant he had one of the posh ones.

I knew you were meant to offer drinks. But alcohol—and cigarettes—weren't habits I'd pick up for some years yet: I had only Mother's selection packs.

'Earl Grey, please.' He politely declined my offer of milk and sugar. This would not have been approved of by Mum. Nor would the subsequent turn in conversation.

'What happened to Julian?'

'Picked up some guy from Magdalen.'

I felt myself flushing, masked it in the kettle's steaming. 'I thought he was your boyfriend?'

'We had a fumble once in the dorm.' Guy was laughing. 'Didn't everyone?'

No. They didn't. *Look at him, looking.* In school changing rooms, I'd kept my head hung. *Backs against the wall, boys.* And oh, the horrors of communal showering.

'You must have had boyfriends?'

No. I hadn't. *If you ever turn out like that you'll be straight out that door.* Girlfriends had been taken to pacify Mother. The strap of a bra was as far as I'd ventured.

'I find that surprising.' Guy took his tea from my hand. 'I mean, you're so good-looking ...' Anyone with more self-esteem might have known what to do with that open ending; I hid behind my *Lapsang Souchong*. Socially more dextrous, Guy conjured a joke-trick from the silence. 'And are these your *Wanderer* wanderings?'

The Wanderer was what we were studying that term. I was still struggling with its Anglo-Saxon. The language in the notebook on which Guy was advancing was a more familiar one. 'It's just some ideas for Cuppers.' I moved to remove it from the desk.

'Can I look?' I stalled, sipping as Guy started flicking. 'Is this *all* your writing?' I nodded acquiescence: it felt like I was flashing. 'It's amazing.'

A little praise steamed my shell open: we talked and talked about *everything*—tea forgotten, skin forming—until Guy clocked the digits on the music system and thought it time to get back to his own room. 'Lectures in the morning.'

I could see the moment moving away from me, like Claudius rising from praying before Hamlet has decided whether (or not) to kill him. 'Or ...' I stuttered when Guy was already halfway to the door. 'You could stay here ...?'

Fortunately, he knew exactly what to do with an opening.

At least, at the time, it felt like that. But I can't, to be honest, recollect much about it. I remember his cock smelling somewhat urinous. I remember thinking *I can't believe I'm finally doing this* (and *I hope my penis doesn't smell of piss*). I remember falling asleep on his chest.

And waking again, next morning, to knocking. Guy was still sardined in the single bed beside me and the door would open any second. I was nineteen then, the age of consent still twenty-one: fear floodlit the room. And shame. Like that time when Mum walked in on me wanking. *What are you doing?* I could imagine her looking down on me in that moment, in flagrante with another man. *What have you done?*

Hearing the key turning, I scrambled for clothing, calling, 'Hello?'

A voice not unlike Mother's bounced back around the corner. 'Thought you'd be in a lecture.'

Shit! I must've missed it: first of the fucking term. 'I ... uhm ... not feeling great. I'm still in bed so ... if you could just, you know ...'

'I'll do the cleaning tomorrow.' I could almost hear Brenda's raised eyebrow. *Did she know?* She could probably smell the testosterone.

As the door clicked shut, Guy burst behind my back. 'I'll do the cleaning tomorrow.' It was an almost perfect imitation of the scout's singsong.

I wasn't laughing. 'We missed the lecture.'

'There'll be others.' Guy drew me back beneath the covers. And—if this were a film—The Smiths' sourly-sweet *Please, Please, Please Let Me Get What I Want* would kick in, the montage of *good times* begin. The sex would get more memorable, and I would come to crave the smell of him, find myself sniffing underpants he left behind one morning. I couldn't wait to be close to him again each evening, spent afternoons staring from windows in the *Bodleian;* it was only his eyes I was seeing. Waking, tangled together, I would run fingers through his tangled hair and Sundays we would just stay there—fucking, talking, reading supplements. It was Guy—who knew everything, or so it seemed—who steered me from *The Times*: before him, I had no idea it was right-wing, or that there was such a thing; my parents read *The Sun*. And—as weeks faded into each other (and, on the soundtrack, mandolins soar)—I would become closer and closer to him, further and further from them.

I'd suggested we go out for lunch but—no—they wanted to have it in hall like I did, *get the full Oxford experience.* My parents had come for a mid-term visit; I wasn't as pleased to see them as I'd have expected a month back. And though—just over a month back—Mum had threatened to hack my long locks off, now that I'd done it, got the Hugh Grant haircut, she too didn't seem as pleased as expected.

'Doesn't suit you.'

I didn't think much of the C&A she was wearing, but didn't say anything.

'What's *griddled* mean?'

Dad was in his usual short-sleeve and jeans.

'It's when they grill it in a pan,' I rolled my eyes at the menu on the table, conveniently forgetting I'd not long since asked Guy that same question. We'd been eating out more than I'd ever eaten out before: back home there'd only been the odd excursion to *Harvester*.

'The salmon for me, please.' Mother was using her posh voice to order; I averted my eyes from the waiter. I'd never noticed their accent before, by then couldn't bear to hear it in my own ears.

My hearing boomed, blood rushing as Guy and Lottie walked in. Guy had been instructed to steer clear; clearly that direction had not been taken by Lottie.

'Hi!'

'Mum, Dad, this is Lottie and Guy ...'

'We've heard all about you,' Dad kowtowed. Obviously, I'd been somewhat selective in what I'd told him, but hadn't shied from revealing that my new best friend was the son of someone he'd seen on his television. 'Would you like to sit down?'

That was the longest *luncheon*. To my perturbation, Guy thought it would be funny to play footsie while Dad asked his usual questions. 'So, what do you want to do after graduating?'

'Act.'

'And can you make a living doing that?'

Guy shrugged. 'My parents have done alright.'

'His father's Teddy Terry,' Lottie reminded us, unnecessarily.

'I thought he was great in that thing ... What was it, Susan?'

Mum, perhaps trying to read the situation, had surprisingly little to contribute to the conversation. But back in my room she was full of questions. 'Is Lottie Guy's girlfriend?'

I've always enjoyed a frisson, like when I pronounced the Queen *should be dead* one evening in the living room. 'He's gay, Mum.' I could feel my temperature rising.

Dad must have gone to the shared bathroom along the landing, because it was just me and Mother: there'd been a corresponding drop in her temperature. 'Oh, he's like that, is he?' She turned her nose up as if I'd just done a dump.

'Is that a problem?' The stench of a lifetime's *when you think about what they do, it's disgusting*'s was now rising.

'And are you like that?'

By that juncture, I didn't much like her. I couldn't but love her. She had always been the best mother, better than all the other mothers, after school she was always there, the tastiest teas prepared and, after the table was cleared, homework laid out there, she always encouraged me to work harder, go further. Until I went too far.

I answered, 'Yes,' and it could never be unsaid.

Dad returned to find Mother sobbing and me, far from comforting, on the far side of the room. 'What's going on?'

'Ask your son!'

'Graham ...?'

The door was still open. I kept my mouth shut, so Mother spelt it out for everyone on the staircase. 'He's a pissing poofter!'

'Whatever he is, he's still my son.'

I could not have predicted my father's reaction. He hugged me, properly, perhaps for the first time. I could not have known then that this emollient gesture augured all would be well in the future: in the fullness of time, Mother might even wear her best hat to my wedding to another man.

Perhaps even the man who would hold me that evening; though his embrace was some time coming. This was before mobile phones: I couldn't just SMS an SOS. I had to leave a note in Guy's pigeonhole, wait for him to finish rehearsing (the Cuppers thing) then down an obligatory drinkie with Lottie (in the *Eagle & Child*, probably) before his knock finally put Moz out of his misery. *I am human and I need to be loved, just like everybody else does.* That night I knew I was.

By extension, back then, I felt more love from Guy's *Mummy* than my own: my first meeting with the Terrys (laissez-faire in a way that only those who've never had a worry, not really, can be) couldn't have gone more knife-through-butterly. But then, it wasn't as though they were meeting their son's first boyfriend: he'd been out since fourteen; there'd been several before me. And Helena—all gamine chic and chunky 'ethnic'—had a way of making *everyone* feel special: the waiter serving us, the entire restaurant. *Wasn't she in ...? And isn't that the guy from ...?* Teddy—who, it's true, did have a certain *Eau de Camp* about him—regaled us with stories of his own Oxford days over brunch in *Browns*—which reminded him of the one on St Martin's Lane, where he was then playing—before (to my relief, savings dissipating more swiftly than I'd been anticipating) *our-treating* us. Then it was over to the bijou *Burton-Taylor Theatre* to see Guy's Pinter with Lottie (who swooned melodramatically at this visitation from another duo of theatrical deities) before they dashed back to town for their own curtain that evening with a *you were marvellous, darling*.

And he was. I was proud. Wowed. As were the Cuppers judges: in their round-up of that first day of the competition they praised especially my boyfriend's *assured performance* (of which, I seem to remember, he gave another that evening). After, his heartbeat boxing my ear, I worried how my own would be received the following afternoon. 'They'll love you,' he assured me. 'How could they not do?'

Each competitor had half an hour. Such was the volume of submissions, performances were spread over five afternoons. The majority were abridgements of scripts known and loved. I had opted for something original instead, juxtaposing Hamlet's soliloquies (*now to my mother: I will speak daggers to her*) and my own coming out story (*Mum, I'm gay*) with words underscored by the music of Morrissey (*I am the son and heir of nothing in particular*). I thought it innovative. Guy thought it *genius*. The judges commended my *well-observed regional dialect*.

Retrospectively, I can see it was wanky and probably a form of therapy but, at the time, I could see only burning injustices. How dare all those straight people tell me they *didn't have a problem with it, so why did I need to go on about it?* How dare all those posh people praise my accent like I'd had some agency in it? And how could the epicentre of intellectual excellence value tradition more highly than experimentation?

You know, some of Morrissey's utterances are true: we really do *hate it when our friends become successful*. At the end of that week, my unique mess was overlooked but Guy's classic rehash got selected for the *Best-of-Cuppers* showcase. To make me feel better about this, Guy claimed it was only because a boy he'd fagged for at school was on the selection panel. For some, networking starts young.

In the *Eagle & Child* after that showcase, Guy and Lottie celebrating *Best Actor* and *Best Actress* prizes, were already planning their next performances.

'Look Back in Anger! You'll play Alison and I'll play Jimmy!'

Even through the emerald of my envy, I could see the notion was silly. Lottie—to be fair—was sound casting for middle-class Alison, who'd fallen for the wrong man. But Guy as working-class hero, angry young Jim railing against a system I found was still in place, firmly, in that closing decade of the twentieth century? I mean, really.

I suppose it was then I started thinking I had fallen for the wrong man. I'd like to imagine it was then I made my first class rebellion, heading to the bar for a round and returning with a packet of Mum's beloved *Scampi Fries* and opening it wide on the table before them, the smell of something fishy instantly infusing the rarefied air around them. And perhaps it was later that evening I made a second, when I fucked him—roughly—like the *piece of rough* he'd once called me. Until he cried out to stop me.

The rough-and-ready accent he affected in that lauded *Hilary* term production was as comic as his imitation of Brenda's back in *Michaelmas*. Unable to suspend my beliefs any longer, I dumped him the week after.

It wasn't that he'd changed, but that I had. Before Oxford, I didn't know what class was, even that it existed. But once I'd experienced it, I found I couldn't separate the gentleman from my resentment of the privilege he'd been born into, so he became collateral in my class battle. *Poor little rich boy never had to fight for anything in his life, take that!* The fact I did it by pigeon-post (that antecedent of text) squeezed juice in the cut. Perhaps I squeezed some enjoyment from that: *fuck 'em, they'll never let me be one of 'em.*

And I never have been. But—though it's been some decades since I pulled the poker from my rectum and stopped despising where I come from—neither have I ever been one of them again. A class refugee, I declined the roles life ordained for me, but castings for those I wanted have proved elusive. Guy—*Daddy* saw to it—walked straight into a starring credit, now has a lovely husband and lovelier hound, as his profile attests. He accepted my friend request. So, seemingly, he's forgiven me at twenty.

TWICKENHAM
Neil Bartlett

Everything is quiet, and I'm fifteen. When I get to the ticket-hall, it looks like I am going to be the first person to walk across the tiles this morning—I know that, because they're still all wet and shining, despite this early heat—so I stop for a moment to gather my nerve. While I'm standing in the doorway, I can hear myself muttering something. Neil, I seem to be saying to myself under my breath; my name's Neil.

Now, my feet are stepping forward across that evaporating skin of water—and now, I can see my hands resting on the shelf in front of the ticket-office window. What am I saying to the man behind it? Ah yes. Of course; Twickenham. I try the word twice, but it doesn't quite want to come out—Sorry, son, the man is saying—so I clear my throat and try again. I'd like a cheap day return, I say—a cheap day return, please, to—but again, the crucial word gets stuck. The man leans forward and asks me to slow things down a bit, so I do what I'm told—and it works, apparently, because now I can see some fingers sliding a sequence of coins under the bottom of the glass, and two cardboard tickets coming back to me. I blush, say thank you—and then keep the two rectangles of cardboard ready in my hand as I walk across the tiles and towards the waiting ticket-barrier.

The water's all gone now.

I remember not looking at the guard—not wanting him to look at me, or make any attempt to ask me why I am there or what for—and then I remember there being sunlight, absolutely everywhere. I can feel my shirt—my best shirt—starting to stick to my back. I ignore it, and sit there on the bench at the very end of the platform and stare. I'm willing that shuddering dot at the end of line to get closer, to burst into being a train and save me.

August. August 1974.

❦

I reckon we'd actually *met* two weeks earlier—at Waterloo Station. And that would have been a Saturday as well, because Saturday was always when I was allowed to go up to London on my own, that last summer at school. I don't remember what in particular I'd gone up for—to see a play, I expect. That was often my reason. My alibi. Anyway, yes; Waterloo Station. We'd both been washing our hands, downstairs, in the men's toilet—and he had very brown hands—very long, sun-tanned fingers—and also this ring; a gold ring, with a small black stone in it. And that sharp black eye had been staring right back at me, even though he—the man—John—wasn't. Except that then, suddenly, he was. He used the mirror to do it—the mirror over the washbasins—and arranged his look so that our eyes really met full-on. No subterfuge, no question; just a statement. I felt a kick, down under the pit of my stomach—and I remember being shocked that he was smiling already. I could feel my face burning, but nothing was said. I just stood there, with my hands dripping and my face reddening, feeling my throat start to knot and clamp up like it always did—and then he went.

I suppose you need to know before I go on that I had done this before—met men like this—but I also want you to know that I'd never—

That I'd never told anyone my name. Sure, they'd asked me, but I'd never replied—because the boy I was when I stared at men much older than me and the boy who everyone else referred to by his name were never the same person.

Because even the idea of them being the same person was enough to make my throat start to seize up like that.

Like I say, it was 1974.

I dried my hands for a bit—and the towel was useless, I remember, all hot and stiff and unhelpful when you pulled it down off the roller to try and find a dry patch—and then I waited for a bit for the door to swing back open—probably washed my hands all over again, I expect—and then I must have pulled the door open myself I suppose and gone back upstairs. There were eyes and feet and hands and mouths everywhere—all of these separate pieces of people, moving absolutely everywhere—but none of them were John, until—

Until I saw him, standing under the clock.

He was standing completely still—his back was turned—and I wonder now, of course, what he can possibly have been thinking. He must have known how old I was, even though we hadn't spoken—I mean there's no mistaking fifteen-year-old skin, is there—and like I say, it was 1974, so both of us were in a very real kind of danger. Was he thinking about walking away?

Anyway ... I stood still as well, I think, for quite a long time, and then—as if he'd heard something—John turned suddenly around. He smiled, straightaway—and the next thing I remember happening is that I walked towards him in an absolutely straight line. Yes—absolutely without hesitation. I mean, there were people, everywhere, but they all seemed to be just getting out of the way, as if John, or his smile, was somehow making that happen.

I'm just going to stop for a minute now, if you don't mind. I didn't think this would be so hard.

We're standing about two feet apart now, face to face, and all of those Waterloo people are walking and talking all around us still, but none of them seem to realise what is happening. John and I swap names—and I can't work out why I'm suddenly able to do that—but then it's John who does all the talking. He tells me that he's working just across the road, in a church that's just over there—he points—and I can hear him saying the church's name as if everybody knows it. Of course, I don't— but I nod anyway, like a grown up—and he says it's a shame, because he's just taking a quick break for coffee, so he can't stop or do anything right now. And I know what that means—I know what the *words* mean—but I don't know what they mean out here, under the Waterloo clock, with so many people about who could overhear them. Then, there's a pause—and then—right out there under that ridiculous great clock—the one that's still there—the one that still always looks to me as if it's about to crash down with some great tearing sound and start killing people—right there, in the middle of Waterloo Station, this handsome, sun-tanned and much older-than-me young man says again that it's a shame, and that another time he'd like to be able to invite me back to his house.

That—I really don't know what *that* means.

Because that's not what houses are for.

John doesn't say anything, but instead he reaches inside his jacket and takes out his diary, which is a little black book with soft leather covers. He finds an empty page, and a fountain pen, and starts to quickly ink something across the pale blue paper. His fingers are strong, and deft, and I stare all over again at how brown they are. Then he tears the page out, folds the gilt-edged piece of paper in half, and holds it out for me to take. He's put his phone number at the bottom, he says.

The next part of my memory has no sound. I guess I tell him that I'll call him—or something, because this isn't a conversation that I've ever had or even rehearsed before—and then John walks away. I can't remember the two of us touching in any way, or shaking hands—just me holding on so tightly to that piece of paper I thought it might break into flames. Eventually, I can hear all the noise of the station coming back into sync with everything else and I can see myself standing there and watching his beautiful back going away across the station until it disappears completely.

John is holding his head right up straight.

💡

Urine, cigarette-smoke and other people's breath. Other peoples' bodies. Also, there was that awful way that a phone-box door swung shut behind you—like it knew it had you trapped.

I was all ready with my coins—and I had my page from John's diary propped open on the top of the metal box where the slot was. I let the kick in my stomach subside, and then, at the very last minute, when I was struggling to get my coin in, I remember everything clotting up inside my throat again.

I remember my breath coming back down the line to me like surf.

I remember thinking should I say my name, in case he's forgotten it—but then—oh Christ, I can hear his voice.

I can actually hear John's voice.

It's easy, he's telling me. If the trains from where I live all go through to Waterloo—he's saying—then all I have to do is change at Clapham Junction. Look up on the boards—he says—look up, and find a train for Twickenham; and then, once you're safely on board, just sit tight and count six stops. There's Putney, and then Barnes, then Mortlake; there's Richmond, and then North Sheen, St Margarets—and then Twickenham. Cross the road, and I'll be there in my car.

I remember a slice of sunshine coming in through the window. I remember the train slowing down—the sign with the name of the station sliding silently past—and the metal of the compartment handle being as hot under my hand as the rib of a panting dog.

❦

It *is* easy. To start with. Walking towards him across the road outside the station is fine—but then, at the last minute, when I climb into the car itself, I lose my nerve and fumble. The strap on the seat-belt is warm and supple—it's hot, like skin—and that takes me by surprise. Also, now the car doors are all closed, I'm back in that telephone box—I can smell it—and also I can feel John looking across at me. I need badly to get something between his face and mine so, as he turns the key, I stare out through the windscreen and start talking—making a conscious effort to keep my throat open, of course—about school, or the train—and all the time I can see the sunshine that's hammering down outside the car windows is putting hard white edges round things and therefore insisting that this is all actually happening. Then, when I do manage to look across at John for just a second—at his hands, on the steering wheel—the little black eye in his ring winks at me as if it recognises me. As if it assumes I know what happens next. The kick in my groin comes even harder this time, and I don't—

I pretend I do—but I don't.

Not in a house.

I remember shifting in my seat, to try and hide myself.

There's my shirt, sticking to my back again.

We turn left. There's a curve in the road, lined with houses—and they're London houses, big red ones, not like the small ones we have back at home—and then there is a dual carriageway. There are some bright, dusty trees, close by the road—trafficlights—and now we're turning left again, because the light's gone green—and then, suddenly, there is a plane—a plane!—so close overhead that it seems to fill the whole windscreen. I duck, and John laughs. He tells me that his house is right under the Heathrow flightpath; sometimes, he says, there are great queues of the things, whole rows of planes hanging up above his house like some sort of giant waiting birds, but that you get used to the noise. Then there are some white-leaved trees again—behind a high wire fence, this time—and then we turn left, and right. Left again—and John says this is just round the back of where he lives. Then, before I'm quite ready, the car's parked and there's that seat-belt buckle again, with its fleshy strap.

John gets out first.

I remember all this next bit as being in very vivid colour for some reason.

First, we're ducking under some kind of wooden arch or pergola, and then we're going out onto a lawn that's dotted with young trees. This seems to be some sort of a communal garden, filling up the space between the two rows of small houses that make up the close or mews where John actually lives—and there is a neighbour, across the way, doing some sort of watering with a hose. Because of the sunlight, the water turns into a spray of something else. Diamonds, I think. This neighbour looks like he's a man of John's age, perhaps even older, and he's smiling and waving and calling out hello—but John doesn't miss a step. He waves right back, and he even uses the man's name, as if this sunshine and me being out in it two paces behind him is all absolutely ordinary. As if nobody needed to know why I'm there or what for—and I must have been looking down at my feet now, because at this point I am noticing that the path across the grass is made up of exactly the same sort of concrete slabs that we have on our back garden path at home. Which also seems impossible. We turn left and I follow John's feet. There are shrubs and flowers on either side of his front path—hydrangeas—geraniums—and also some sort of big white daisy which I know I recognise from our garden at home but whose name I can't quite remember—and now I must be looking up again, because I can see that John's front door is painted black, whereas our door at home is painted in just an ordinary kind of white. The paint looks like it might be hot. Like your hand could sink right into it. There is a brass door-knocker, and the numbers are all in brass too, which is something else that is different. John unlocks the door and then he stands aside—there's a step you have to take, he says—and he's right, you have to step up and over something to get inside John's house, a sort of a raised threshold. I can see this, but my feet won't move. It's like the tiles again, at the station—except that now John is saying You go first, and I'm saying, Thank you.

Inside, everything is dark—a bit too dark, after all that dazzle, and the sparkling water falling over his neighbour's flowers—and I can't quite make things out. I can see a dining table, with too many chairs, and also some sort of a big wooden chest or cabinet, something very large and locked-looking. Most inexplicably of all, there's a piano—really—a great, big, black grand piano—something I didn't know anybody had in their house—and it seems to be collecting all the light in the room. The lid is a pool of oil—and there's a sheet of music on it, floating. It looks like something somebody must have lost. And there is something else, something almost as big as a person, wrapped in a blue cloth and leaning against a wall, something which I can't make sense of at all. But I don't ask—I mean, I don't ask for any explanations. I think my name a couple of times, but it doesn't really help.

John's keys move in his pocket and the noise makes me come back to myself.

He goes first up the stairs.

On the landing, it's the bathroom, first—John points that out in case I need it, I suppose. And then the next room along is his spare room, he tells me—the tiny one, the one that we never really went into. Through the doorway, I can see piles of grown-up clothes and some open suit-cases sitting on the bed. And then here, at the end of the landing, is the door to John's bedroom.

He opens it.

Everything is white—white walls, white wardrobe doors—and there is a long, tall, sheet of mirror that's got me trapped inside it. I turn away. Everything is a bit too close for comfort in here and it feels like our two bodies fill up the room almost entirely. There are some thin white curtains across the window by the bed, I notice and they're moving very, very slowly.

I can see fingers, undoing buttons—but I'm not sure if this is John undoing my shirt, or me undoing him.

Now, we are taking off our trousers—and now I stop and turn away again, because John is bending over and taking off everything, and that's something else I've never seen before. He stops being brown all over.

Next, there is a duvet—we only have sheets and blankets, at home—and John is leaning over and dragging this great white fat thing off the bed, pulling it onto the floor and leaving it there in a heap. He pulls it off the bed just like he tore that page out of his diary—in one go. Like he does this all the time.

There's that burning on my face again. That spasm, in my throat.

Now—now I can feel the bed-sheet, very cool and smooth against my skin. The white window-curtains along the side of the bed are right next to me now—easily within reach, should I want to stretch out a hand and touch them—and they have shadows moving through them in waves. The window itself has been left ajar, and the air that is coming in from outside feels both warm and cool at the same time. John starts to touch me—on my foot, first of all, because now I am lying on my back, and John is standing at the bottom of the bed—and I know that he's looking at all of me, up and down. I try to look back at him—I really do—but I can't—not yet—because of the burning on my face—and so I turn my head and watch the shadows moving through the curtains instead. They are moving very gently and the air that is touching them is touching me all over too—and now, finally, I do look at John. And now—again—the first thing that he does is smile.

The first part of our lovemaking I remember as happening in complete silence; but later on—after half an hour, perhaps—I can hear myself starting to make lots of noise. Really. I'm making sounds that I don't think I've ever made before—and they bewilder me. They arrive in the room without my even being sure that it's my own throat that is making them, and I think I flounder a bit at this point, and maybe even call out for help. When this happens, John doesn't stop. He is using his mouth on me now and he is doing it better than anybody ever has before. Somewhere low down inside me, I am beginning to feel sensations that are too large to stay put; I can feel them getting impatient. They need to be acknowledged, somehow—and as my back starts to arch, I realise these feeling or sounds of mine must be like those planes John says are always lining up over his house—except that these planes aren't high, they're deep. I start to pant, and then—I suppose—I start to sing. John still doesn't stop what he's doing, but with his spare hand he reaches up and lightly brushes two fingers across my open mouth. The fingers slip inside me and he hooks them against my lower teeth. I understand. John is reminding me that the bedroom window is still ajar and that the water may still be turning to a spray of diamonds above the flowers that are just across the way there. But he isn't telling me to stop. He is telling me to keep going—quietly. He is telling me I can signal to those waiting planes any time I want to, and bring them in to land. He is telling me that nothing needs to stop me now, least of all myself. He is telling me that, at last, the sunshine and my throat and my voice, are mine.

Neil, he says, not looking up from his work. Neil.

I come.

※

We all have to leave our childhood selves behind, of course—to abandon ourselves—and I sometimes wonder if that's why we're all so obsessed with stories that take us back somewhere and then snap round to reveal some terrible wound or abuse that is supposed to then somehow explain everything that ever happened to that person afterwards. Well, just to be clear, this picture of my fifteen-year-old self involuntarily arching his back in a sun-filled August bedroom is not a picture of abuse at all. Listen to the sounds that I'm making through John's fingers—long, straying notes, played *pianissimo*, fingered right up high on the neck of a double bass. They're wonderful.

Wonderful.

※

Lots of things can happen between two people afterwards, but this is what I remember happening after that very first time between me and John.

I remember our both using the bathroom—John was the one who taught me not to be ashamed of that, amongst so many other things. Then, back downstairs, when we were dressed, I was looking at that piece of music which had been left open on the piano-lid—and the notes were all just birds perched on wires to me, haphazard. John came up quietly behind me, and told me in that marvellous voice of his that he played in an orchestra, on the double bass—and here he gestured across the room and introduced the big vertical package leaning against the other wall to me as formally as if it actually was another person, one whose company he loved—and then he told me that the music I was looking at was the score of the piece he was currently learning. That's what he'd been doing when we met, he said—rehearsing, in that big old church just across the road from Waterloo. The flocks of birds were all the different parts, he said, and that one, second from the bottom, was his. He said another time—the next time—he'd unlock his gramophone and play a recording for me, so I could hear how all the parts fitted together. Then he shook his keys and said it really was time for me to get back in the car and begin my journey home. I wanted to ask him what it felt like, to be able to read music—to know, when you sit down, that all the music is actually already there in the air of the room somewhere, just waiting for you to join it, or be part of it. I wanted to ask him if life was like that—if everything was actually there waiting for you already, but that you just had to learn how to read it or play it, or maybe even just be in the right place at the right time with the right person.

Right now, I could dial his number. I mean, I could get up from this desk and find my phone and my fingers wouldn't even hesitate. Not at the zero, or the two, or those three unexpected eights in a row at the end.

※

John and I carried on seeing each other for thirty-four years—almost until he died, in fact. He got to watch me grow up, which delighted him, and his was the first body I ever got to see change and grow older. I don't know how many times he picked me up at Twickenham station and took me back to his house while I was still at school—perhaps half a dozen times, perhaps not even that. Later, when I was at college, I used to go and hear him play sometimes, and afterwards, driving home through the night, we'd talk the miles away, and those nights would make me feel that I really did know how everything worked already.

John died of AIDS—of the plague. Not right at the beginning, but after it had been with us for about the first twenty of its disgusting years. In 2005, I think, or maybe 2004. We'd lost touch, by then; he'd moved to Scotland for work, I was in London, or on the road—and the two of us were down to Christmas cards as our main means of contact. Indeed, I only heard he was dead two months after the event, when a mutual friend sent me a copy of his obituary from a music magazine. The picture that accompanied the obituary was lovely—John was smiling, of course, straight into the camera and still tanned from whatever tour the orchestra had just been on. He always did somehow find the time to keep his skin dark and his arse bone white.

About a year after he died, I tracked down and ordered a CD of John playing Bach in a church in Edinburgh; I opened the Amazon envelope, and read the notes on the back of the CD until I found his name—but I wasn't able to actually bring myself to tear off the cellophane and put the disc in the machine. Hearing those beautiful sounds being made by the same hands and fingers that had once played me would have been too brutal an experience.

And that's it, I suppose; I think I've remembered everything that's left. It's late, almost half past four in the morning, and somebody is waiting for me upstairs. I've been reading this through for one last time before ending it and while I've been doing that I've been struck by how many different kinds of silence there are in this story.

Maybe silences are actually best thought of as places. Places we may need to go back to, if we are ever to understand how we got from there to here.

Putney, and then Barnes, then Mortlake; Richmond, North Sheen and St. Margarets.

Twickenham.

BLEACH
Neil Lawrence

I thought Dad might've taken my side. Even if it was only out of guilt. Surely, *his* recent experiments with a woman half his age would help him remember being sixteen? But no.

'A week with Auntie Glynis can't be *that* bad,' was all he had to say.

Never mind I hadn't seen her for twelve years. Never mind he'd never visited her *eh*ver. As far as I knew, he only took the homewrecker to locations they called 'luxury'. But Auntie Glynis lived in Waunarlwydd and, tragically for Waunarlwydd, *The Valleys have Eyes*—for which it was to be the location—had never made it to filming. Waunarlywydd was to be my punishment.

I was being packed off to the narrowest bandwidth this side of the Outer Hebrides and, not coincidentally, the end of my personal life.

◉

'Why can I trust your sister but not you?' Mum asked, before we were even out of the driveway and on our way to the station. 'Your sister's always careful what *she* does.'

I pulled down the sun visor and gave Dinah an evil look through the mirror. Dinah's silent smugness echoed from the backseat. *Careful at not getting caught,* I thought.

'She does *sly* stuff,' I muttered, pressing a fingernail into my arm. I felt a subtle kick to the small of my back letting me know Dinah's reaction.

'Maybe. But she doesn't embarrass us like *you* did, does she?'

Us? There was no *us* anymore. Hadn't Mum got that? Two parents in one house makes an *us*. But I didn't say anything. Instead I clicked the seat back as far as it would go, hopefully digging right into Dinah's kneecaps.

'You think I need watching, is that it? Because I'm male. You think I'm up to no go good behind your back. Is *that* it?'

'You should just be more careful, that's all,' Mum said, in a smaller voice.

💡

I'd expected Auntie Glynis to turn up at Swansea station carpark wearing sludgy wellies and driving a Land Rover. Instead, she was leaning on a Mini Cooper in red high heels. She hugged and kissed me with so much enthusiasm it took five of her Poundland aloe vera wipes to clean the lippy off.

'Lent the tractor to Farmer Evans' boyos, did you?' I said, aiming for snitty.

She produced fake gold sunglasses with 'Gicci' written on the side and put them on *very* slowly.

'Your mum didn't warn me you was funny,' she said.

She opened the Mini's door and threw my case onto the back seat. The car reeked of cheap air freshener. *Pineapple*, I thought, but it was so synthetic who could tell?

'Mum says I'm here to help look after your vegetable garden,' I said, '*and* your chickens *and* your dog. But you probably don't need any help at all do you? I *know* this is my punishment. So, skip the lecture yeah?'

All she did was laugh. I wasn't gonna have that.

'I know about those Cardiff bikers of yours as well,' I went on. 'Don't you have a thing for chest piercings?' I focused my gaze through the windscreen. 'And if you think I'm taking over the odd jobs *they* normally do for you, well ...' I gave her my own laugh.

But damn it, Auntie G was laughing louder.

'Bikers?' she said. 'Were you born clueless or did you catch it from a toilet seat?'

I had to stifle a chuckle. She was *not* going to break me.

I hunkered down for the long drive.

I'd been expecting bushes in bloom, flowery lanes, green grass and sheep pellets. But on a dual carriageway everything looks dirty: the shops were grey, the mums greasy-haired, their offspring crustier than their mothers and greyer than the shops.

'Classy 'hood,' I said.

'It's a bit shite, to be fair' Auntie Glynis said, with the faintest of Welsh accents.

''xcuse me?' I said.

'Were you hoping I'd mount an impassioned *defence* of this fuckhole?' She laughed again.

'My advice: drop the sulk,' she said, 'You're 'ere now. Make the most of it. Or shut up. Or both,' she said, 'And frankly, I'd rather let the chickens repair their own shed than give you a jackhammer to get poundin'. I've got toothpicks with more girth than your arms.'

She didn't know I had already learned to do many things with the right sort of jackhammer.

I must have smirked because she laughed. 'Excuse the reference to power tools. Probably not appropriate in the circumstances.'

Now *she* was the one smirking.

What had Mum told her?

❦

Inside her bungalow, an oversized worm on legs waddled into the hallway.

'My baby!' Auntie Glynis winced as she kneeled; several of her joints cracked and her leather pants squeaked. Classy.

'What the *hell* is that?' I asked.

'A dachshund,' she said calmly. 'His name's Bleach.'

'Okay,' I said. 'That makes sense.'

At the sound of my voice the thing minced toward me, and started to circle around my legs, Malteser eyes blinking. His ratty little tail wagged so furiously it shook his booty.

'No!' I said, 'Did you teach your dog to *twerk*?'

Aunt Glynis was not amused.

'I'm not a dog fan,' I said, to clarify. 'No offence but if a person is in need of stimulation that's why God invented apps. Animals are just *sad*.'

'And are you such a person?' Auntie G asked, giving it the full plum.

Then she looked right at me. *Into* me. So close it made my skin prickle.

Fortunately, Bleach's panting was loud enough to be heard in the pub at the end of the road. That gave me an out.

'I won't make friends,' I said. 'Not with him. It. Whatever.'

Auntie Glynis was still looking. Her lower lip was pushed out like: *thinking*. This was going on *too* long.

'How long have you had Bleach?' I asked.

She patted her hair. 'Not long. He's a replacement.' She paused. 'Dogs are a bit like men,' she said. 'They need keeping on a *tight* leash.'

The muscles in my back locked up.

'Is that what you do? String them along?'

'So *you* don't like them, then?' Auntie Glynis said. Bleach was now nosing at my leg. '*Dogs*, I mean.'

'Boundaries!' I snapped to whoever might pay attention.

Up close Bleach smelled like Weetabix and manure.

'Is there something you wanted to *say* to me?' I asked. 'Is there something Mum told you?'

'Listen chicken,' she said, in a soft voice, 'Lots of girls have the same trouble as you when they get into teenage years. They start to feel that *pull*. See what I mean?'

'What?'

She put her sunglasses on the table. 'Do you think I didn't get jiggy at seventeen?'

'Jiggy?' I said, laughing. 'Who the hell says 'Jiggy'?'

Her smile shrank. But not much.

'I know what Grindr's for,' she said quietly. Her voice was all weird and sad, like Mum's had been in the car. Her eyes looked like Mum's too. 'What I'm saying is look after yourself—set up some cowin' privacy setting to protect you *and* your family and don't point 'location finder' to your own back garden.'

Well that told me. I clamped my jaw shut to stop my mouth gaping.

'Half term's the perfect time to reflect. And you can stay out of harm's way here. See what I mean?'

The silence went on long enough for me to again see the garden security lights turning on and Mum's astonished face as I got up off my knees.

'Take Bleach for a walk,' Auntie said. 'He's been cooped up all day ... But before you go ...' She extended a hand, palm out. 'Fresh air, not fag ash.'

I handed the pouch over. She went to the bin, opened the foot pedal with a *clang*, turned the pouch upside down and shook every ounce out. 'No more shag for *you*,' she said with that saucy grin.

I stomped down the hallway, Bleach skittering behind. Once outside, I slammed the door hard enough to make the letterbox rattle. Ha! She hadn't asked for my Rizzla.

Was it my imagination or did I hear her voice, from inside, singing: *drama queen*?

Bleach was barking. *That* was a certainty.

'Shuttup, dickhead,' I muttered.

His ears went up. The fucker was grinning. He thought it was funny. I forced a smile off my own face.

Then he exploded out of the gate and onto the main road.

I *had* to go after him. Who was the dickhead now?

Despite his sausage shape, he was surprisingly speedy and it wasn't until reaching the bend in the road that I caught up with him.

I tried, with all the grace of a drunken ballet dancer, to scoop him up and caught sight of a large shape looming ahead. A surprised-looking man on a tractor had to swerve to miss us. Fortunately, Bleach had come to a standstill. Maybe badly kept vehicles burping out toxic fumes weren't his thing. Maybe being plastered across the road wasn't either. Whatever it was, I made a grab for the dog, holding him close to my chest.

Up on the tractor, the man halted his ride, shook his head. His cap fell off and I got a glimpse of thick, steely hair. For a moment, I thought—but no, he was too old. Even for *me*.

'Something to do?' he shouted.

What the fuck did *that* mean?

I dropped to the verge as he 'sped off'. Bleach was licking my face, a wriggling, furry Peperami. When I gave in finally and giggled, he slipped his tongue inside my mouth.

'Get off!' I spluttered, 'You're disgusting.'

Not as disgusting as his breath though. Bleach didn't care. His eyes were fixed on mine. He seemed to be grinning. Then he gave me another tongue sandwich.

Five minutes later we had reached the public land Auntie Glynis pointed out on the drive in.

'Right you little bugger,' I said, lowering Bleach onto the grass. 'Run! Like the overgrown caterpillar you are!'

And off he scampered, back legs and front barely in sync.

I sat on the grass and watched. Bleach was soooo oblivious to the whole tractor near-miss thing. What if it had been a car? Some pumped up boy racer or tosser in a pimped-up Beemer, or worse yet a Merc ... What if it had been one of them? Then ...

Bleach, who had now removed his nose from out of the largest of cowpats, trotted back to check on me, with a frenzy of sniffs and licks.

'You should be more careful?' I cooed.

A breeze crept up my trouser leg making me shiver.

Who did I sound like?

I *knew* the answer. And maybe she *did* have a point.

That guy? Polishing him off like that—the danger of it ...that was the *thing* ...the turn on. Getting caught was the unfortunate humili-ation. But all Mum could say was that I was like my father. 'Always thinking with his todger.'

Back at the bungalow, Auntie Glynis was bent over a chopping board. When I brought back Bleach cradled in my arms, she looked up and smiled.

'Ran off, did he?'

I nodded.

'I nearly soiled myself ... I'll have a bath if it's alright with you, then maybe ring Mum? Would that be okay?'

'Does that mean ... you need laundry done?'

I treated her to a look of ice. 'Not like *you're* thinking,' I said. *Boundaries.*

Five minutes later, the steaming bathwater was so welcome. The soap, soft and orange-scented, covered my arms.

I sank back and let go. I tried to ignore her horrible splashback tiles. The colour of avocado, or nose doings.

I stopped moving.

I loved looking at myself in the bath.

I hated looking at myself in the bath.

☙

Back in the bedroom, dry and towel-wrapped, I stood by the window.

Up the road, in the spot Bleach tried out his tractor-dodging, was a man, tall and broad, coming towards the bungalow, his steps confident. I could see dark hair, full lips, stubble you'd run the flat of your tongue over. At the gate, he stopped, noticing he was being watched. Taking time to roll and light a cigarette. Then he glanced up.

I held his gaze but remembered Mum upset in the car. I *would* ring her.

I turned away from him. Only once I had shirt and jeans back on did I risk looking out the window again.

The man had taken the turning at the end of the lane leading past a pub called *The Rose Inn*. I picked up my Rizzla packet from the bed.

If I caught up in time ... he might ... share his tobacco?

'Fuck it,' I muttered. I was starting to sweat.

I could go for a little walk *first*. *Then* I could ring mum and tell her I was fine.

LAST VISIT
Alex Hopkins

He went alone, arriving at 10pm. His mother had always lit the porch when he visited; it was now dark.

He parked the car and entered the house, walking to the lounge, reaching for the light switches. Crystal beads bathed the room in gold.

His mother had died in her armchair. A neighbour had found her body.

He stood in the space between her now empty chair and the one that had been his father's and lingered for a moment, the silence falling on him. Then he went into the kitchen, which was cluttered with filthy pans and plates. It was the room he most associated with his mother— her refuge from his father—and it appalled him to see it like this.

The drinks cabinet looked untouched since his father's death. His mother had hardly drunk since that awful night of truths and recriminations. Most of the bottles of liquor were unopened and the Scotch was waiting; he poured himself a large glass, gulping at it.

He went upstairs, walking past his childhood bedroom; he couldn't bear to go in. Instead, he headed towards his mother's bedroom, but couldn't face that either, so he continued down the dark corridor to the guest bedroom where he stood looking out at the black lawn. Then he undressed, lay down, and prayed for sleep.

He rose at 6am, dizzy with tiredness and, for the first time in years, craved a cigarette.

He made a strong coffee before moving into the lounge. And it was then, seeing her chair in the shards of morning light, that it hit him: she was gone. He swayed, as if his feet had been kicked from beneath him and reached for the side of her chair. As the tears came, he closed his eyes, holding his hands out in front of him, reaching for the joy this room had once promised, but then moved them back to his sides, clenched his fists and took a deep breath. He couldn't break. There was too much to do.

Clearing the garage was the easiest task to start. He rummaged through boxes of memories, finding objects long forgotten, reminders of his first five years—the years spent with his parents before he was sent to boarding school. He remembered the day his father had delivered the news in a cold, flat voice, not even looking at him. He knew it was his decision to send him away, his cruelty once more crushing his mother.

He had lost count of the times he had wished his father dead. Every time the other boarders ripped apart the tuck box his mother had lovingly packed for him, every time they trampled on the currant cake she had baked, every time he had been jeered at on the rugby pitch, every time he had been called fag and pansy and queer and shit stabber, every time he had been spat at, every time he had cried himself to sleep, every time he had been woken at midnight and dragged into the bathroom and kicked and punched in the face, every time he had been ambushed in the cricket pavilion, every time he had been held down and burnt with cigarettes; each and every time, he had wished his father dead.

But what he now found reminded him that it hadn't always been that way. He discovered things that he could hardly believe had once belonged to him, touching them carefully as if searching for their stories: Dinky diecast metal cars, toy soldiers and tatty photograph albums. There he was holding his mother's hand beside the greenhouse, his father in the background, picking runner beans; a moment he couldn't remember, but a snapshot from days he had never wanted to end, that had left him hungry ever since.

At 8am, he summoned the courage to go into his mother's bedroom, tossing skirts and blouses into piles, dumping everything in bin liners, carrying them downstairs, discarding them on the kitchen steps, before swinging around, striding back through the house, up the stairs again, for another load, and another after that, his heart pounding, sweat pouring down his face.

He carried a bottle of paraffin to the bottom of the lawn, making a fire by the pond, in the same place as he remembered lighting the fire that long-ago summer, during those few days he had spent with Simon. For the next hour, as the pink morning light fell through the trees, he moved feverishly between the fire, the garage and her bedroom, heaving bags, cardboard boxes and wooden crates through the house, across the lawn and to the fire. He burnt everything.

Finally, he entered his old bedroom once more. Her gowns were in the big oak wardrobe and mothballed, covered in plastic: marbled velvet, Paris chiffon, Duchess satin and silks with flashes of gold and silver. It astonished him that his mother had held on to them. He wondered if she had ever come in here, opened the wardrobe and remembered. He hoped so.

He remembered when he had first found the gowns, forty years ago; he had been eleven. He had brushed them against his arms, imagining how it must feel to be wrapped in something so beautiful, so delicate. When Simon visited, they had both been fourteen. He recalled the trepidation in his voice when he'd asked his mother if Simon could stay, and how she hadn't hesitated. Of course, my darling, she'd said, smiling, he'd be very welcome. His father would be in London; it would be safe, he'd thought.

He sat on his bed, isolating the spot that it had happened. It had been night time, and he had opened the wardrobe, revealing the gowns to Simon; he had only wanted to show him how his mother used to dress, prove that she had once been beautiful but, before he could stop him, Simon was parting the clothes, reaching for the emerald silk dress dotted with silver butterflies. Simon, no, he'd said, no, don't, please, but it was useless; there was no telling Simon, which was one of the reasons he'd loved him, and suddenly Simon was climbing out of his clothes and into the dress and they were both laughing, Simon pointing to a black satin gown with a golden brocade like broken half-moons around the waist, and snatching it from the hanger, throwing it at him. Come on, Simon had said, your turn, his smile lighting the whole room. He had looked at Simon and hesitated for a moment but before he knew it, he too was removing his clothes and slipping into the dress as if he were trying on another life. Let's dance, Simon had said, dance with me, and so, moments later, he was walking cautiously towards him, unable to believe that this was happening. Simon was pulling him into his arms, and they were moving around the room, swaying and giggling, and at that moment he felt that this was everything; this was all he would ever want. He didn't hear his mother's footsteps, but suddenly there she was, staring at them draped in her precious dresses at precisely the moment that Simon pulled him to him, harder, this time kissing him softly between the eyes. Oh, she'd said, just the one word, but then she'd smiled her usual smile, goodnight boys, sweet dreams, she'd said, quickly walking away.

The next day he was terrified, but she hadn't seemed any different with him. That evening she had helped them light the fire by the pond, leaving them alone as they barbecued sausages and chicken legs. The night ended with them sitting at the foot of her chair as she knitted, smiling down at them as they played scrabble. Everything had felt possible.

After Simon left, he had been sitting on his bed, sitting where he was now, when she finally spoke to him about it. I'm happy that you've got a friend, my darling, she'd said, and then she cast her eyes to the floor and paused before speaking again. But your father must never know. I'm sorry, but that's how it must be.

He and Simon had one more year together, though Simon never visited the house again; he was never mentioned in the house again. But they ran and picnicked and made love in the fields and woods surrounding the school; they laughed and talked and cried and dreamed. They protected each other, just for a little while. Then Simon's father took him away to the other side of the world, and again there was nothing but silence and emptiness and pain.

He couldn't think about it anymore. Anger coursed through him; he rose from the bed, grabbed at the gowns, ripped them from their rails, hurled them into heaps, took them downstairs and left them outside. He intended to burn them along with everything else, but he found that he couldn't, not yet.

Exhausted, he returned to the house, to the dining room, where he sat at the table, in the same place he'd sat throughout his adulthood—opposite his parents. He thought about the meals they had eaten here, so many meals accompanied by the polite conversation that had made him want to scream until his throat tore. He thought about all the things unsaid. He thought about the day that his mother had told him, delicately yet unequivocally, that his dreams and longing must be bundled up and consigned to the house's dreadful mound of secrets. He thought about how he had never found the courage to challenge her, how he detested himself for it, and her. He remembered the hours he had sat at this table in the years ahead, answering her questions about how he was, what he was doing, without ever talking about how he really felt, without speaking of the men he loved, the men he was watching die in their dozens, their beautiful bodies and minds pulped by a disease that neither she nor his father would mention.

He thought about the night that he had come to the house immediately after his father's death, and the immense relief and excruciating guilt he felt knowing that he was finally dead. Might it be different now? he dared wonder; now the man who had terrified them both was gone, could there perhaps be something after so long of nothing?

He remembered the first anniversary of his father's death; they had drunk too much, and it had all come out. He thought about the furious, pained words he had used. You're ashamed of me, I sicken you, don't I? My life, what I am, it repulses you, he'd said. No, no, she'd said, no, my darling, I only wanted to protect you from him. Protect me? he'd shouted. She'd started crying, sobbing as if her body were breaking apart. I'm sorry, I'm sorry, it's my fault, she'd said again and again. I should have let your father have his way, kept you with us; it's my fault, she'd said. But I didn't want him to hurt you. I knew you were different, special, she'd said, speaking softly now. I thought you would be safer away from him, that's all. He'd stared at her. What do you mean? He'd said. She'd flinched, her body shrank, and when she'd spoken again there was a tremor in her voice. It was me, she'd said. What do you mean? he'd repeated, his voice rising. It was me, she'd said, who decided you should go to boarding school. He'd sprung back, looking at her as if she were a stranger. Suddenly it had made sense; that was why his father hadn't been able to meet his eyes that day he'd told him about the school; he had never wanted him to go. You, he'd spat at his mother, you. Yes, she'd said in the tiniest of voices, me. She'd moved slowly towards him, placed a hand on his shoulder, but he'd swiped it away, and she'd gasped. All these years you let me believe it was him, let me hate him, he'd said, fighting to control his voice. He'd paused, trembling, looked at her steadily, brutally. You sent me away, mum, he'd said, and she'd buried her face in her hands.

In the few years that remained to them, he'd tried to move beyond it, he'd tried to understand, though it wasn't enough, and this time he knew it had been his fault; he'd kept his distance, visiting too infrequently, every three months or so, barely phoning her in the meantime. He had adored her and never forgiven her. He had punished her; he had let her die alone.

He sank his head towards the table and cried, silently, just for a little while. Then he walked outside, picked up the pile of gowns, moved down the lawn to the fire, which was crackling and spluttering in reds and purples, the smell of petrol filling the air. He began to throw the dresses into the flames, watching the past crinkle away. None of it matters now, he said to himself, it's over now, but then there were just two gowns left: the emerald silk and the black satin. He brought them to his face, breathed them in; he closed his eyes and saw himself and Simon: Simon in the silk, as green as his eyes; he in the satin, smooth like happiness on his skin. He felt Simon's kiss again. It was the first time he had been kissed, the purest of his life. Then he saw his mother in the same clothes, a lifetime ago. She had done what she'd thought was best, he now understood, but sometimes the way we choose to love perpetuates the damage we seek to diminish. He would keep these two dresses, he decided; he would cherish them, just as his mother had; they were all that was left, yet they held so much, just enough.

He sat on the dewy grass, pulling his legs to his chest, sitting as he had with Simon that summer night when the crickets chirped, the fire roared, the chicken sizzled, and his mother sat in the house waiting for them. Everything should have been possible.

When he opened his eyes, the sun was breaking through the clouds like splinters of gold; he could feel the promise of its heat on his face.

A REVIEW OF "A RETURN"

Juliet Jacques

Review
Film Diary I: A Return (2020)

J. G. Singer's latest work is an ambiguous, ambivalent chronicle of the small, suburban town where the filmmaker grew up, and an intriguing look into who gets excluded from such places and why. However, it doesn't say as much as it could, even when it reveals more than it intended. Words by *Phil Hamilton*.

When *Syntagma* journal asked if I wanted to review J. G. Singer's new film—an hour-long walk through their home town in Surrey, shot on 16mm with Singer's narration and an ambient soundtrack—I was hesitant. I've long been interested in Singer's work, not so much because I share Špela Milanič's conviction, expressed in her review of *Summer Days* (2018), that Singer is 'the most promising queer experimental filmmaker in contemporary Europe', but because I knew Singer in our youth. That would not be a problem in many instances—I would happily interview Singer (who uses they/them pronouns) or include their work in any survey of recent queer film. But a review presents an ethical consideration, demanding objectivity as it does. In this case, I think it more interesting, and potentially productive, to write *through* this moral issue than to recoil from it, hence my accepting this commission. I hope that you, the reader, will indulge me, and I hope J. G. Singer will forgive me.

With its title betraying the influence of great film diarists such as

Jonas Mekas or David Perlov, *A Return* opens on a train. The image flickers and fades in, awakening the viewer somewhere between Earlswood and Salfords on the London–Brighton line. With that characteristic 16mm light burn around the edges of the shot, Singer shows us the Royal Earlswood Hospital, or the Asylum for Idiots as it was called when it opened in 1853—the first purpose-built establishment for people with learning disabilities. 'Who knows how many horrors took place in this castle,' reflects Singer, telling us about two cousins of the queen who were hidden there and listed as dead in *Burke's Peerage*, decades before their actual deaths. Described by architectural critic Ian Nairn simply as 'not nice', the listed building looms over the surrounding countryside and now serves as luxury flats (of course) with a Union Jack flying over the top—a whitewashing of a complicated past that perhaps reveals more about *A Return* than Singer intended.

The film *really* begins when Singer gets off at Horley station, offers glimpses of the private company logos and reminiscences about British Rail despite being too young to remember it. Unlike their early works about London, where Singer moved 'as soon as I legally could' (for a degree at Goldsmiths, naturally), the narration does not strive too hard for the effect of Patrick Keiller, noting simply that 'History does not happen here.' But there are personal histories, and people with histories, as *A Return* explores. The first of these is quite amusing: Singer sees a man sat in a car waiting outside the station, picking his nose, who they immediately recognise as 'Mr Norton, who threatened to expel me in Year 10 because he thought I'd put glue in his coffee. I hadn't, but I think he'd just never liked me because he thought I was too feminine, and a bit of a smart-arse.' Then, a lament: 'So did everyone else.' At this point, the man in the car realises he's being filmed and angrily turns towards the camera; the shot ends abruptly, most likely with Singer running away like a naughty schoolchild.

There are a few establishing shots to tell us more about what kind of town this is: a large Waitrose and an old but well-maintained department store; a sign for Horley Tyre & Exhaust (that may have inspired the pun that opens Shena Mackay's 1986 novel *Redhill Rococo*, set in the next town up, where the protagonist sees 'Redhill tyres and exhausts' from the train); and the big Wetherspoon pub, in what was once 'a grand cinema, back in the Thirties'. So far, so unremarkable. Singer takes us to the secondary school—the only one in the town—to poke at their memory further, having already set up an unhappy time there with that earlier anecdote. It's break-time: children are eating, talking, playing football or basketball, with the five-storey tower block that hosts the Science labs looming over the playground like the Royal Earlswood over the neighbouring villages. 'Perhaps I could have given this life more of a chance, as my parents were always telling me to,' Singer wonders, over the noise. 'I'd made my mind up to leave before my first day here, and so I grew up in exile in the only place I'd ever called home.'

The camera shakes: perhaps Singer did not use a tripod as they wanted to be able to get away quickly if seen shooting, but the jerky effect conveys two things. The first is that this is not a major work, but one made quickly and cheaply when more ambitious or elaborate filmmaking is impossible. The second is the nature of Singer's personality, at least as an adolescent: jittery, anxious, trying to assert their own opinions, tastes and desires while being deeply concerned with peer acceptance and struggling to work out how much of their gender non-conformity to display. We were in the same year at this school, both taking our GCSEs in 1998 and then going to sixth-form college in Reigate, before I moved to Brighton and Singer to London. Singer talks about alienation, boredom and loneliness, leading to a deep-seated depression. I recall these feelings well, as we shared them. How could we not, in a town like this, with its run-down high street, its lack of anything to do besides under-age drinking and chasing the dragon at house parties, the constant fear of being beaten up by resentful teenagers with little to occupy them and less to hope for?

Singer stops lingering on the playground, and talks about the early 2000s, when they and other queer people took vicious abuse in a national moral panic that culminated in a mob in Newport driving a paediatrician out of her home (and an avalanche of complaints against Chris Morris' *Brass Eye* special on Channel 4, satirising the media's role in this campaign). They take a walk that we often did together, home from school, either over the rusty railway bridge or through the subway (which, Singer wryly tells us, inspired a song by The Cure 'that's six lines long'). Wondering what became of the school bullies and if they even *want* to know, Singer mentions a fight that they were supposed to have here, 'twenty-four years ago' with 'a boy from Year 10' that 'I was later told got set up because I was bent'. Wisely, Singer didn't show up, hiding at my house instead, not long after I'd become their only friend, and not long before I became rather more than that. Filming the trains from the bridge, Singer reflects on how often they left during their teens (partly because it was so easy to bunk the fares back then) and on their permanent departure in 2000, which seemed to freeze the town's development in Singer's mind, almost as if it didn't exist when they weren't there.

Horley *has* changed, of course but glacially compared to the nearest cities. Singer notes the Gatwick Islamic Centre, pointedly named after the nowhere-place of the nearby airport rather than the long-established town populated overwhelmingly by white, middle-class people who always return Conservative MPs and councillors, shown on a board in the centre. (If Singer had kept up with local news, they might have heard about people vandalising the Centre back in 2012, throwing alcohol and eggs at it and scrawling graffiti on it as worshippers observed Ramadan.) They stop at a bookmakers, which used to be a record shop in the 1990s, where the staff introduced us to the kind of artists whose works now make up the soundtracks for Singer's films: Autechre, Fennesz, Mogwai, Underground Resistance, etc. Singer tells us briefly about 'the only thing in the town I ever loved', and how it closed down 'when Tesco and then Amazon started selling CDs and the shop couldn't keep flogging singles to kids on their way home from school to subsidise them selling weird electronic records to people like me'. There's an air of smug superiority to this, coming from Singer's relief at successfully leaving a place 'without culture' and becoming something like the person they wanted to be. They show us the old library, closed down and unoccupied, but not the larger one recently opened at the other end of the high street, but one doesn't have to know this to suspect the filmmaker is more concerned with weaving a story about the self than their surroundings.

After pausing at the memorial and thinking about the role that local and national mythology around the two world wars, and rhetoric around patriotism and terrorism more generally, played in binding the Conservative (or anti-Labour) voter bloc in December's election, Singer enters the recreation ground (or 'Rec' as we called it). This hosts the annual funfair and fireworks, with a skate park and a tennis courts, and used to have a little gazebo that, as Singer recalls, had 'No Gays' daubed across it almost as soon as it opened. Singer focuses on the empty space where it stood, using double-exposure (a bit of a cliché in this type of film) to take us back to the past, with two people kissing inside a similar wooden structure (presumably filmed elsewhere, although Singer doesn't say so), looking nervously to camera in fear of being seen and, almost certainly, verbally or physically attacked.

The dialogue stops and the music intensifies in *A Return*'s most powerful sequence, as Singer fades to the same people in a dark indoor space. Both would be read as male: one helps the other to dress as a woman in a wig and make-up, soft pink dress and stockings, and then they kiss again. It reminded me of Carolee Schneemann's *Fuses* and other 1960s experimental films, as Singer shows the full pleasure of this sexual act and then cuts to close-ups of a hand moving across stockings or caressing a false breast, lips touching and bodies pressing. Readers might have guessed by now that the cross-dresser was Singer and the male figure was me, in the most loving moments of a furtive relationship that began in our final year at school and ended in our first year at sixth-form college.

The film captures the incredible joy of the secretive sex, which took place at my little flat on the Langshott estate when my mother was out (and often used her clothes), but not Singer's constant vacillation on whether they wanted a relationship, nor their refusal to allow any public expression of it even after they came out, at college. It makes no mention of how Singer began dating a woman in summer 1999: my problem was not, as some of my friends suggested, that Singer had been 'pretending to be gay' because 'it's cool' (trust me, I still have a scar on my head that says it wasn't, not in our town) but that it began when we were together, with no agreement about whether our relationship was open, and if it was, *how* open. For all the time we'd spent together, I was swiftly dropped; Singer's relationship with the woman didn't last long, as they met a man as soon as they started at Goldsmiths. I don't know if Singer is with anyone now, but there are no more mentions of romance or relationships in *A Return*: perhaps their artistic career crowded out everyone and everything else.

Singer finishes the film walking along the River Mole—as we often did, holding hands when we felt certain no-one could see. As they wander through an alley past an old pub to the yard of the fourteenth-century church, they reflect on reconciliation, wondering how much of their identity is built on their rejection of the town and its rejection of them. The light is fading and the multi-coloured burn gradually consumes the 16mm stock, before whiting out and bringing the film to a close, scored by a beautiful ambient piece by German composer Wolfgang Voigt—specifically, *Königsforst 6,* to which I introduced the filmmaker on its release back in 1999. Hearing one of my favourite pieces of music in this context, I thought about the catharsis for which *A Return* is aiming. Its conclusion felt hollow to me, as Singer never expressed anything but contempt for the town when living in it, and I doubt the sincerity of the apparent peace made with it at the end: this makes the film feel like the cinematic equivalent of sticking a Union Jack on top of an asylum and rebranding it as luxury flats.

Perhaps I'm not the best judge. Like Singer, I've moved on, first to Brighton and then Berlin, and have had several long-term relationships since then. But I still remember how they never really apologised for the way they treated me as a teenager. And then it occurred to me: could this be intended as some form of belated apology? Because who is this film *for*, if not for me? And is all art, at its core, primarily for the person who makes it?

SCAFFOLDING
Giselle Leeb

These are the bones that Jack built.

I imagine the doctor works late into the night to solve my wounds. I can see he would like to crack me. I know, as in a nightmare, that he is solving not me but an abstract problem. And when he's finished, I'll disappear again—all he can see are the wounds on the surface of my skin.

He has persistence. He would like to drill down to my bones. And when he has done it—which I have every faith he will—he'll forget about me. I'll be gone, except as a case study in the journal article that will finally make him famous. My name will be a footnote in history and no one will bother to read it.

This is the skin that lay on the bones that Jack built.

The doctor is droning on.

'Vitamin C deficiency causes open sores,' he'd told me on my first visit. 'Untreated, it can lead to skeletal abnormalities.'

When he thought my case was simple, he couldn't wait to get rid of me. He chided me on my diet and advised me on which supplements to buy. He didn't even write a prescription.

He probably didn't expect to see me again, but I kept coming back. I had to. The doctor's lectures grew longer as the wounds on my skin and the frequency of my visits increased. I knew he thought I was wasting his time and the NHS' money, that I wasn't bothering to take the vitamins.

It was a special day for the doctor when I reported pain and swelling in my joints to accompany the deepening wounds. He took a sudden and unexpected interest in me. Well, in my body. Scurvy is virtually unknown these days, at least in Europe.

'What is happening?' I asked him, practically in tears.

He carefully explained: in cases of scurvy, the collagen maintaining scars over old wounds degenerates faster than normal skin collagen ... or something. The scars break open. The wounds come back.

'Nothing to worry about, the vitamin C will kick in soon,' he said.

'I've been taking the pills. I haven't missed one,' I said.

But he still didn't believe me and arranged for me to take the vitamin C under supervision.

I do remember a moment, after he'd verified I'd swallowed the pills for several weeks, when he turned from the evidence on his computer screen and actually looked at me, properly looked.

He ignored my tears. Or perhaps he just didn't notice them. Tears, I imagine, are not on his professional—or personal—radar. But I could see the greed for knowledge shining out of him, and I knew then it was bad.

Now the way he looks at me sometimes, I feel like he is asking me something, and he doesn't know what he is asking.

This is the wound that broke the skin
That lay on the bones that Jack built.

I also don't know what the doctor is asking, but he is wearing down my patience.

The wounds kept reappearing, as if they'd never healed, as if my life was going backwards.

The doctor's real interest began when I correlated a specific wound with a childhood incident. It was a simple explanation of how the wound had occurred:

I slipped on a patch of ice and cut my hand on a jagged rock buried in the snow; it was a freezing day and nobody came—and did this make the pain a little worse?

Of course, the doctor didn't comment on my associative ramblings. His interest was not piqued by the emotions attached to the event; his initial aim was simply to find similar correlations and record them.

But the duration of my appointments increased from ten to fifteen minutes after that, then to twenty, and eventually to what felt like an eternity. Only much later did I find out the doctor was neglecting his other patients and risking his job.

It was round about then that he brought up the journal paper. It was in the ideas stage, he said—in a very kind voice; of course, he needed my permission.

This is the scar
That sealed the wound that broke the skin
That lay on the bones that Jack built.

The doctor and I didn't talk about personal things at first, as is only natural in a doctor–patient relationship. Probably best, too, to avoid ripping off old scabs.

He asked me to expand on the circumstances of the incident; he needed a little more for his paper.

But, 'Psychologists are not doctors,' he said, when I added to my original account and mentioned—impassively and factually, I thought—that I'd sustained the wound on the way home from my first enforced visit to a psychologist. There was something wrong with me and my parents wanted it fixed.

'It's not personal,' I replied, but he had turned back to his screen.

Meanwhile, my remaining scars turned red, ready to break their seals and burst open at the right moment. It's astonishing just how many scars—those unreliable wound-covers—there were on my body once I started counting.

I felt desperate. The doctor was no help. I began to match each of my wounds to its corresponding memory on my own. I needed to know the full extent of my previous injuries—that is, what the endpoint would be and how bad the pain would get before I reached it. In doing so, I became convinced the scars attached to traumatic memories were breaking open first.

Of course, I didn't tell the doctor. Given his disdain for psychology, he wouldn't have believed me.

This is the boy that made the scar
That sealed the wound that broke the skin
That lay on the bones that Jack built.

I felt like the scars were letting me down. I—my body—had made them, but now they were failing; just another thing I had somehow got wrong.

The doctor's interest in me intensified as even more of my scars sprang open. I could sense his eagerness by the way he started doing things by the book all of a sudden. I imagined him reading an old, forgotten doctor's manual with instructions to lean back in your chair—not too far back—and observe the patient surreptitiously, perhaps ask a few questions, while secretly looking for signs of mental disturbance.

Nonetheless, the doctor remained resistant to psychology.

I admit it was hard to get the facts straight; my memories were hazy at times. I understood how the doctor must be feeling.

The doctor had a lot to think about as my case, and his paper, progressed. I imagined him at home, shutting the study door on his nuclear family to work on the article, alone and happy in his wingback chair, his one little treat.

This is the dad with the crumpled scorn
That thrashed the boy that made the scar
That sealed the wound that broke the skin
That lay on the bones that Jack built.

It was inevitable—I realised much later—that the doctor would ask me a personal question.

The physical evidence was overwhelming: my skin prickled, scars blooming into wounds one after the other like sick flowers, every single wound I'd sustained intent on reappearing. But something was missing: the doctor needed a theory to complete his paper. And when he asked me again about the incident on the ice, I could see him turning over an idea in his mind.

Some of the wounds had, as he put it—delicately he thought—a human origin, as opposed to just tripping and falling, banging your head mistakenly on walls, doors ... ice ... that sort of thing. A direct human cause. Or, it might be more accurate to say, the wounds had been made by someone else, on my skin, on me. 'Was there,' he ventured, 'somebody with you on the ice that day?'

The doctor had finally, reluctantly, entered the realm of psychology.

I rubbed my finger back and forth over one of the few unbroken scars left on my arm. There was no point in answering his question; a successful man like him wouldn't understand about my father. It would just make it harder for him to finish the article that will make him famous so that he can buy lots of wingback chairs and spend more time on his own, or with the lovely family I'm sure he has, if that is what he wants to do.

This is the mother all forlorn
That kissed the dad with the crumpled scorn
That thrashed the boy that made the scar
That sealed the wound that broke the skin
That lay on the bones that Jack built.

I was right not to answer. In our next consultation, the doctor's face fell when I inadvertently mentioned my mother. I felt such guilt for complicating things for him.

My case is something like a dead elephant I happened to see on the telly the other day: four months after the animal had been shot by a poacher, there was just a swathe of dried-out skin collapsed over her bones. There was nothing in between.

In other words, wasn't the doctor—wasn't I—leaving out something important?

The doctor was obsessed with bones. He forgot about the flesh, and all the stuff that goes with it, the feeling stuff. I can understand that better than most, although I'd rather not dwell on it.

'Any previous broken bones, or fractures?' he started asking as my wounds deepened. It wasn't just old wounds that reappeared, he explained, but also breaks in bones. 'Even the bones are held together by collagen,' he told me. 'The bones are the scaffold of the body.'

The doctor was fully committed by then, even more eager for a cure than I was. When my symptoms worsened, he admitted me to his private clinic, his sideline to the NHS. Here, people paid handsomely and the doctor always smiled.

I couldn't afford it, but he didn't charge. After all, the article was far more important than a month's worth of public school fees or extra tennis lessons. The doctor needed it to become famous and make more money.

I was starting to feel ... dehydrated ... dried out. I didn't want to get closer to my bones; they are, the doctor fails to understand, something best left unacknowledged. They alone, of all my tissues, escaped the early beatings and have not had to deal with any breaks. And they make things, vital things of which I have only the dimmest comprehension. Red blood cells? Corpuscles? Something, in any case, that keeps my body going.

Too distressed to read, and bored, I lay on my bed, my wounds suppurating while an IV dripped vitamin C into my arm, and made up the rhyme to pass the hours. Actually, I started it after my first visit to the doctor, but I didn't understand it and put it away for a while.

I didn't make it up, I modified it. It's one you most likely know. In my family, such as it was, it was passed from my grandfather to my father, and then to me. Maybe it started with my great-grandfather. I'm not sure how far back it goes.

I almost hoped writing it would change something. I don't know why I thought that.

I leave it next to my bed, perhaps hoping the doctor will read it. My only chance of that is if he sees it as a symptom of some kind; he wouldn't be interested otherwise. So far, nothing. I've started to use bigger, clearer handwriting.

This is the doc all tattered and torn
That noted the mother all forlorn
That kissed the dad with the crumpled scorn
That thrashed the boy that made the scar
That sealed the wound that broke the skin
That lay on the bones that Jack built.

I've realised that none of this is at all scientific and I've given up hope of a cure.

The doc finally noticed my rhyme. All of a sudden, he was very interested and now he refuses to stop talking, mostly about himself. It's like he's borrowing my thoughts, telling me about how his father hit his mother, who never stopped trying to help his old dad be a better person, or something. About how his mother kept telling him it wasn't his dad's fault that he hit the doc too, he couldn't help it, it was just that he'd been beaten by his father, the doc's grandfather, who had, in his turn, been beaten by his father, and so on ... And how he finally understands that his fascination with the healing power of bones led to his medical career.

'So, perhaps worth it, in a strange way. If I could go back and choose, would I prefer to have been adopted? Would I be a doctor if I had been?' the doc asked.

I wish I could feel more compassionate, but it's my rhyme after all.

The doc stole it. There, I've said it.

The doc is still trying to finish his paper. I don't think he's in a fit enough state for it though. He seems perpetually tired.

I fed him a few facts about my early life, some true, to speed him along.

This is the patient all shaven and shorn
That treated the doc all tattered and torn
That noted the mother all forlorn
That kissed the dad with the crumpled scorn
That thrashed the boy that made the scar
That sealed the wound that broke the skin
That lay on the bones that Jack built.

After the doc finished his paper and I'd read it, I felt that he finally believed me. Once I had something definite to hold onto, I could let go, and immediately started to get better. Like anyone in recovery, I prefer not to think of the darkest days.

I'm not completely out of the woods. The paper wasn't enough for the doc. Whenever we're alone, he lies on the empty bed next to mine and asks me questions.

I wish his interrogations would stop. He can't really expect me to feel things all the time. Let go, like I did, I want to tell him.

Regardless, it's time for me to put my life back on a solid footing. My skin is healing up nicely, while the doc's has begun to show open wounds.

The doc comes into my room. He hangs his white coat on the back of a chair and lies down on the spare bed. I watch him lying there, bathed in the sterile stripes of sunlight coming through the window. I imagine his skin peeling back, splitting him open. I can feel the strands of collagen loosening, like relaxing in a bath of warm tears.

He looks into my eyes and it would almost be true, if unscientific, to say that we experience, for a moment, the wounds, the life, of the other, our scars small islands in oceans of pain.

But the doc is crying. He looks helpless.

I stare at the red, raw patches on his arms. And I feel that I've suffered enough. The past is the past and I want to blot it out.

The doc leaves the room to wash his face and I try on his coat. It's a good fit and I feel so secure. But when he returns and sees me, his eyes hold an incoherent question that I somehow can't bear.

I judge it best to ignore it. I need to get away. 'I'm due to check out in ten minutes,' I tell him.

He starts crying again.

I do have a heart. I usher him quickly into his office and seat him in the patient's chair. I whip through the filing cabinet and find a depression questionnaire, the PHQ-9 or something.

The doc bats away the form with his feeble, wound-encrusted arms. The wounds are showing down to the bones, I note.

But I know how to cheer him up. I switch on his computer. 'Hang on,' I say, and I google. 'There are two-hundred and six bones in the human body,' I tell him. 'It all starts with the bones.'

DILATED PUPIL
Ollie Charles

The smell of stale beer and vodka lingers. My brain is dizzy with anxiety and heavy, as if pushing a big weight in the gym.

It's late, most people are asleep in their beds, except us. There are no windows, nothing to connect us to the outside world, only the blazing lights that swallow us whole. We dance like brilliant monsters, gorging on every bit of energy we have and downing shots of anything we can get our hands on. Our bodies scream, our hands wander.

My eyes register the other bodies, worshipping the curves of their muscles. Twisting and turning to the pulse of the music, my head fills with their hard bodies, their thick arms, their broad shoulders.

My heartbeat quickens as the lights change colour; blue, green, purple, orange. Sweat trickles down my forehead, although I can't be sure whether it's mine. All I can hear is the fierce pounding of the DJ's beat.

This will be our secret, won't it? No one would believe someone like you, the voice says.

Every time I feel a hand on my shoulder or breath on my neck, my heart stampedes, a herd of horses, and I wonder whether it's him coming back for more. Most of the time he's just the voice, whispering. But sometimes I see him, standing in front of a classroom, acting as if there wasn't a monster thrashing under his skin, waiting.

Panic starts to rise and I feel a shudder up my spine. I need to breathe. In. One, two, three. Out. One, two, three.

I dance. There are men everywhere, snakes slithering, looking for prey. We wear glorious masks to hide who we really are.

These days my body rarely feels like mine. It feels as if I'm locked in a jail with a sentence that has no end. And it fills me with shame, afraid to tell anyone, afraid I'd be sent away.

One of the dancers pulls me closer, his hands around my waist, squeezing me tight. I keep counting my breaths, as if focusing on a test, trying to calm myself. He has large hands, which move across my back. I feel his cock grow hard and my nipples stiffen. The urge to kiss swells. Our tongues dance. I think he's enjoying it. Spits mix like an incendiary cocktail and I get caught up, thinking everything is okay. A momentary sensation. That's when I see his face, staring at me, his lips curled upwards, a disturbing sneer.

I hear someone near me laughing.

You'll never amount to anything. No one will ever love you.

A calloused hand tightly gripping my shoulder as I sit in class, a long fringe framing his dark eyes, silently staring down at me whilst I dig my nails into the fatty part of my leg and I keep looking forward.

The kissing stops and I pull back, bumping into the bodies around me. The room spins, I have to get away.

The distance to the door looks impossible to reach. Hands grab at me, hands trying to pull me back into the animal enclosure. I feel a shooting pain down my spine. It feels hard to breathe, as if I were running a marathon.

You'll never feel any better than you do right now.

How would you know how I feel? I say.

The first sense I register, as I come to, is my hearing. A violent bass drop, making the sticky floor vibrate. I notice a drip, drip, drip.

My blurry eyes start to refocus, like someone turning up the dimmer on a light switch. I reach my hands out on either side of me and feel cubicle walls, grimy and covered in tiny scrawl that I can't make out. As I move, I feel the cool of the porcelain toilet on my legs and above, the flickering light like the flame of a candle about to be blown out. The skin around my neck feels hot to touch.

I hear a door slamming open and for a moment the music from the club washes over me.

Fuck yeah, I hear someone moan.

I realise it's the cubicle next to mine. Then I hear a second voice, a restrained whine.

Fuck yeah.

Then I see the body sitting on the ground in front of me, in my cubicle, hunched over itself so I can't see the face. Its long, dark hair is slicked back, I notice a ragged crack of congealing red in the soft bit of the back of the head.

I start to shake, tears falling down my face. I want to scream but nothing comes out, like in a nightmare when you're being chased. Who the fuck is that?

A heavy, metallic smell fills my nose and my throat fills with blood. My eyes feel dry. I start to retch, heaving for air to fill my throat, my lungs, but all I can see is the body, discarded like a piece of junk. I pull my denim shorts back up around my waist. They're ripped.

I dig my nails into the palms of my hands, scratching, until it starts to sting, bleed. The skin on my arms feels rough, like sandpaper, blistered. I blink, one, two, three times. The body still remains. Did I do this?

I try my hardest not to touch it, not to even make direct eye contact, as if it were some Greek myth that might turn me to stone.

I look up and see the door to the cubicle. Are there any cameras in here?

What am I meant to do? Call someone? Tell someone what happened? But I can't remember what happened, and how am I meant to explain who this is when I don't even know.

Would you really forget about me that easily? The voice is back.

An empty classroom, except for the two of us. Outside the sky is filled with stars, illuminating a path home, beautiful.

I step around the body and swing open the cubicle door.

Did you hear that? one of the couple in the next stall ask.

It's nothing, there's no one in here. Come here. Let me fuck you.

Fuck yeah.

In front of me is a wall of mirrors. I'm looking back at me from the other side.

Are you alright? I ask the me I can see.

My eyes, framed by deep bags, stare back. My face looks blotchy, my raw lips are peeling. I bite down on a small bit of dark, hardened skin and, as my teeth pull, I rip off too much and yelp in pain. I feel a sharp stinging sensation and a bubble of blood bulges from the middle, which I suck back up into my mouth. The sensation is delicious agony.

My phone vibrates in my pocket. The couple in the cubicle are grunting and moaning.

The screen screams with light, like staring at the sun.

Where r u?

I wish I knew how to respond.

In the mirror, I notice the body behind me shiver and shake. It starts to sigh and moan, like a wounded animal after a car collision.

The grunting noises from the couple in the cubicle grow louder and louder until I can hear nothing else, and the makeshift walls of the cubicle start shaking, as if they may buckle at any moment.

The body's mouth gapes open, starts moving.

What the fuck are you staring at?

It's the voice again. The voice from the classroom, the voice that has followed me in my memories, the voice that I was told I should trust.

The body dribbles. A stark red. Like rain down a windowpane.

Every muscle screams at me to flee, but I remain frozen. The monster in the mirror holding me captive, arresting me for what feels an eternity. I'm unable to turn away for fear of an impending attack. I gasp for air, steady myself, prepare to retaliate.

I watch as the body pulls itself to its knees, its fringe caught between the browning blood dried on its forehead, where skin flaps gaily.

I choke down phlegm, throwing my neck back as I heave, trying to compose myself. I feel a quiver down my spine, a flash of pain. I instinctively reach for my forehead, which feels damp. The tops of my fingers are caked in a brilliant red, framing the dirt beneath my fingernails.

The body slides its head across the cool rim of the toilet bowl, resting. A teacher should have your best interests at heart, your appropriate adult. I stare hard at the body's sad mouth, it's sunken skin, furrowed brow. A crusty sliver of blood beneath its nose is reflected in the dim spotlights and I notice a dampening in its trousers. The body musters enough strength to pull a small bag of white powder out of its pocket.

Flash to sitting in his classroom, him offering me a line of coke, holding my head down on the desk, applying pressure to my neck, my back, kicking the backs of my legs so I lose balance.

Flash to him always staring at me. When I wake in the morning, when I allow someone else to touch me, sneering, never letting me forget.

Flash to my head spinning as I gasp for air, struggling against his tight grip on my neck.

The mirrors, which line the wall watch, wordlessly. The mirrors are portals to an infinite number of other worlds; Wonderland, Oz, Neverland. They are full of other versions of me, dancing in different ways, saying different things, making different decisions. They all wait and stare.

Did you do this?

The body feels the wound on the back of its head.

I don't know what I did.

The couple in the cubicle walk out one after the other. One looks down towards the ground, unable to make eye contact with me or his lover. He walks to a sink and starts to wash his hands. I want to grab hold of him, put my hands on his cheeks, hold him tight. I want to tell him that everything will be alright.

Fucking hell mate, you alright? the other asks me.

I'm great, never felt better.

Mate, did you hear me? He's stood at the sink on the other side of me.

Why won't he go away?

Do you want me to call someone to help?

Help who, I think.

Neither of them sees the body.

At what point do we start to believe in the jagged shards of our memories?

My trauma is bright red. What about yours?

SEROSORTING
Justin David

Clean only?

This is shorthand he's not yet come across. Rupert stretches, discreetly pressing nose to armpit. He's the wrong side of fragrant but natural is what most men push for these days.

He draws on his fag and leans back on the window of the barber's shop. His eyes move from the stud on his phone screen to the stud, on the other side of the street, haloed in red neon from the 24-hour launderette—*BuffLondon54*, an angel of pleasure in a pristine white vest, tanned arms sleeved in black ink. The straps of his rucksack sit just where a bondage harness might cut into flawless equine muscle. The man is waiting for a bus—twelve metres away—literally, according to the app. A bus arrives. For a moment, it looks as if he might board and Rupert feels a tug, a craving in his loins. When the bus moves on, the man is still there cruising him.

Between them, pedestrians drift by—day-glo hipsters, hi-viz construction workers, high-spirited mothers falling out of *Pepper'n'Spice* with take-away dinners, women in hijabs, old Turkish grandfathers heading to the Community Centre. Aren't we lucky, Rupert considers, to be part of this collective who so easily rub along with each other, sharing communal spaces—the café, the market, the library, the restaurants? Isn't that wild? This community is testament to a very profound connection we all have with each other. Or, at least Rupert likes to think so.

They lock eyes and *BuffLondon54* smiles from beneath the peak, white teeth flashing in the middle of salt and pepper stubble. Rupert's ass twitches with a faint tingle of possibility, like the zest of an amuse-bouche awakening the taste buds.

It's the second or third time Rupert has seen him round here—at various times of the day, never dressed for anything like work, unless of course he's a rent boy. Though, truth-be-told, no one has solicited on the street this side of 1996. All that caper is carried out online these days.

He's probably in a committed relationship, judging from the wedding band on his finger. *Rupert, you're in grave danger of sounding like your mother.*

The last time Rupert spotted *BuffLondon54*, he was with friends, laughing raucously in the Dirty Duck on Dalston Lane. His preppy-daddy appearance clashed terribly with the velvet pelmets and tasselled lampshades of the shabby-chic public house, though he seemed eclectically at home. *BuffLondon54* had mischievous and frisky eyes and the lithe body of a sportsman. *BuffLondon54* had followed him into the toilets where, shyly, Rupert had declined to engage.

The phone vibrates in Rupert's palm. *Into?*

He holds his fag in between middle-finger and index, and types with his ring finger. *Long sweaty sessions. Flip-flop.*

Accom or trav?

—abbreviated abbreviations he's quickly become used to now that he's two years single again and daring himself to plunge into these deep carnivorous waters. Brevity is key to encounter these days. No small talk. Keep the prelude quick and business-like.

Either. Looking for later, his thumbs reply.

Rupert hasn't ruled out the prospect of another serious relationship. Ultimately, he yearns for companionship. But he can still remember the sound of the door closing behind the last one for the final time, after he had delivered irreconcilable news.

For now *fun* will be enough.

For now, it's brevity that excites him—not a languid stroll inside the calm waters of romance but the shock of being, within a few exchanged phrases, oubliette deep in a carnal encounter. Each call into the darkness stayed with him, despite them being fleeting and anonymous.

The phone vibrates: the image of a muscular torso laced with further tattoos appears on his screen. It wouldn't be the first time he'd been tricked by a fake profile photograph. He was once tricked into thinking he was going to meet the captain of the English rugby team by someone who resembled Stan Laurel. Yet, here is proof, if ever he needed it, of a head attached to the corresponding body—rugged looking, optimistic demeanour, opalescent eyes. On *BuffLondon54*'s neck, the sunburnt gooseflesh of an older man, one of Rupert's more unusual tastes.

Phone buzzes again. *My place? Party and play?*

It's one of his good days. He's having a good day.

He notices the lights of the junction change from red to amber to green and the circulation of the traffic begins again, as if a valve has been opened, allowing it to rush once more into the veins of central London—cells perhaps oblivious to the anonymous exchange taking place on this street corner. His mind explodes with the possibilities on offer. Rupert imagines entering this man's personal space, exposing himself, peeling off that white vest, breathing in the smell of skin beneath stubble, surrendering to chance and maybe vulnerability.

The man pulls the peak of the baseball cap down over his eyes and let's his hand fall in front of his belt buckle, punctuating this anatomical sentence by allowing the tip of his thumb to outline the seemingly endless shaft of his penis to the crotch of his jeans.

Up4it, Rupert types. *Barbers first*. He smiles across the street and points into the full-length barber's shop window, as a blonde customer exits, hair cropped short and clean shaven; there's a little pink at the nape of his neck. Rupert checks the shopping list on the man's profile once more: *Fucking, sucking, nipple play, lots of body contact, sub-dom role-play, sometimes like to get high with a guy during sex, clean only*. He jams the phone back in his pocket, looks once more across the street at him. What the fuck is *clean only*? Rupert takes one last drag on his fag before flicking the stub into the gutter and turning into the barber's shop, now that it's his turn in the chair.

This room is cared for with the unfussy love of its owner who has dressed it with quaint artefacts: little cobalt nazar beads and amulets hanging on the corner of mirrors, a carved wooden coat stand and a budgerigar tweeting loudly inside an ornamental cage. All of this contrasts with the flat screen television that has played continuous Al-Jazeera for the seven years that he's been coming here. Though, in all honesty, the whole place could do with rewiring, and the grout around the tile of the sinks has seen better days.

Rupert's always been quite introspective but lately these ponderous, analytical moments are hitting him more frequently. Perhaps it's a side effect of being single. Perhaps it is just to do with getting older. Perhaps—

'Hoşgeldiniz' the barber says.

Rupert smiles and nods.

In the seat next to the window and the birdcage, the fatherly, tubby barber places a towel across Rupert's lap and covers him in a cape of protective nylon.

'Head? Wet shave?' he asks.

'Yes,' Rupert nods.

'Beard?'

'Shaping and a trim,' Rupert replies, sinking into the cushioned chair. They are verbose as always. 'How have you been?'

'Oh, busy. Warm weather bring more customers.' Brevity is the barber's charm. It's always the same. They exchange pleasantries in Pidgin English, usually about the weather or a comment on the mood of the budgerigar—whether it is singing or not. But mainly Rupert sits still and the barber works in silence. This fortnightly visit is an opportunity to vague out, only right now Rupert is still aware of *BuffLondon54* out there in the darkness.

The barber rests his hands on him, looking at Rupert in the mirror. 'How are you?' he asks, massaging Rupert's shoulders a little. He feels the barber's onion breath on his cheek. The smell of it mixes with the pongs of hair lotions and products that stand like a cityscape along the washbasins and work surfaces. He gets to work. First, he gets rid of the excess hair with a swipe of the clippers across Rupert's beard ... red hair falls to the floor. The barber starts filling a little bowl with hot water into which he sinks his shaving brush. While he's preparing, Rupert looks down at the red shavings from his own hair, mixing with the blonde hair from the previous client. The intermingled hair is caught by the fluorescent light of the shop; it's almost as if all the hair could have been from one person, one body.

He watches the barber plunge the brush up and down into the soap until it foams up like meringue. He puts it against Rupert's head and rotates the brush in little circles until his entire head looks like the top of an ice-cream cone. The barber snaps a clean razor out of its wrapper and clicks it into the handle. Rupert feels the blade rest tentatively against his skin and hear the frit-frit of it like pine against sand paper. The blade moves methodically in controlled rows across his head. The barber leans close. He checks in the mirror the evenness of his work, flicks foam and hair into the sink. Closer. Row after completed row, thin wisps of hair vanish from Rupert's head, exposing his slick, vulnerable scalp.

For a moment Rupert feels intensely horny and he imagines himself in the chair with *BuffLondon54* running the blade across his head. He never understood why there's something divinely sexy about a sexual partner shaving one's head, but there is. Something to do with trust? Something to do with submission?

While all of this is running through Rupert's mind, his eyes have become unfocused.

'Sorry. Sorry,' the barber says.

Rupert realizes that to the barber it appears that he's staring at the black mildew growing on the wallpaper around the washbasins.

'I try make better but just keep coming. Better accept just part of building. Damp everywhere. Part of us. Just like the mice. This their home.'

The damp patches are creeping all over the interior. Some blotches are worse than others, but it's literally everywhere. Riddled.

Rupert is perplexed. He looks up at the barber's reflection in the mirror.

Rupert senses the eyes of *BuffLondon54* on the other side of the street. As he turns his head quickly to get a better look through the window, he feels a frictionless slice upon his forehead. At first, he thinks he's imagined it. His head looks clean without a blemish but the blade is sitting in the epidermis and the barber is grimacing. He closes his mouth and moves the blade. A trickle of blood starts to seep out, releasing a two-year old trauma that Rupert had up until now kept hidden.

'Sorry. Sorry. Stay still.'

Rupert can't move. He can't speak. His pulse increases. Dizzy. He wants to tell the barber ... but ...

The barber dabs gently with tissue and removes red liquid. Rupert, paralysed, watches the barber's naked fingers moving around the blood, in slow motion. There's a tiny nick on his thumb, perhaps caused only by a pair of barber's scissors. It still looks fresh. What if ...? There is this obsession with blood, every time Rupert cuts a finger, grazes a knee, has a nose bleed. His blood. Her blood. Your blood. My blood. Stay away from the fucking blood.

The world fades. Rupert can hear the sound of the budgerigar but it seems very distant. The barber is unmoved—cool as a nurse in a white room, staring at two little blue dots.

Panic shoots through Rupert. *This test is reactive. I'll just go and get the second test.*

Out of breath.

Can't breathe.

Heart pounding.

Need to get out. Need to get off this chair. He can't move.

Try to look normal. Try to breathe.

Will he have a heart attack? Will he die? Panic consumes him. Sweat breaks out on his brow.

The barber looks up at Rupert in the mirror, sees him out of breath. He knows something is wrong. 'You okay?'

Rupert manages to nod, gulping for air at the same time. He stares at the stain on his forehead that can never be erased.

'I sorry. Okay. Okay. Just little cut. Nothing. See. I clean. Blood stop.' He squeezes Rupert on the shoulder and smiles. 'Relax.'

Rupert nods again but it all comes rushing back to him ... how he felt contaminated, dirty, unclean. Ah!

Un*clean. Clean.* Un—

He feels the phone vibrate persistently in his pocket and the budgie berserks inside its cage.

The barber finishes. He tidies the edges of Rupert's beard, the outline of his mouth below the moustache, the hairs on his cheekbones. He trims the unruly hair around Rupert's ears and eyebrows and splashes on that damned cheap cologne that he's always too polite to decline.

He pays with a twenty. Doesn't wait for the change. Leaves more hurriedly than usual. Just get out.

'Your change,' the barber says as Rupert voicelessly approaches the door. Rupert waves it away. 'Thank you. Have nice weekend,' the barber says.

Rupert nods. He tries to smile at him but can't. He steps outside the shop, tears in his eyes, the test results stuck like a broken heart in his throat, as if it were yesterday, the weight of the last two years swishing around his knees like water in a sinking rowing boat.

He pulls his phone from his jeans pocket and reads the last message.

We're set. I've sourced everything from a mate. V, G and M. It's going to be a banging night. Can't wait to get you naked. Ready?

Rupert touches his forehead, feeling that un-healable incision that is now on the outside, as well as the inside. Pedestrians drift along the pavement. All around him, he sees the same gash upon the foreheads of people passing by on the street, a little trickle of blood from a fresh cut, and their grubby stains of mortality ... an infection running through us all. We are *all* unclean.

He looks over at *BuffLondon54* who's been waiting on the other side of the street all this time, still perhaps not waiting for a bus, but with a now rather satisfied look on his face. He removes his cap for a moment to scratch his head—no mark; this confirms what Rupert has been thinking—that *BuffLondon54* has seemingly been spared, and there is the disconnect. Rupert glances back at all the people passing by. All the stigmata he thought he'd seen have now vanished from their faces.

He swallows the severed heart, which sinks heavily to his

stomach and he's reminded that he must get home to take his tablet *BuffLondon54* gestures with open palms, his satisfaction turning to confusion as Rupert turns and walks the other way.

IT MAY CONCERN
Keith Jarrett

Maybe his name was Rumpelfuckinstiltskin. Or something worse ... like Bill. My fixation was beginning to concern me, and now I was starting to worry about worrying about the absence of his name. Seeing as we'd first met eight or nine months ago, it had gone way beyond the point where I could just *ask* him.

Sunlight burst through the hallway as I flicked through the stack of letters on the ledge. *TO THE HOMEOWNER. TO WHOM IT MAY CONCERN.* A few flyers mixed in. Takeaway menus. Offer leaflets from a nearby supermarket. I would have known if he'd told me already; of this I was—almost—certain. I'd noted down scraps of what he'd said to me in the dozen or so times we'd met, all the pieces of information he'd given away, most of it fluff, inconsequential details. He worked in an office. He had friends for dinner sometimes, which meant he was at least able to cook. What did he cook? He'd changed the subject but disclosed his mistrust of microwaves.

Maybe he was a spy or a terrorist, or something else equally sinister. A Tory politician? My imagination was running wild, and I needed to rein it back in.

The toilet flushed from across the hall and I jumped. I patted the pile of bumf—all unaddressed—away and tiptoed back from the hallway and into the kitchen, enjoying the feeling of the underfloor heating on my soles. He must have washed his hands quickly, if at all; he pounced into my peripheral view within seconds of my moving into a plausible position.

'Just getting some water!'

I approached the taps, glanced at a glass teetering on the edge of the draining board. He kissed my forehead, the wetness of his lips suggesting he'd splashed his face in the sink. He grabbed me close.

'You look a mess.'

'Ok ... *thanks*?'

He had that self-assured way about him that could never be messy. I stared down at the hair on his belly, the towel he'd half-heartedly tied around his waist; his cock peeking through the gap.

'That's a good thing. We kind of got a workout in there.' He laughed. 'Here!'

A kitchen rag appeared. He smudged at the crusted bits of our cum. I batted him away.

'I'll probably grab a shower, if that's all right?'

I tottered over towards the bathroom, from whence the nameless one had come.

'What about your water?'

'Oh yeah ... thanks.'

I held out my hand while he poured from the tap. It tasted of London grit. I'd been raised not to trust anything that didn't come out of a bottle or a can; where I was born, if you had taps in the kitchen, you most certainly didn't drink from them unless you boiled it first. Old habits, I guess. I beamed anyway and gulped it quick. His smirk was mysterious, a winner's smile. I pecked at his lips and swished away to the bathroom, trying not to look *a mess*.

I shouldn't have even bothered with a shower, but I needed to clear something in my brain. I retraced my thought patterns as the lukewarm spray submerged me. I'd tried looking for letters, I couldn't find his wallet, no cards, no ID lanyards hanging from the key hook, or in his pockets. I pushed the safety button in and turned the heat up.

It was an old grand house, renovated in that tasteful, bland way that people interested in property values like. Nothing to offend and nothing to reveal. Maybe I should have just enjoyed the moment, the blankness of it all, allowed myself to be the most conspicuous presence in the house, the neighbourhood. I let my eyes rest on the blue and white tiles while the scalding spray galloped down my back, then I closed them.

At some point, he must have entered the bathroom, de-towelled, and stepped in. I felt the change in temperature first, a bite at my neck, then lower, as he stooped to wrap his arms around me. While the distraction wasn't *not* welcome, I was still working on a plan, and so it took a while for me to change gears. I twisted round to return his kiss, threw my neck back like a porn star, moaned into the sterility of the tiles, enjoying the echo. Once I dived into the drama, the momentum took over and I forgot my self-consciousness, my *messiness*. He brought it out in me. This was why we'd seen each other again after all these months, I guess, despite the creeping unease I felt. It certainly wasn't because of his house, or his personality.

After a couple of minutes, I led him back to the bedroom, because: a) the images of me slipping and dying and my blood flowing away down the plughole weren't too sexy and b) the environment. He was that much older and wouldn't live to see as much of the destruction of the planet as I would. I turned off the tap and we dripped all the way across the carpet and soaked his sheets. No way would this be possible at my place.

This second time, he came inside me, whispering my name. He'd never done that before. I tensed with the guilt that this could never be reciprocated. My eyes grew hot in frustration and so I tried to return to the moment, to the gradual slowing of his thrusts, the aftershock. As he softened, his cock slid out, slug-like. I smiled into his hand. He kissed my neck again.

It was getting late; the sky had lost the brightness of an hour before. I dreaded how the weekend passed so fast. Tomorrow, work would drag again, too soon for me to have recovered from the drudgery of the week before. I raised myself up from the bed and made leaving noises. He insisted on giving me money for a taxi, with 'a little more extra' because he didn't have anything smaller than a fifty. It felt a bit sex-workery, but I pocketed the money and got the tube home. It would have felt equally dishonest to refuse; I just hated being offered in the first place.

💡

I have always been aware that names predetermine events, how so much of one's life is inevitable once pinned to a name, a foreshadowing of sorts. My own name had gone through its own metamorphosis; I'd swapped a letter round to loosen it from the shackles of gender. My last name had no such luck, but it had also been twisted in the distant past, perhaps a misspelling on a plantation ledger, branching it off from the original Scottish root that landed in Caribbean soil.

As I was mumbling to myself about this, three un-uniformed police pulled up. I was searched and questioned again. They could have at least given me a lift to the tube station.

The following day I returned to the office and donned my headphones. Editing interviews, sharpening the sound. Arranging the captions. Cutting. Replaying. Trying not to self-hypnotise with the monotony. It took three cups of coffee to achieve optimal concentration. Any more could produce panic, any less and the mind wandered too easily. The guy on loop in my ears was a cockwomble. It was difficult to listen to someone you have taken an instant loathing to. Repetition made it easier; becoming accustomed to the cadences, the hesitations, the vulnerabilities of the voice. After playing the interview for the tenth time, and the caffeine wearing off, I decided I would take him home to finish it off. I spent the rest of the morning deleting 'reply all' messages and changing my email signature.

My work allies were busy as it was launch day. I mildly liked everyone else, but we didn't have much interaction and I was mostly left alone. I ate my sandwich at my desk, browsing through the news and all the junk I'd saved to look at later. Somehow, I ended up searching for his address—him of no name, that is. I searched for the house next to his address. No owners came up, no matter how deeply I investigated. I whistled when I learned the estimated house price. I hovered the little yellow man onto the grid and walked through the streets online, several thousand pixels worth of front-gardened houses and semi-detached palaces full of anxious new money. Reinforced car-tanks. Tinted children and tightly wound-up windows. Double-locked doors. I let my imagination run wild before I noticed the clock. The little hand had overtaken the big hand and it was well past the end of lunchtime.

Later, the bus home was slow. I skimmed the news on my phone to pass the time and regretted it. All grim: murders, earthquakes, injustices, and the bickering men in charge of everything. Nowhere seemed safe: there was nowhere I could escape, no desert island I could run off to and live, preferably with a hot guy, with a name and few hang-ups. I turned my alerts on, replied to the more appealing dick pics, put on a happier playlist.

At home, I flung down my bag, put out the bins and hoovered till gran came back. We ate some warmed-up leftovers with the television soundtracking the silence and I finally went up to my room. Sleep took hold of me with my clothes still on. I dreamt of all the guys' names called out on a register: Eric, Federick, Luc, Faizal, Ciaran, Kareem, Sahir, Shawn, Daryl, Derek, Dee Jay, Nelson ... All the guys I'd known since I came out, and when I came out again. All the guys I'd dared to club with at college. All the guys I'd failed to get close to. I woke up a couple of hours later. It was clearly still bothering me.

Late through the night, unable to fall asleep again, I replayed the interview from work, and continued editing until I was fairly pleased with the result. My job was thankless, the kind you only take notice of when it's not done well. No one notices the hours, the monotonous graft, all the effort made in order to be seamless, invisible.

Tired, but still sleepless, I put my headphones down and listened to the traffic outside. I looked through his pictures. I tried to do a reverse image search. No joy; they were nearly all screenshots. Nearly ... but for one.

I wished I hadn't been so thorough.

I fell asleep again, numb.

On the way to work the next day, they'd cordoned off part of the street; a boy had been stabbed. I had no time to get my usual fix from the coffee shop before getting the tube so I had to wait till I got to the office and grab one from the canteen. By the time I reached work, my head was throbbing.

My manager asked if I was ok, casually, while walking past my desk.

When my manager asked someone if they were ok, this was not to be taken as a good sign. I kept my head down for the rest of the morning.

⚐

He messaged late on Friday; he'd been out for a drink. *Are you free?*

Why not? One last time. It would make no difference. *Sure, give me an hour.*

I can get you a cab.

I pulled on a jock, a t-shirt and some jeans, preened a little in the bathroom and announced my departure to 'meet work colleagues'.

My gran raised an eyebrow and sighed, but I was not a child. I'd move out when I could afford it, or I'd stay till she died. That was the deal. She knew I wasn't about to get anyone pregnant.

In certain traditions, if you name something, you can fix it to you. A song I'd learned sometime ago became a whistle under my breath: '*Si te preguntaran dónde es que yo vivo, no le dé mi nombre ni tampoco mi apellido ...*'

In many places, it was impolite to speak a person's real name. If you knew the name of someone, you could call them back to where you were, whether they wanted you to or not. *Take your name out of my mouth.* In various religious traditions, God had many names, or infinite names, or none that could be spoken by humans. I knew this because of Wikipedia and my Aunt Alba, who used to tell me stories. I also knew this the way trees know how to make skeletons of themselves in the autumn.

⚐

We fucked on the settee, the television lights flickering behind our

147

backs and making patterns on the wall. We flopped back onto the cushions to catch our breath afterwards. He zonked out almost immediately and I tiptoed to the bathroom. I troubled my reflection in the mirror. I needed to know for sure. As long as he was still asleep, I could search upstairs.

Before I could even begin any further escapades, he called out for me.

'I'm in the bog!'

'All right. Shall I get you a drink or do you want a cab?'

I asked for the latter, irritable, having been so close to the confirmation I craved.

⚲

The driver was over-familiar, too inquisitive. I was anxious to be home, to return to my work, to the unruly voices that needed to be fitted into neat ten-minute segments.

⚲

The disembodied voice is a curious thing. I hadn't really grown up with the radio, but there were some personalities I knew and could put a face to. There were a couple of others I could guess at, people I'd heard in the car on the way to school. I'd imagine their faces puffed with anger as they argued with callers, alternating between immigration and gays, gays and immigration. By the time I started getting the bus to school, it was Muslims instead of gays.

I liked to believe that you could hear a genuine smile, you could hear cruelty, bitterness, passion, intelligence. All of these were evident in subtle inflections, emphases, accents. You could hear when someone was making too much effort to disguise their humble origins, their ulterior motives. At the same time, you could throw yourself into the gaps, into what you couldn't see.

I liked to believe the gaps held the most potential; I still do. In this world of the unspoken, my grandma and I lived on diverging orbits. We gave each other space.

Enlarging his image on my phone screen in the dark—the one I'd tracked to a social media post and then, through its likes, to a profile, and then a company website—I studied his face. *Perhaps he had a twin?* Someone once told me desperation was the damaged shadow of hope. Until this moment in the dark, with only the phone's glow as a guide, I'd always underestimated shadows and their stretching prowess.

I read out his particulars from his bio again, so many of the things he'd been deliberate about hiding.

To calm myself enough to sleep, I imaged a thousand other scenarios in which I would have felt just as uneasy. For the sake of possibility bingo, he could have been: a reactionary columnist, an internet troll or, yes, a Tory politician.

Or what if he'd simply been an awful son, friend, husband? What about all of the people in my life who'd simply remained silent?

⚲

The following weekend, I broke into his house. I didn't mean to.

This is how it occurred: my phone pinged with his message. He was free later on but was out shopping. I didn't reply, turning it over in my mind. One last time?

Sure, I replied, after a while.

I *wasn't* sure. I was curious about my own hypocrisy.

It was just supposed to be a walk around the block but I didn't want to be inside with my thoughts and so I kept going. The sun hung low. Music blared from the flats on the other side of the street. The traffic was heavy from all the road diversions and Saturday shoppers. Agitated families blocked the road. I veered through the park to find peace.

There was nothing to do. It had rained heavily that morning, so the grass was wet and there was nowhere to sit. The museums were busy or expensive. I had no desire for more coffee. The library was being renovated. My friends were newly coupled and either not free, or free later, or too annoying to be around.

After two hours of meandering, the streets took on a familiar upwards slant. I only realised as I was approaching his house that I'd arrived, hours before I should have.

Some people have voices in their heads. If I'd had one, it could have told me to turn around and head back home, or anywhere away from the house of this man who I didn't really know. I had no such voice; this much is evident.

Also: he was supposed to be at the shops. Also: the door wasn't supposed to be ajar.

❦

Of course, his wife's account of the whole run of events was entirely different. Who can blame her for being startled when a stranger walked into her house like they owned the place? When she found the stranger ruffling through her possessions? Who can blame her for thinking me a thief, or worse?

And what did it matter? Perhaps it would have been better if I were a burglar.

❦

In the alternate space where I live, I blocked the man's number and continued my weekend oblivious. I prefer this reality to the noisy cell I inhabit now. I prefer that world's microwaved dinners and its silently disapproving grandmothers who were gradually becoming accustomed to seeing their family in a new light. In this alternate space, I am curious for knowledge—and names—and all that comes with it, but I understand it carries a weight.

Also, in this alternate world, I would have no need to muse on all the coincidences that brought me to this moment. How banal the reality was, how unremarkable the omissions! I think now of how one person's office resembles another's. How listening to voices—as I did—and writing speeches—as he did—fall within similar spectra. How his words had placed themselves inside mouths that snarled at lives like mine. How I searched for the ugliness I thought I deserved and still found myself surprised.

PARTNERING

Aisha Phoenix

Celina spent the best hours of the day programming, stopping only for steaming cups of ginger and lemon and instant noodles. Working at home, she never saw anyone and no one saw her, which meant she didn't need to worry about whether they'd find her nose too broad or her skin too dark. By the time she'd finished on Friday evening, the light had drained from the sky.

'Damn! ... Car,' she said, as she checked the time on her Universe.

'I don't know how to respond to that,' her wrist computer replied.

'Car,' she said again, pulling on the pair of trainers that moulded to her feet.

She grabbed a coat, snatched up her bag, and rushed out. If she was lucky, she'd just make it to the club during happy hour when entry and rentals didn't cost a world of credits.

On her Universe, she tracked the car's progress to her apartment block and cursed it for making her wait outside for five minutes. Then she cursed their 'intelligent' navigation system for sending the car down the back streets. In the days of drivers, at least she could have dictated the route.

The car was warm with the scent of fake leather. While it crawled over speed bumps, Celina got out her pocket mirror and applied lipstick, blusher and eyeliner, using her little finger to smooth away smudges. She finished by massaging oil into her scalp to give her short hair a nice sheen. She held the mirror at arm's length to admire her work, even though she knew no guys would be looking at her.

When she arrived at the club, it had just gone nine. There was a white couple in front of her. The woman had her arm around the man's waist and she was leaning against him. Celina saw the way they gazed at each other. That would never be her. She didn't need anyone. She pulled herself straighter and turned to look at the flickering white fairy lights in the display in one of the bars a few doors down.

When she got to the door, the iris reader announced she would be charged twenty credits—twice what she would have paid had she been two minutes earlier. She descended to the Dressing Room floor in the glass lift and sat on one of the smart thermo benches to pull on her dancing shoes. The bench began to warm her legs and she looked at the groups of young women joking and laughing as they changed together. A number of them had their bellies on show and they adjusted each other's hair and outfits. Although she was less than a decade older than most of them, Celina felt as though she was from a different era. She'd never had a group of friends like that, women she could be herself with and relax into. One of the women was taller than the rest, with bright yellow heels accentuating sculpted calves. She had coffee-coloured skin and black hair, pinned up in a thick twist on her head. When she laughed, she tossed back her head and beautiful creases appeared around her eyes.

It cost Celina four credits to check in her coat and five to leave her bag. At the rental window, instead of requesting her usual Advanced Pro, she sighed and opted for the much cheaper Basic Plus. Next time she wouldn't be late.

'Today, you're dancing with Frank,' the automated voice of the kiosk hologram said.

She was used to Alejandro and Mateo, but Frank would have to do.

They made their way down to the dance floor, past the rows of men waiting at the sides, and she thought of how it used to be, back in the day, when she and all but the prettiest women, stood about waiting to be asked to dance. She missed nothing about those days, but the guys were not so happy to see them go. She'd heard the grumbling at the bar and been subjected to lewd remarks about her needing a *real man*.

'Ready?' Frank said.

She took his left hand in her right, resting the other on the dance-bot's shoulder. The DJ was playing timba, her favourite. They started doing the basic step with a few cross-body leads and side steps thrown in for good measure. It was much easier than she was used to, but with a Basic Plus, what would you expect? She focused on styling and added in some more complex footwork to stave off the boredom. Frank didn't seem to notice, just kept plodding along rigidly in time, a smile fixed on his face.

The dancefloor was already quite crowded. There were lots of women with Basic Pluses and some with Improvers. Celina couldn't see any Advanced Pros, but the women who usually hired them tended to arrive much later. Dotted about here and there were some casual dancers without bots, most of whom were not very good. Although these couples were responsible for all the mini collisions on the dance floor, they were laughing and smiling. From the way they held each other, Celina assumed they were new couples still bound by infatuation. She studied the women. Most of them were white; some were tanned. They were pretty enough, but nothing special. Most of the guys weren't that special either, except for one who could really move. She wondered whether she would be dancing with someone like him if she had lighter skin.

By midnight there'd be more couples, those Celina called *the Professionals*, who colonised an area near the stage and danced exclusively with each other. When she was partnered with Mateo or Alejandro she took no notice of them, but with Frank, she imagined what it would be like to join them.

After dancing to five tracks, Celina became aware that she was being watched by a thin man in a green shirt standing at the edge of the dancefloor. Over Frank's shoulder she saw him nudge a larger guy; they both looked at her and laughed.

'Please would you get me some water?' She spoke slowly to Frank, careful to make herself heard over the live music that had just started up.

'Of course,' Frank said. 'Coming right up.'

She watched the bot walk away. He was tall and well-toned with broad shoulders. She let her eyes rove over the men hovering at the sides. Most of them were her height or shorter and no longer in their prime. She left the floor and headed to the toilets.

As she passed the bar, she saw the man in the green shirt walk into Frank, spilling her drink down his front.

She continued towards the toilets, but glanced back over her shoulder. The man in green was in the middle of a group of guys crowded around Frank. They seemed to be jostling him. For a moment, she hesitated. He was a bot, he'd be fine. Celina pushed through the throng of jeans and dresses and disappeared into the Ladies.

She didn't go into one of the cubicles, just stood dabbing at the sweat on her face.

'Having fun?' the woman in the yellow heels said, coming out of a cubicle.

Celina smiled at the woman's reflection.

'I love your hair,' the woman said, as she washed her hands. 'It really suits you.'

'Thanks.' Celina gave her cheeks a final dab. 'I like yours too.'

When Celina came out, Frank was outside waiting for her. He held up a cup of water. 'Shall we go to the chill-out zone?'

She shook her head and downed the drink in one go. She'd found it very unsettling the first few times Mateo or Alejandro had known exactly where she was in the club. They were just tracking her Universe.

When they were back on the dancefloor and Frank said, 'Ready?' Celina expected more basic steps and cross-body leads. What she got instead was one basic followed by a series of fast spins. Frank was no Mateo or Alejandro and his movements felt awkward, almost jerky, but he was able to execute the moves.

From the corner of her eye, she saw the man in green laughing with his friends. Had they hacked Frank? The bot's steps got increasingly complex, but so did Celina's. She started to grin as she felt the adrenaline rush she usually got from Alejandro or Mateo spinning her across the floor. She caught the eye of the woman in the yellow heels, who smiled.

When the next track started, the man in green was right there, dancing with a young brunette woman next to Celina and Frank. He was trying to upstage every move Frank made. Track after track he danced, until his green shirt was dark with sweat and his face glistened. When Frank spun Celina five times in a row, the young woman dancing with the man in green made a T with her hands and left the floor, wiping her face as she pushed through the crowd. The man in green followed her.

As Celina queued for her coat, the man in the green shirt came over. 'Nice moves.'

'Thank you,' she said, eyeing him warily.

'But ...' he began.

'Here we go,' she said, under her breath.

'Don't you miss the connection you get when you dance with a real man?'

'Not really.'

'But do you connect with those things?'

She shrugged. 'They always dance in time, they don't touch me up or step on my feet. It's quite exhilarating, actually.'

'That's not what I meant. Don't you miss the energy and tension ...'

'I came here to relax, not feel tension,' Celina said.

'You know what I'm getting at.'

The queue was hardly moving and the sweat on Celina's back and chest, along with the air conditioning, was starting to make her feel cold.

'Most of the time I didn't feel *energy* or *tension*,' she said, crossing her arms in front of her chest and avoiding his gaze.

'I'm sorry to hear that,' he said. 'Dance with me. I'll show you what I mean.'

'I'll pass,' she said, putting out her hands as a Warmer rolled slowly by, wafting hot air.

'Come on, just one dance,' he said, leaning in towards her.

She shook her head and stepped back.

'It won't kill you.'

'She said she didn't want to dance with you.' The tall woman with the yellow heels was standing a couple of feet away, her eyes fixed on the man.

The woman turned to Celina. 'I'm a member. You can skip the queue.' She led Celina past the line of sweaty bodies to another cloakroom entrance. 'I'm Elle, by the way.'

Elle scanned her Universe to open the door, just as the DJ started to mix in one of Celina's favourite tracks.

'Mi Vida!' Celina exclaimed, grinning.

'Shall we?' Elle said.

Celina looked up at Elle's shining eyes and dimpled cheeks.

'Sure,' she said.

They left their coats in the cloakroom and went back downstairs. The dancefloor was empty save for a few women dancing with bots.

'I could never dance with a machine,' Elle said, taking Celina's hand. 'Technically they're great, but they're not sensual.'

Under the warm magenta lights, Celina was struck by the way Elle's hips moved, the speed of her feet, and the little half smile that played at the corner of her mouth before she launched Celina into a series of turns. As they moved around the dancefloor, Celina felt weightless in a way she never had with Frank, Alejandro, or Mateo. She was five again, the world spinning around her after exuberant playground whirls. Elle turned Celina in towards her and when the song ended, they held each other's gaze.

THE BIRDWATCHERS
Julia Bell

After sex, warm and stretched and feeling lithe, alive, again, they took their breakfast in the garden. Elise and her partner, Mira, often enjoyed sunny summer mornings on the deck that faced onto the small, private garden of their apartment. A plot that Elise had gently tended over many years, overhung with fragrant jasmine and clematis. Consequently, they never took much notice of the neighbours. On one side was a Turkish couple who mostly used the garden for laundry or barbecuing kebab and, given that they couldn't understand what they were saying, it was easy to phase out the music of their voices. On the other side, the ground-floor flat had been empty for months, the collateral in a messy divorce, and the garden was overgrown, brambles and nettles creeping under the fence.

So, it was a surprise then, as they sat with their sweet tea, naked under their thin robes, ready like cats to enjoy their coiled moment of satisfaction, to hear the sound of voices on the other side of the fence. Speaking English, she caught a word or two: *popular, contract.* And then the loud drawl of the estate agent, *of course the garden could do with a little work but it's a blank canvas!* Mira raised her eyebrows and shifted in her seat. Something about the loudness and the proximity intruded on their privacy, and somehow the relaxing moment was lost, causing Elise an irritation that lasted most of the day.

A few days later when taking out the rubbish, Elise saw a large white removal van parked in the street outside. She lingered at the gate in case she could glimpse whoever was moving. Over the low dividing wall, she could see the front window next door and as she turned to go back indoors, she thought she caught a flicker of movement, the blur of the drop of a curtain, a ripple of fabric. She shivered and nodded in the direction of the movement, feeling a bit stupid for being caught at the gate being nosey.

Over the course of the next few days where there had once been silence there was suddenly the noise of people living. Thumps of furniture being moved, muffled laughter. Elise noticed it at first, then it sank into the background and she didn't think about next door again until the weekend, which was Mira's birthday.

The weather was warm and sunny, so after a lazy few hours in bed, Elise got up and laid out the table in the garden for brunch, while Mira took a shower. She carefully arranged the table with a vase of freshly cut flowers from the garden, the presents in an artful pile. She took a photo and posted it to Instagram, wishing her beloved a Happy Birthday so everyone could see. #Blessed. Everything was so pretty and so perfect, she concluded, spooning coffee into the cafetière. When Mira came out of the shower she took a photo of her too.

'Not so early, God. You're obsessed with Instagram.'

'I'm just happy, that's all.'

Mira sucked her teeth and turned her attention to the pile of presents. 'What the hell is this?' Mira held up a long box which had been delivered by UPS a few days earlier.

'I've no idea. Sanchay sent it, I think.'

Mira's cousin worked in Silicon Valley and every now and then would send them expensive new technology. At Christmas it was an Apple Watch, before that a Fitbit. After taking them out of the box and playing with them for a bit the novelty usually wore off and they lay abandoned around the apartment.

'Oh God,' Mira groaned. 'It's one of those voice-controlled things.'

'Alexa.' Elise recognised it.

'Why are digital assistants always women?' Mira tutted and opened the box. 'Sanchay does this to me on purpose! He thinks I'm frightened of technology so he sends me these things to make me deal with it. I'm not frightened of it, I just don't like it, there is a difference.'

But they amused themselves nonetheless, plugging in the speaker and trying to get it to work.

'Alexa, play Björk.' Mira said.

'*I'm sorry I don't understand.*' The disembodied voice echoed across the garden.

She repeated the instruction to the same response. 'She doesn't understand my accent! She's racist!'

'No, it's how you pronounce Björk. It's not supposed to sound like you just puked.'

'Oh whatever. Bee-erk, bee-ork,' Mira tutted and waved Elise away. 'Alexa, what's your favourite sexual position?' She said a bit louder.

'*Sorry I didn't understand that.*'

'She's a virgin.' Mira giggled, sipping her coffee.

Exactly at that moment a loud sneeze from the other side of the fence made them both jump.

'*Shiiit.*' Mira covered her mouth.

'Alexa, play some jazz,' Elise said, and quickly the sound of Miles Davis covered their blushes. But they sat there for a few seconds without speaking, a little disconcerted.

The sneezing was followed by rustling and then the sound of vigorous scraping and scratching—the crisp ring of metal against stone. Whoever was next door was doing the garden. Close to the house, the fence was high and overgrown with climbers, so it was impossible to see who was on the other side, but the panels towards the end of the garden were lower and topped with trellis which meant it was perfectly possible to look through into next door. Elise resisted the temptation to go to the bottom of the garden to look.

Over the following weeks, Elise continued her work at a busy family law firm, Mira teaching her undergraduate classes and writing poetry. The weather was unseasonably rainy so they didn't spend much time in the garden, but Elise noticed that bags of garden clippings, accumulating by next door's front gate, bramble stems snaking out of the top of the bags. Also, there were suddenly a lot more birds in the back garden. First the small birds—the sparrows, the blue tits, the blackbirds, then the bigger, louder, birds—magpies, crows, some moronic pigeons and a couple of screechy green parrots, all lined up along the fence taking an interest in the garden next door. Then one morning, a flock of starlings descended on the gardens in a screeching cloud, distracting them from their breakfast.

'Ew, what the hell?'

Elise stood up and clapped her hands to try and startle the birds. She didn't mind a variety, but she minded the flocks: there was something pestilent about so many of them all fluttering together at once over the garden. So much movement made the air turbid and hyperactive. She went to the end of the garden and peered over the fence. She saw that the garden next door was indeed cleared and that a bird food station had been rigged in the centre of the lawn. It looked industrial, cages of peanuts and fat balls hanging off its branches like the parts of an infernal machine.

'Maybe I should have a word?' Elise said, 'it looks like an aviary over there.'

'And say what? I'm sorry but you can't feed the birds.'

'But it's not very healthy. All that bird shit.'

Mira shook her head. 'In Hindi we have a saying. You should not have an argument with the crocodile if you are living in the water.'

'You think they're crocodiles?'

Mira shrugged. 'Well, we don't know, do we? It's London. What do we know about our neighbours?'

A few days later walking home from work, she saw a couple on the pavement outside their house. He was slight and short with a shaved head and glasses with thick lenses that were almost old fashioned. Stood next to him was a woman who Elise thought was probably much younger than her hunched shoulders made her appear. Their dynamic, even from a distance, gave off a troubling quality, the air around them inexplicably heavy. As Elise approached, he didn't seem to move or blink, just watched her with a steady eye. Without even asking she knew who they were.

'Oh hi,' she said when she got close enough to speak without shouting, 'you must be next door!'

His nod was not especially friendly. Neither of them smiled.

'Well done on the garden! It was a bit of a mess.'

The woman looked up and Elise could see watery blue eyes and skin stippled with acne scars.

'Well, I'm Elise.' She found herself adopting the voice she might use with a child. 'Your neighbour.'

They both blinked at her.

'We know. We've been meaning to contact you,' he said. His voice was rather high with the trace of a rural accent, Norfolk, maybe.

'Oh.'

'About your plants.'

'Yes?'

'They're growing through the fence.' She wasn't sure why but it sounded almost as if they were accusing her of something. 'They're out of control.'

'Well yes, there's been no one living there for nearly a year.'

'We need to cut them back.'

'Oh of course. No problem.'

'We need the light,' she said.

'Well, no worries. Chop away! Let me know if you need anything,' Elise said, in a way which she hoped conveyed only in emergencies and went inside.

She didn't say anything to Mira about this encounter. Neighbours. They were a London hazard. Wherever possible it was usually the best strategy to try and ignore them.

On the next sunny day, setting up the outside table for breakfast, she noticed that the jasmine and clematis were looking a little thin. In fact, she saw as she looked, they had been cut back so severely that there were now holes in the canopy and the branches were drooping into the garden. Broken stems poked through the gaps in the fence, frayed and mangled as if they had been hacked.

'Bloody hell.' She noticed too, that panels had been nailed across the trellis to stop anyone looking through.

Even Mira noticed. 'What happened to the plants?'

'*Next door,*' she mouthed. 'Said they wanted to cut them back.'

'That's a bit *extreme.*'

A magpie landed on the top of the fence chattering loudly, making them jump.

'Too many bloody birds. I can't put the washing out anymore. One of them shit on my blouse.' Mira waved her hand at the magpie until it flew off with a squawk. 'We should shoot them!' she said, loudly.

'Or get a cat,' Elise said.

Mira raised her eyebrows approvingly. 'I'm all over that.'

There was a sound of a door opening next door and a cloud of startled birds, lifted up from the garden.

They tried to eat their breakfast but found it difficult to relax. At first, Elise thought it was perhaps the breeze, a low hissing, like the rustle of wind in the leaves of the bamboo, but it got louder, although still indistinct, voices, speaking quietly but insistently. It made her skin itch.

She nudged Mira with her foot. 'Can you hear that?' she said, mouthing the words, her voice barely above a whisper.

Mira wrinkled her nose. The sound got a bit louder, more obvious. Like someone was hissing instructions. It was impossible to hear what was being said, but there was a difference in the tone, one voice deeper than the other.

'What was that about?' Mira asked, when they were back indoors.

'I don't know. They're weird.'

'I think you're right though. We should get a cat.'

Returning from shopping a few days later, Elise could see figures on the pavement.

'Is that them?' Mira asked.

'I think so.'

'You didn't tell me she was gay.'

'What do you mean?'

'That number one cut. So lesbian.'

'She's not—' but they were too close to have this conversation. She wanted to say, just because she's got short hair doesn't mean she's gay, but also, the last time Elise had seen her, the hair wasn't so short. It was cropped, not shaved.

'Hi.' Elise said, wondering if she should pause to make small talk, but she didn't even know their names.

The woman looked at the ground and he held on to her arm, tight enough for it to look like a squeeze. He nodded at them but didn't say anything. There was something peevish about his face, she thought and his eyes were furrowed as if he spent a great deal of time frowning. But more than anything Elise was unsettled by her hair: it was shaved roughly, as if with a razor, or by someone in a fit of great feeling. It looked hacked, uneven, tufty at the edges. She was set to just walk past them, with no more than a polite nod when Mira stopped.

'Hello!' she said, brightly. 'I'm Mira. I live next door.' Elise cringed, she recognised that voice of coercive friendliness. Mira was expert at it, especially if she wanted to find something out.

But the two of them just stood there. Not offering a greeting by return or even a name. He just stared right through Mira as if she hadn't even spoken, the woman pushed her tongue inside her bottom lip, which made her expression seem suddenly aggressive. The atmosphere was unexpectedly hostile.

'Ah.' Mira said. 'I see.' And she pushed Elise gently forward. 'Come on, let's get this shopping inside.'

Once they were safely indoors Mira exploded. 'What was that?! Oh my God, they have maximum bad energy!'

'I know,' said Elise.

'They're so rude! And her hair! *So* lesbian.'

'Women can have short hair without being gay.' But Elise couldn't stop thinking about her hair, the shorn strands of it fluffed around her ears.

After this, sitting outside became a performance. The moment the patio doors were open and next door were present in the garden, the air seemed to change. Everything took on a prickly, self-conscious quality. Elise found she was hyper aware of the sounds of their movement, even though they were clearly trying to be quiet, there was an atmosphere of stealth and the whispering—the whispering!—all of these things, made their presence so much louder than if they had been shouting, or even just speaking quietly. And then there was that sound, the clinking of a chain, and a new noise which came to punctuate their mornings: a harsh electric buzz.

'Oh no, they've got one of *those*,' Mira said.

'What?'

'A NutriBullet or something. When I lived in halls that noise would wake me up every morning. Someone with a bloody bullet.'

A large pigeon strutted the fence eyeing her imperiously, squirting all over her flowers. Next door. They were becoming annoying.

The following day Mira returned from work with an empty cat basket.

'We need a spirit animal to help us with this conundrum,' and she nodded her head toward next door. She had arranged it with an academic from her department who had accepted a job overseas. 'It's a pedigree. Bengal.'

When they went to collect it, Elise thought it looked like a small leopard. It had a lithe, glossy body with distinctive dark spots and stripes and startling yellow eyes. It was called, rather unimaginatively, Simba. The owner, Diane, was a middle-aged woman with a kind smile who was clearly sad to be giving up her cat.

'She's really curious, so she'll want to be allowed out. But put a collar on her because she'll go for the birds if you're not careful.'

At this Mira looked at Elise and winked. Elise tried not to laugh at her audacity. It was the thing that had so attracted her to Mira in the first place, her refreshingly un-English directness and ability to stand up for herself. Not taking anything lying down. Elise knew she had a tendency to be too passive and it secretly thrilled her that Mira was sometimes so decisive, so argumentative.

'But aren't you worried about her being stolen?' Mira asked, picking up the cat, which twisted in her arms until she was forced to hand it back to the woman.

'Well, I only let her out during the day. She knows to come in at night.' Diane took the cat from Mira and stroked it, her face turned and looked quite sad. Elise felt like she was intruding on a private moment and looked away.

'Don't worry we'll send photos.' Mira said, 'and you know, if you do come back, we can always negotiate custody.'

Diane laughed and sniffed. 'You're so kind.'

So, Simba came home with them, meowing loudly in the taxi all the way. If she was honest, Elise was a little apprehensive about it. She had always resisted the impulse to get another cat, even though she had in the past lived with many. She liked her house to be tidy and just so. The idea of dealing with cat hair and animal excrement again made her nervous.

'It's OK, we'll get a cleaner.' Mira said, as if reading her mind.

The cat seemed to settle into its new surroundings incredibly quickly. Diane was right, it was an intelligent creature, it didn't go and hide under the bed, instead it stalked around the house rubbing up against the furniture to mark its territory. It shat in the litter box and ate a bowlful of cat food before curling up on the sofa next to them, as if it had always lived in their house.

For the next few weeks they kept the cat indoors and Elise almost forgot about the neighbours. The harsh scrape of their Nutri-Bullet had even faded into the background. Mira booked a glazer to come and put a cat flap in the back door and they bought a collar, and got her microchip updated from Diane's address.

'Such a handsome hunter.' Mira said, stroking the cat under the chin, so that it closed its eyes with pleasure and purred loudly.

'With such a noble face.'

'We're such clichés,' Mira said, 'lesbians who get cats instead of children.'

Elise laughed. 'Maybe it's a nice cliché, and anyway, ew, I don't want kids.' But she still took a photo for Instagram of the two of them holding the cat like a baby.

The next sunny weekend morning they opened the patio doors.

'OK, let's do this.' Mira said.

'Do you really think this is a good idea?' Elise said, holding the cat who was wriggling against her grip.

'I'd say so,' she said, pointing at their garden furniture which was covered in bird shit. 'We're going to have to clean that if we want to sit out.'

Elise gently poured the cat from her hands down onto the patio and watched as it tore its way through the undergrowth, sniffing and pissing and marking out its territory.

'This garden, it's perfect for a cat.' Mira said. 'So much to see and explore.'

To begin with they let the cat out tentatively, closely supervising every visit outside. But once the cat had a taste of the outdoors it became vocal and restless, and started scratching at the woodwork around the door.

'Look at that mess! I'm sorry I'm going to have to let her out.' Elise unlocked the cat flap. 'Don't get lost,' she said to the cat.

It took about a week before the inevitable happened. The first kill was small, a blue tit, the second one bigger, a blackbird, and then a magpie which the cat wasn't able to drag through the cat flap. Elise was at first disgusted by the mess—the splayed, livid flesh and the feathers, so many feathers! and the sad fold of the neck—but then she was sort of pleased, thrilled even. It had rebalanced something.

It was Sunday afternoon when the doorbell went, Elise looked through the grainy intercom screen. 'It's them.'

When she opened the door their dour, angry faces instantly soured the atmosphere.

'Your cat,' he began.

'You need to keep it indoors. It's killing the birds,' she continued.

'It's also killing all the mice that are attracted by all that bird food,' Mira said, without a pause, an edge to her voice. In between the birds, the cat had brought in three mice.

'I'm so terribly sorry, her collar keeps falling off,' Elise said, but she felt Mira nudging an elbow into her ribs. Was she already being too accommodating? Probably. 'It's a Bengal you see. They like to hunt.'

'Well, you need to keep it *indoors*.' The woman was looking at her with such venom that it was hard to withstand the sudden force of it.

Her hair had grown back a bit since Elise had last seen her, but she couldn't help but notice her earrings, six or seven studs which crept up her earlobes catching the late afternoon light, flashing like a warning. She seemed somehow bigger, more muscled and aggressive than before, Elise wondered if she'd been working out.

'The decline in the British bird population is directly related to the numbers of domestic cats,' the man said, as if he were speaking from a leaflet.

'Well, you can't control a wild animal,' said Mira, 'but thank you for letting us know,' and she slammed the door shut. 'God, they're so horrible!'

'But you can't just slam the door on them like that!'

'I just did.' Mira stalked back into the kitchen and picked up the cat. 'How could anyone hate you?' she said, nuzzling her face into its flank.

'But what if they do something?'

'Do what?'

'To the cat. You hear stories. And it was a robin this morning. I wanted her to frighten the birds, not decimate them.'

'Well, we just need to get her a better collar with a bell on.'

But the next afternoon, they were disturbed by the sound of hammering and pigeon spikes appeared along the top of the fence in a narrow line all the way to the bottom. The garden felt suddenly smaller, meaner, spikier.

'Oh.'

Elise picked up the cat and coddled it.

'Well, I guess that will stop her,' Mira said. Then leaning towards the cat, 'Just leave next door alone, OK?'

But the truth was it had ruined the outdoors for them, although Elise didn't really want to acknowledge it. They began to sit in the front lounge with the windows open, instead of in the kitchen with the depressing view of the garden. Elise began to think that perhaps it was time they moved.

The weather changed towards summer and it got warmer. Living without the patio doors open became impossible, until one Saturday they were suddenly surprised by the sound of loud rock music and laughter coming from next door. A party.

'I didn't know they had any friends!' Mira said drily. The smell of a barbecue wafted over the fence along with a cloud of charcoal smoke. Even the cat, sniffing the air once, scuttled back inside.

The noise went on all afternoon and into the evening. People were getting quite drunk, Elise thought, judging from the noise, which was escalating, along with the noise of their stereo—a long litany of bad 80s AOR rock—from Genesis to Eric Clapton. It wasn't the kind of music they would have chosen for a party, but whatever.

Around dusk it started to ease off, though the music thumped on, this time Cher segueing into Pat Benatar.

'Their music taste is kind of gay.' Elise observed tartly. 'I had an affair once with a woman who was obsessed with Pat Benatar. I'm not joking, she'd been to ALL her concerts.'

Just as she was moving to close the door, there were voices, really close to the fence.

'What's with all the spikes? You got a pigeon problem?' The voice was raspy, male.

There was a short laugh, then a voice she recognised.

'No. A lesbian problem.' Her voice, even louder, meaner. She thought of the dangerous glitter of her earrings.

She motioned for Mira to come, putting her finger on her lips.

'Ohkay. But the spikes are a bit extreme. What are they trying to do?'

'They have a cat. It's been eating the birds. What else can we do if they won't keep it inside?'

'Ah.'

'I mean one of them... she's always hitting on me, isn't she darling?'

Then his voice, distinct, the burr of his accent more noticeable somehow. He sounded a bit drunk. 'Can't keep her eyes off you!'

The other voice laughed. 'You sure that's a problem? Couple of randy lesbians living next door. You could put that in the sales pitch!'

A laugh that sounded like a bark. 'I'd rather die!'

Elise was frozen, not quite sure she could hear what was being said, or quite digest the meaning of it either. Seriously?

'Oi!' before she could stop her, Mira was up on the bench, roaring but even with this height advantage she couldn't quite see over. 'Just for the record. Not even if you paid us!'

There was silence then. A cough, a scrape. Someone whispering something and suddenly the music went inside, doors, windows, closed.

They stood in the kitchen staring at each other.

'What the fucking hell was that?' Mira was pale with rage. 'They can't get away with that!'

Elise didn't really want to acknowledge it, but she was shaking. 'They just did.'

Mira paced the kitchen, they discussed calling the police. 'But what do we say? How can we prove it?'

'We need to write down everything.' Elise said, opening a note on her phone.

They tried to go to bed, but neither of them slept. That uncomfortable prickle across the skin, the acid in the stomach, the throbbing vein in the temple. In the end they both took a sleeping pill.

In the morning, they sat in the kitchen, neither of them moving to open the doors in spite of the weather. As if rebuking them, the cat was already stretched out on the bench in the sun.

'We need to talk to them.' Mira said.

'Why? What was that thing you said about crocodiles?'

'I just need a recording of them being homophobic.'

'But they're not going to say what they said yesterday to your face. That's the point.'

'But they might ... If I have a recording we can go to the police.'

'Do we have to?'

'How can we not?'

And Elise knew there was no point in trying to stop her but as they were dressing, she glanced out of the bedroom window. There was a big truck outside and there were men carrying boxes into it.

'Look, they're leaving.'

Mira stood next to her and they watched for a while. Elise felt relieved and then something else, a familiar kind of ache, the bruise of the injustice that would never be corrected. But although neither of them acknowledged it, there was no point in confronting them now.

They went back downstairs, gratefully throwing open the patio doors. The first thing they would do would be to get rid of those spikes, Elise thought. A few hours later they were gone. Elise could feel it, even though they hadn't seen the truck drive away. There was something about the air. It's deadness and lack of static. People gave off energy, and she had been living next door to their transmissions for so long she could feel when they weren't there. She stretched out on the bench. Thank God for that, they would have the garden back at last.

But still, next door would linger for a while, in all the places where violence likes to hide, in the hiss of an accusation not quite heard, the exclusion of close laughter, the sudden, neurotic flutter of a wing.

OUR KIND OF LOVE
Paul McVeigh

Cruelty was the currency on the streets of Belfast back then and that made the McAuleys rich among a prosperous people. Everyone in Ardoyne kept their distance, even the IRA. Perhaps that's why the McAuleys eventually turned on themselves and why the boys stayed away from Mary. Lucky for me.

How did I get away with it? Because it started so young it was harmless. Because we were a joke between them when they had no other bones to chew. Because, mostly, I wasn't to be taken seriously. Sure, wasn't I a big fruit after all? And the older we got, the more eyes minded from their corners, the more I played up to the idea. Took all the abuse it got me so that I could be near to her.

We shared many moments of love Mary and I. God knows it was the only touching she felt that wasn't violent. In our final year of school, her mates would make faces when they spotted me watching through the gates at lunchtime but they laughed nice too and waved. Any other lad would have been chased away but the nuns liked me. A good altar boy they knew me as and 'not like the other boys'. Not really a boy, even. All was on track until we turned sixteen and traded school for the Shamrock Lounge.

Mary met Finn at the Shamrock, one of Ardoyne's working men's clubs where women sat on one side and husbands sent drinks over from the other. It was understood that the longer the drinks kept coming the longer the marriage lasted. My spot was in the no man's land of the bar, with the few tolerated misfits. It was a Saturday night and every pair of lungs in the room pumped smoke into the air like we were all part of some cancerous machine. My eyes stung in the dark box of a room, with a low ceiling and living room wallpaper wet with sweat. Mary sat at a table with her gang; Theresa, her older sister, Geraldine, aka Duracell, her ginger mate from school and Anne, the obvious looker of the bunch, with her long blonde hair and doll-blue eyes.

The girls pulled Mary onto the floor. The gang clearly loved dancing, except Mary, who'd pull at her clothes and scratch at her arms. She positioned herself with her back to the wall; her friends a swaying barricade between her and the world. They laughed and sang to each other. Anne posed, flicked her hair and eyes, too beautiful to look at a fixed point. Geraldine danced by rubbing her thighs together, back and forth to the music. It must have gotten pretty hot along there with all that rubbing and men's hands were often drawn to the warmth of her fireplace.

Finn was a quiet kid from somewhere in the country. No personality to speak of. No friends. No confidence. He had nothing except the respect of others because he worked hard and said nothing. Not a bad word about anyone passed his lips and in Ardoyne that was rare; tearing people down helped us relax. Oh, and, of course, most importantly about Finn, his da came from farmland money. He was a daddy's boy, by all accounts, whose da made a laughing stock of him when he wanted and Finn seemed ok with that either because he was a bit backward or because he was a bit smart.

I saw Finn at the other end of the bar watching the girls dance and thought nothing of it. After all, he was surely looking at Anne like every other man there. I saw the tight grip of his fingers around his pint glass and the twitching muscle of his jaw. Whatever he was holding inside of him took a lot more effort with each drink.

The girls clung to each other leaving the dancefloor and thronged to the bar. Mary looked at me and smiled. It was warm and private and spoke of us; a promise of the love we planned to share. A better love. Gentle and safe. One that would protect us from the world. It was the other thing that died in the shooting that night.

I don't know if this is true or the imaginings of afterthought, but I remember again clocking Geraldine's thighs and how she pressed her skirt to her legs and arse. On her way to the toilets someone made a passing comment and she turned to them, her face bright red with embarrassment. The gunman came through the main door, Geraldine was blocking his way. Screams and broken glass joined the sounds of the bullets hitting the walls and tables. I hit the deck and shouted, 'Get down!' at Mary.

An IRA man returned fire from a hatch leading to the men-only bar, and the shooter, exposed in the doorway, fell back against the wall and slid heavily to the floor. People rose from behind the upended tables, while others held onto each other to steady themselves. The moaning wasn't human.

How Finn did it, I don't know. Why, baffles me even more. There was nothing to save. Any fool could see that. But he went to Geraldine. He put his lips to what was left of her mouth and breathed into it. My Mary fell in love with him right then and there, while his lips were on her dead friend. I saw it with my own eyes. I saw it in her eyes.

I doubt they'd ever even met before. I would have known as she was rarely out of my sight. But I can see now the outcome was inevitable. After that night, Mary avoided me. I didn't get it at first. I put it down to grief. I gave her space. Then I saw them go walking. God knows how she stuck him. He never said a word when I followed them. I wondered if she knew, as she paraded him round the district, if she was letting me see it was over between us forever and that Finn was the one for her. I couldn't blame her, for wanting something more.

They would stop at an entry and touch in the dark. He was shy and useless. What did she see in him? They hardly even kissed, just held each other while she talked. He always walked her home. Never brought her to his. Never tried to sneak into hers. An awkward little country boy who thought a cock was something that woke you in the morning. He was loyal, I'll give him that, not a chaser like most of the men, but not as loyal as me. I'd never even looked at another woman. But then, by this stage, I wondered why that was. And that maybe they were right about me.

On her big, noisy, ugly day, Mary was transformed. Pride made her pale skin burn like white fire. I watched. And the brighter she burned the darker I became. Of course, I was invited to the reception, everyone was, at the best hotel in Northern Ireland. It was also the world's most bombed, which made me smile. Finn's family showed off their money. Why they were living in Ardoyne if money was around was a mystery. In a place where everybody knew everyone's business you never asked anyone a direct question. And this is why Mary's family accepted him. Money. Though that made them resent Finn deep down, on the surface, at least, it made them act their version of nice. The thing about being around money is you're always wondering if being close to it will somehow make you richer. Coins falling like crumbs from the feast.

If I'd any interest in getting involved, back in the day, I might have arranged a surprise as a wedding present. Not an actual bomb but a phone call, an evacuation, a scare. Instead, I watched them laugh. I saw Finn light a fag at the emergency exit. Mary saw him and smiled from a place my kind of love couldn't touch. Smoke drifted in from the open doors where the men stood talking football and shite. They bundled in, hands in pockets, barking laughter, bodies straining against, or drowning in, ill-fitting shirts and jackets. Finn's da joined them, putting his arm around his son's shoulders and pulling him away from the group, up Glengall Street.

I wanted to be invisible but felt like I was expanding, about to explode, like a dark star. I needed outside to get some air but wanted to avoid the men. I went through the hotel foyer, out the front doors, away from the busy entrance and stood at the corner looking across at the rich facade of the Grand Opera House. Around the corner, I heard Finn talking to his Da.

'I know I haven't been a good father to you,' his da said. 'I know that.'

'Don't, Da.'

'I haven't. There, it's said. But I'm going to give you the best advice I ever got.'

I couldn't help but lean forward to watch them though the netted window curtain. His da spat behind him into the street while tucking in his white shirt, forced loose over his fat belly.

'My da told me, and I'm passing it on to you,' his da said. 'Hit her tonight. A good one, mind. So she knows. That's what I did to yer ma and sure look how happy she is.'

'Da, those days are gone,' Finn whined, like he was trying to get out of doing some household chore.

'Thirty-odd years of marriage can't be wrong. And get it right the first time and you won't have to do it much after.' His da stubbed out a fag on the pavement, then wagged his finger. 'Come on, now, we enjoy this aul day. It friggin' cost enough,' he laughed.

I stepped flat against the wall while they headed back in through the emergency doors. I had to tell her. I ran back the way I came, weaved through the smiling guests and kids chasing around the legs of adults. The room shouted, laughter rattled like gun fire, my back teeth sent warning shots up my jaw as they ground into each other. I leant on the door to the ballroom to stop myself swaying.

I watched her dance to some cheesy disco crap. Her gang around her like the old days. Her sister Theresa home from London, Anne who stayed behind like her, and the one missing, for a minute, there, and then gone to wherever ghosts go when not appearing at weddings.

Maybe he wouldn't do it, I reasoned. Maybe he'd ignore his da.

The happy couple danced. A crowd gathered around them clapping. Cheers blew them across the floor and out to the stairs signposted to the Honeymoon Suite. I followed. They waved and turned, climbing upwards. The party moved back into the ballroom dancing and laughing.

'Ach, don't be all maudlin,' Anne said, linking arms with Theresa and smiling at me. 'It's not like you could have married her, is it?'

I had wanted to go up there but something occurred to me that made me hold back. If he did beat Mary wouldn't it be to my arms she'd run?

The relief took the wind out of my sails and I fell onto the chair behind me. I looked to see whose table I'd joined. Finn's mother was alone, rigid in her seat, fingers with boney joints locked together on her lap, face tight and cross. An untouched dinner looked up from the table, and she placed a white napkin over it, like something had died right there in front of her. The gravy seeped through, making a face on the cloth for a moment before it bled out to an unrecognisable stain.

THE RELUCTANT BRIDE
Iqbal Hussain

As he drives past the *haveli*, his mother's warnings flit through his head:

    'Don't relieve yourself under a tree at night—you might disturb a jinn.*'*

    'Never bathe after sunset—who knows what spirits you'll attract.'

    'The feet of a churail *point backwards.'*

The burnt-out mansion has lain empty for decades: unloved by buyers and shunned by locals. The crumbling towers and minarets loom like pitchforks against the near-full moon, while bats wheel in and out of the shutterless windows.

He detects movement through the gates and his hand clutches the *taweez* around his neck, before remembering he lost it years ago. Devoid of its protection, he touches his earlobes instead.

As he navigates the country roads, he drums the dashboard and launches into an old film song, his nasal tones cutting through the phut-phut-phut of the engine.

Having plied his trade at night for so long, he would struggle with the madness of the day. Even in these small hours, he finds passengers: a broken-down car; a partygoer missing the last bus; an urgent dash to the hospital. The money may not be much, but he lives simply.

Something large darts across his path.

'What the—'

He swerves, mounting the pavement, straight for a pair of ornamental wrought-iron gates. The *haveli*. Distracted by his singing, he has somehow ended up here again. He slams the brake and releases the handlebars. The steering column jabs into his chest. Smoking *agarbatti* and assorted talismans litter the interior.

All is silent, apart from a high-pitched ringing deep inside his ears. Then, with a rush, he returns to the land of the living. He tentatively unfurls himself and the horn stops blaring.

Before he can inspect himself, he is arrested by a sound that chills his flesh: a woman sobbing. He shakily swings his legs out of the driver's seat. Peering across the road, he sees nothing but endless fields of corn, rippling in the wind.

'Hello?' he calls out. '*Kaun hai? Aap theek ho?*'

The crying ceases. From a distance, the lowing of an ox carries through the air like the plea of a dying man. Then a figure emerges from behind a giant peepal tree, stepping into a shaft of moonlight. For the second time that night, he stops breathing.

Before him is a woman in full bridal dress. A highly decorated red *dupatta* cowls her head. She is bedecked with gold: a *tikka* sunburst pendant over her forehead; a nose chain across her cheek; swathes of necklaces around her throat. In the cold light, her scarlet gown is the colour of dried blood.

He remembers stories about *churails* resting under peepal trees. How they lure the unsuspecting by hiding their ghastly features in the guise of an attractive woman, sometimes a man. Her face is in shadow. He glances down, but her legs and feet are swathed in the folds of a *lehenga*.

As she approaches him, she stumbles, throwing her arms out and sending her gold bangles clattering. Her hands are withered and burned. He flinches, and she draws back.

Guilt floods through him. 'My mother—may Allah be merciful upon her soul—would not let me leave you here. Please, come.'

She opens her palms to show they are empty. What he thought were burns are in fact elaborate patterns drawn in henna.

He gathers her meaning. 'No, no, no. I wouldn't dream of it.'

She scans the road. He reassures her they are the only ones abroad at this hour. He understands it isn't proper for a lone woman to be in a vehicle with a strange man—at any time, let alone at night.

With the *lehenga* concealing her feet, she glides towards him. Halfway across she stops, pressing the back of her hand to her mouth, her sniffs replaced by a gasp. He turns away. It has been many years since he has made use of a looking glass, but he knows what she sees.

He calls over his shoulder. 'Sister, please, it is not safe. You don't know who you might meet.' He swallows an urge to add 'or what'.

♦

Normally there is at least a silhouette, but tonight there is just blackness.

'*Beware the person who casts no shadow or reflection.*'

Adjusting the mirror, his fear gives way to relief as the woman shifts into view. Her head is dipped, her painted hands upturned on her lap as though in prayer.

He is reluctant to drive around his usual haunts. Even at this hour, they may come across someone who registers the rickshaw and its unusual passenger. A woman's reputation can be smeared by a gossiping tongue. Instead, he ploughs deeper into the countryside, aiming for the nearest big town. The petrol gauge is at midpoint—he will need to be mindful, as there will be few places along these long, remote stretches at which to refuel.

He sees her look up and gaze out of the glassless window. She gives her hand to the night. The flickering moonlight picks out eyebrows inset with jewels, lips dark as pomegranate seeds and a pale complexion, otherworldly.

Clearing his throat, he asks if there's somewhere he can drop her off.

Several seconds pass before she answers. 'I have nowhere. I have made my bed and I must ...' She leaves the sentence hanging.

He is thankful the night conceals his blushes. 'No problem, I will keep driving.' His nasal delivery compares poorly against her rounded tones. He tries to soften it. 'Forgive me, sister, but who ... why ... what happened?'

The air ruffles her *dupatta*. 'My education, my dreams, my hopes— they all counted for nothing in the end.'

The headlamps light up a semi-circle of barely a metre in front, the rest of the road remaining in darkness.

'It should have been the happiest day of my life,' she says. 'I was betrothed to him since I was a little girl.'

He pictures two school-aged children, holding hands, giggling and skipping. She swiftly disabuses him of this notion. 'He is twenty years older than me.'

His grip falters and the rickshaw bucks like a skittish horse.

'Today was the first time I met him,' she says.

'You know, it is not so unusual.' He speaks with exaggerated cheeriness, waggling his head. 'My own sisters saw their husbands only two or three times.'

She snaps: 'And that makes it right?'

He shrugs. He has never thought about the question of right. It's just how it has always been.

'He is handsome,' she says. 'Fair of skin. Well-respected.'

'*Wah, wah!*' he exclaims, hands momentarily raised in the air as though weighing up her good fortune. 'My mother—peace be upon her—would say he is a first-class match.'

She glares at him in the mirror. 'But I do not love him.'

The mention of love sparks memories: fragments of a face he once knew flash onto his windscreen before disappearing into the night.

'Love!' The woman spits the word out like it was a bitter gourd. 'All they care about are dowries and how much gold their daughters will get.'

'Come, sister, our parents just want the best for—'

'You're a man—what would you know? All this!' He glances up at the mirror as she sweeps her hands angrily over her bridal gown. 'It is the fate of women to be seen as chattel.'

'There must be something you can—'

Without warning, she screams and smashes an arm onto the ledge, the vibration travelling through the metal and into the springs of his seat. She screams again and again, each time punctuated by the crash of heavy bangles.

He slams on the brake, throwing up dust devils, before rushing out to check on her. She cowers in the back, twisted at an unnatural angle, sobbing. Blood trails down her forearms. He blinks and the blood morphs into tendrils of henna.

Her tears are accompanied by another sound: the banshee-like howls of wild dogs. He surveys their surroundings, but only discerns vague forms in the inky night. The hunting calls build, suggesting the dogs are on the move—in their direction.

Someone—or something—whispers in his ear. He yells and spins on the spot, flapping his hands by his head. There is no-one there. The woman is still curled up on the seat, still weeping.

Once more, his fingers reach for the long-lost *taweez*.

Scuttling back to the cab, he twists the throttle to its maximum, putting distance between themselves and the dogs.

۝

'Can I take you to your family?' His throat is dry and he has to repeat himself.

She springs upright.

His grip tightens on the handlebars, the old scars on the back of his hands raised in ridges.

Her hair has worn loose, slick strands framing her face. In the mirror, her kohl-rimmed eyes flash into his and he is forced to look away. 'Only if you want to deliver me to my death,' she snarls.

He is reminded of dialogue from the melodramatic films he used to watch. But there is truth in what she says. By abandoning her husband, she has put the *izzat* of both families at stake. Women have been pushed down wells for lesser 'crimes'.

The moonlight highlights her nose, mouth and chin, the *dupatta* shielding the rest of her face. Her lips are parted, the tips of her teeth glinting. He hears his mother's warnings. Silently, he sends up prayers for her and recites the *kalmahs* for himself.

۝

'The *haveli*: our very own tragedy.' She lurches forward, making him jump.

With her breath on the nape of his neck, he struggles to concentrate. 'Please, sister, it is better if you—'

'That poor boy. His sweetheart. Trapped inside,' she intones, as though reading from a headstone.

He shivers. Women unnerve him, and this woman in particular. He prefers the company of his male passengers and has formed friendships with some, even if pursued more from his side than theirs.

'A prejudice borne out of Partition,' she continues, settling back with a thud.

He tilts his head. 'Partition?'

'No boy of his would marry an Indian girl, and less so for love. They say he struck the match himself ...'

The straight road, the hypnotic lilt of her voice, the drone of the engine: her words recede as his imagination takes over. His ears resound with the whoosh of ignited kerosene. Soot clogs his nose and throat. He feels the desperation of the doomed lovers as burning timbers and searing heat block their escape.

A pothole jolts him awake.

The woman is talking about her husband of one night, a powerful landowner. With her own family's fortune from cotton, the match was deemed auspicious by the soothsayer all those years ago.

She spent her marriage morning submitting to various beautifying rituals from an army of servants and sisters-in-law. The scents of sandalwood and jasmine fill the cab.

'The one thing they couldn't give me was love for *him*.'

Only when the clock chimed midnight was she allowed to retire. She avoided looking at the marital bed strewn with petals. While her husband bade goodbye to the last of the guests, she escaped by climbing out of the window, scaling the banyan tree outside.

She disappeared into the dark streets, hiding in shadows to avoid the few cars and even fewer pedestrians out at that time. She kept moving until she ended up, exhausted, at the derelict mansion.

'And that's when you found me.'

⚲

He climbs out, stretching his arms overhead, breathing life into stiff limbs. His spine rat-a-tats like a burst of firecrackers.

A brooding of adobe houses lines the road, windows reflecting the fiery sunrise like the ruby-red eyes of very many devils.

He glimpses movement behind him. It is the woman, though it doesn't seem possible she could have left the cab so quickly or so quietly.

'Don't stray far, sister.' His voice cuts through the quietude.

Scrutinising her, he sees no sign of pregnancy—*churails* often being ghosts of women who died in childbirth. Her feet remain covered. As the sun travels up her scarlet and gold outfit, she is turned into a living ember. He exclaims in wonder.

She turns around, her face fully illuminated. His mouth drops open. The early morning heat warms his back. The woman circles him, like a moon around a planet, and he is compelled to track her. He steps out of the shadows—instantly bowing his head, unable to meet her gaze.

With a jewelled hand, she lifts his face. She caresses the grooves and folds, as though to make the pain go away. He can't stop his tears.

She presses her lips upon his wretched cheek.

He is back in the burning *haveli*. His ears fill with the roar of the fire. Closer, the cries of someone huddled into him: his beloved Rekha. So, this is how it came to pass: crouched behind an armoire, in each other's arms, resigned to the deathly embrace of the choking black smoke and merciless flames.

As the night replays in his head, he sobs uncontrollably. 'I was not able to save her. I failed her.'

The woman touches him tenderly on the arm. 'What is it? What is the matter?'

Her voice pulls him into the present.

The woman slides off a bangle and offers it to him. 'Thank you. For everything.'

Dazed by lingering memories, it takes a few moments for him to respond. 'No, no, no, my mother would never allow it.'

'Please, let me repay my debt.'

The bracelet slips from her hand and rolls towards him. As she stoops down, her eyes widen. She lurches upright, retreating backwards, transfixed by his feet.

'Sister, what is the matter?' he says, scooping up the bracelet and holding it out to her.

She trips. He reaches out to steady her—even though she is now halfway down the street. His arm stretches out, as though it was made of rubber.

The screams that follow reverberate around the houses. Lights flick on and windows fling open.

'Get away from me, you monster!' she screeches.

In his rush to calm her, he forgets about his feet, normally hidden in the footwell of his cab. While he has learned to perfect the human form in every other respect, his feet point forever backwards. He finds himself walking away from her though his body and face are turned towards her.

She shrieks and takes off. Her skirt drags over the ground, raking stones and throwing up a train of dust.

He turns around and goes after her, his head looking over his shoulder. 'Please, sister, I did not mean to distress you.'

From around the bend, a truck: a thundering, malevolent, belching *bhooth*. He commands it to stop, but it is too late. Amid an explosion of hydraulic brakes, the fleeing red figure disappears under the wheels of the juggernaut.

A sense of helplessness swamps him, followed by a realisation: it is not she who is the ghost.

Doors and gates clang open. Dogs race out. Cries of '*Ya Allah!*' and similar exhortations fill the air.

Above the commotion, a child's voice: 'It's a *churail*! Look at its feet!'

As heads swivel in his direction, the man shuffle-skips to the rick-shaw, throwing himself into the cab, twisting the key, wrenching the starting bar. It won't catch. Stones bounce off the metalwork. Several strike him, but none draw blood.

With a final frantic effort, he yanks the vehicle into life and hurtles down the road. In the rear-view mirror, he glimpses the truck driver amid the villagers. He is crying, beating his chest, swearing the woman appeared like a ghost from nowhere.

Half an hour later, as the sun breaks free of its moorings, he stops. Abandoning the rickshaw, he seeks sanctuary in the peepal tree: the same tree from which the woman stepped out all those hours ago. Daybreak finds him back at the *haveli*. Today, he realises why.

The old mansion was his home in life as it is now in death. It took the bride-in-red for him to remember who he was. Her kiss has unlocked memories he had long buried.

A great heaviness has been lifted off him.

'It is time. You are ready to come home, my son.'

He is startled out of his thoughts by the voice.

'Mother! Is that you?'

He rubs his cheek, which is tingling from where he was kissed. Heat fans out from his face and floods his body. 'Mother—where are you?'

His body is on fire. He has forgotten what it is like to not feel cold. 'Mother, I can see you! And who is with you? Rekha? Can it be?'

He laughs, the boy he once was. The burden he has carried melts into the morning sun.

THE WEIGHT OF MY REVENGE

Kit de Waal

I wanted to hurt him back and the truth would serve me well for that. It needed no embroidery, no clothes nor shoes and looked its best naked, like a winter garden.

The truth hung heavy in my coat, made me lean and veer but still, from time to time, I would take it out, weigh it, spit on it and whetstone it sharp on both sides to wound going in and wound coming out.

I watched time like a sailor's wife, easy in his absence, until I became invisible to him, blurred at the margins, forgotten. Then, as if by chance, I let the truth out of me, in company, when he could not cry out or collapse and I watched him bleed and walk away.

I took the truth that night and watched it fall from the bridge and pierce the river's skin.

It had cut my pockets to shreds and I was no lighter.

COUP DE GRACE
DJ Connell

I'd come to Paris to deal a deathblow. That's what I told myself. We'd been limping along for months. The strain was hollowing me out, making me jumpy and defensive. Worse, I was becoming petty and I hated being small.

I found the park near the train station and was delighted by its box-cut trees and green benches. It was late afternoon and the sun was bathing the small, fenced world in gold, making anything seem possible. I towed my suitcase through the gate and onto the grass island. The sign said this was *interdit* but in typical French style, there were more people on the grass than on the dusty pebble path. I stretched out beside my suitcase and would have fallen asleep if not for a manic child in a synthetic cape running at high speed, shrieking and waving a plastic sword. The noise should have annoyed me but I found the chaos comforting, a distraction from the task I had set myself.

The next morning, the park looked completely different, empty and unhappy. It was too early for Parisians who had inky espresso to drink and children to get to school. I circled the grass island now damp with dew, and settled on a bench facing a bed of waxy yellow flowers. My hands were trembling from lack of sleep. As I wedged them under my thighs, I recognised the force of my father's genes in the shape of my leg. He had been a short man, built solid and strong for forking hay and mending fences. My mind, eager to extract itself from the despair that had engulfed me the previous evening, seized on a joyous memory of him walking through the dewy grass of a hay paddock, calling my name and laughing. He could do no wrong, my father, even when what he did was at odds with what seemed right.

As a child I'd watched him slaughter sheep on the square concrete pad behind the barn. The family had to eat, he said. The killing was a duty, something he did with tight lungs and gritted teeth. My job was to bring them in, running zigzag over the uneven ground, shouting and waving my arms to guide the ewes into a network of pens.

My father's knife was a wooden-handled weapon with a thin curved blade. He called it the 'gully-gully' and kept it in the kitchen drawer with my mother's wooden spoons and potato peeler, a sinister presence among the mundane tools of women's business.

The blade was carefully sharpened on a whetstone before being carried stiffly out of the house and down the gravel path to the pens where anxious sheep huddled, eyes bright with fear. I was told to wait at the gate while he seized a Border Leicester by the scruff of the neck, dragging it out of the enclosure and onto the concrete square. There he straddled it, my signal to back away. The sheep's head was abruptly pulled back against its spine and quickly, very quickly, my father ran his blade across its throat.

The blood.

What blood!

It flew in an arc, a red ribbon suspended in the air for four, five seconds. It was the heart, the treacherous organ tasked with keeping the animal alive, that ultimately pumped its host dry of blood and drained the spark from its eyes.

Now in the cool stillness of the Parisian morning, I could feel the pump and slosh of my own heart. It, too, had turned traitor.

The reunion the previous evening had disintegrated into an epic argument, brutal and wounding. The air had boiled with accusations, hissed in sharp whispers to avoid alerting a family in the next hotel room. There was shame in what we were doing. It was dirty and wrong to be so cruel. We had loved each other. We probably still did.

The last word hadn't been spoken when she'd dozed off next to me, rolling close out of habit. I'd moved to the edge of the narrow hotel bed, chest burning, trying not to be touched or to touch, struggling to breathe.

The park gate clanged. I looked up, startled. It was still very early.

A moment later an elderly man appeared. He was walking in a deliberate manner like a sailor accustomed to movement underfoot. There was a worn look about him, the way his trousers tented at the knees and his jacket flapped open. He was in his late seventies, I reckoned, the age my father had been when he died. There were several benches in the park but I knew immediately he would choose to sit beside me.

A faint whistle issued from between his discoloured teeth as he touched down on the wooden slats. He turned and lifted his woollen hat. It was faded blue with an embroidered band, like a Greek fisherman's cap minus the visor.

'*Bonjour mademoiselle.*' He raked his fingernails through his thinning hair.

'*Bonjour monsieur.*'

'English. You speak the English?' He smiled, exposing a gap where a premolar had been removed.

'Yes.'

'I also. Speak the English.'

I nodded, reluctant to engage.

His head bobbed again and in his eagerness I understood that he was lonely, perhaps desperately so. I found myself smiling against my will, wanting to reassure him.

He was not French, he told me, relaxing into the contours of the bench. Vladimir was his name. Born in Yugoslavia. They called it something else these days but he still called it *Yugo*. Not that he would ever go back. What for? He'd lived in Paris forty years and worked at the Citroen factory. The retirement was good from Citroen. Well, it was good enough. He shrugged. He'd been a nightshift worker and had problems sleeping. Insomnia was a curse.

'You also,' he said, glancing at my smeared makeup and rumpled clothes.

'Yes, sometimes.'

I'd slipped out of the hotel at first light still wearing the clothes of the previous day. My lover had been asleep, her arm stretched across the bed, fingers curled as if beckoning.

'My wife dead. One year before.' The old man looked at me, expecting something.

I nodded.

He nodded again, wanting more.

I closed my eyes and thought about the woman I'd left sleeping in the hotel room. What was wrong with me? Why couldn't I simply break up with her, drive the knife home and be done with it? I wasn't my father's daughter. But then, I was. I'd been his special girl, constantly at his elbow, eager for his nod of approval and grateful for attention. It was good to be grateful, I told myself. It made life easier.

I looked at the old man. 'I'm sorry to hear about your wife.'

I was, too. Pity was another companion. It was the ache I experienced on seeing a dying plant on a windowsill or a dog being handled roughly. I now felt a familiar ache for the old man, as if I was responsible for his suffering or at least for lessening his burdens. This caring for the bruises of others was what had me trapped. I wanted out but couldn't bear the thought of my lover returning to Edinburgh with a broken heart. I'd viewed her parting from every angle, searching for a way to soften the blow. If I could only force her hand, I reasoned, there would be no turning back. Let her be the victor. I'd have something more precious, freedom without guilt or regret.

'Dead by cancer!' the old man blurted out.

I nodded.

'My wife,' he repeated. 'Dead by cancer.'

'I'm sorry.'

I pictured his elderly wife, thin and yellow. She was propped up on pillows, listening to Vladimir rattle saucepans in the kitchen. He was making a hearty Serbian soup with chunks of carrot and white beans. Herbs were circling on its surface. I paused. Did they put chicken stock in soup over there? I could see farms with cows and pigs but no chickens. There were sheep in the Balkans, plenty of them. I'd seen sheep country in old war footage, good fertile pasture blown to smithereens by bombs and landmines. I imagined the killing that had gone on during that terrible war, men going about it behind barns. A swift blade across the throat.

'Thirty-seven year.' The old man pointed to his marriage finger. There was no ring, not even a mark.

'That's a long time.'

'Married?'

'No.'

'Better.'

I didn't think it was better. It wasn't a document that had me pinioned.

I was too soft, my father said, shaking his head in disappointment. He scolded me for bringing home wounded animals. You've got to put them out of their misery, he warned. You can't let an animal suffer. The rabbit with a broken leg was whisked out of the shoebox, its neck snapped with a conclusive twist of the hands.

I'd been living in London for a year when I got the call. It was time, they said. He could go any day.

From my father's bedroom window I'd seen the dog running with something in its mouth. A duck, a beautiful female mallard snatched from a pond filled with spring rain. The bird was limp but still alive when I pried the dog's jaws apart.

My brother appeared in the barn as I was making a nest out of hay. 'You've got to put the thing out of its misery,' he said. 'You need to harden up.' His tone was righteous and mocking. Life and death were men's business.

I turned my back on him, arranging the wounded bird on the nest like a still life.

The duck was in the same position the next morning, stiff and cold. By the end of the day, my father had also died. The arranging was carried out by an undertaker. It had to be done while the body was still warm, my brother explained. You couldn't let it become rigid. It wouldn't fit in a coffin.

The old man nudged me with his elbow. It was an ugly intimacy, an intrusion.

'Drink?' He pointed to me and slapped his chest in a jovial way.

'No, thank you.'

'Wine, French. Best.'

'*Merci, non.*' I held up my hand. He was pushing his luck. Lonely people often did.

'Wine good. Sleeping.' He made a wedge with his hands and placed them next to his head.

'*Non. Merci.*'

'You only think people are weak,' my father had warned. 'They take advantage. You can't save the world, girl. Sometimes you've got to be cruel to be kind. Put them out of their misery.'

The old man nudged me again. 'Bed, good.'

I stood up shaking my head, smiling in a final way. Viewed from above, the old man looked even more worn out and fragile. His trousers were threadbare from constant wear.

'Wine!' He shouted, his voice deep and oily. His hands moved in an agitated manner over his knees. He hit his chest again before rapidly sliding a hand down to his crotch. He squeezed himself.

'Sex. Good!'

I staggered back as if slapped but the old man had anticipated my retreat and caught hold of my wrist, tugging me towards him. I tripped and almost fell, arriving inches from his face. The smell of unwashed hair and clothing rose from his body. There was garlic on his breath.

He chuckled and the sharp flicker of triumph in this tiny laugh pierced me like a slaughterman's knife. My vision blurred as a new, raw perception ballooned out of me, out over the empty park and beyond Paris. I saw where I'd come from and where I was heading. I saw the hopes and mistakes that held me together, the missed signals and opportunities, my flaws and failings. Heavy-footed, I would continue to trudge the same path, making the same mistakes. I would learn nothing.

As my perception shrunk and collapsed back into me, I experienced a burst of heat and light. The old man let out a yelp of surprise as I twisted my wrist from his grasp. My hands had formed fists but it was the hard edge of my elbow that I drove into the side of his face, shattering his dentures and sending shards of opalescent plastic flying from his open mouth. His eyes flashed, wide with surprise and fear. His head slammed against the bench and snapped forward to flop over his chest. It dangled at an awkward angle for a moment before his body slumped sideways, twisting on its way down to hit the slats of the bench with a soft thud. The collar of his shirt had pulled open to expose the pale, dimpled skin of his throat. The old man's face was upturned, a single dull eye open.

How quiet it was. Quiet and still.

I took a deep breath and looked past the park bench to the row of box-cut trees, my eyes drawn to the vivid green of early summer leaves. In a few weeks their colour would deepen as the trees put in the hard work of summer, their roots drawing riches from the soft earth, channelling minerals into the solid shapes of trunk and branch.

In the distance, a car horn sounded.

The park gate clanked.

I stepped back and stumbled, leaping over the yellow flowers to get my footing. Pebbles crunched and scattered as I hurried out of the park.

A LIFE THAT ISN'T MINE TO SEE

Kerry Hudson

My wife doesn't like it. She doesn't understand, *One day you'll get caught. One day you'll get the ever-loving shit beaten out of you. Creeping around at night. Or you'll get arrested. There are laws you know. You're a headteacher, you can't go taking chances.* I tell her I'm playing squash and take my kit out of the house in a sports bag.

I've got two hours. I head right to Victoria Park. The canal. It's never easy—that's part of the pleasure—but there the light reflects off the water onto the tow path. The buildings throw shadows. I find a quiet bench just beyond a bridge. Just dark enough. A nice element of surprise.

Now I hear footsteps—kids. Walking towards some basement club in Dalston, I suppose. Platform DMs and cans of Red Stripe swinging from their lithe wrists. I let them go—imagine the noise, the fuss they'd stir up. Next, a slow, squat dog walker in an anorak who'd probably be all too delighted to see me waiting for her. I almost choose a cyclist with neon stripes flashing up their lycra, bike lights beaming through the darkness. That might have been special actually. But they're too fast—gone before I even fumble with my strap.

I'm feeling a bit defeated when I walk back past the Tesco Express to see her. I do understand my wife's point about this, about *this one* especially. But isn't all the best work compulsive? And she's there like she always is. Tonight, in the frame of a smashed in phone box, her hip leaning against the lower shattered pane, the piss yellow light falling on the sharp edges of her face. She doesn't even know I'm here. It's easy with her. Just like we're collaborators. I pull out the camera, focus in close. Snap.

☼

I don't tell anyone I'm a headteacher. Instead I try to hold myself like the other, younger artists—confident and casual and as though I've still got my whole life to be taken seriously and this is just a laugh really, an excuse to knock back some cheap, warm wine. It's true it's just a group exhibition. Just a small gallery in a renovated warehouse in the not yet gentrified edges of Clapton. But people seem to really like my stuff. I watch them stop, see their hands gesture towards the pictures, exchange a sentence or two. There's three of her. She's by the ATM curled under lasagne layers of sleeping bags and stained duvets. I caught her in the early morning bending to pick up a cigarette in the carpark, her loose tracksuit bottoms shivering at her ankles in the wind. In the middle, *that picture*, as my wife— though I suppose I don't get to call her that anymore —referred to it. The photograph captures it all. Her in that yellowed light, sockets dark, eyes closed in what I imagine is the closest thing to joy she knows, her lips around the glass pipe as smoke drifts across her slackened features. If you asked me, I'd say it looks like peace.

And as a woman who's been looking at my pictures steps towards me, I think that's what I'll say to her. But what she says—looking at me directly, with so much tension in her shoulders that I don't need to look down to know her hands are shaking—is 'what's her name?'

And she keeps asking, her voice raised above the self-congratulatory chatter and wine bottles chinking, so other people look over too. 'What's her name? What's her name?'

☼

Of course I stop and stare. Of course I recognise her, even without the ripped tracksuit bottoms. Her hair is pulled back into the thin ponytail, she's wearing black trousers and a grey polo shirt. She's standing in the middle of the aisle, reading the back of a bag of crisps.

She looks up at me and smiles shyly, 'I read there was loads of sugar in some of these flavours and my kid won't eat anything else at the minute.' I don't say anything. Don't move. She makes that *do I know you?* face that pretty young women give to older men when they want them to go away. She looks down at my basket: microwave curry, half tins of beans, a single bread roll in a too big cellophane bag, a pint of milk, two packets of cheap biscuits. It's fleeting but I catch it—pity. She smiles again, 'Sorry, can't I get past then? I'm running late, so ...' Her Argos name badge says Susan. I step back, 'Of course, sorry.'

I say it again to her back though she can't hear me. She's rushing—to her job, to her kid, to a life that isn't mine to see. 'I'm sorry, Susan.'

PIXMALION
Polis Loizou

The first post of his I see:

He stands, painted white, against a brilliant blue. A sheet draped around his waist. This falls, coyly, to expose the raised white V at his groin and the white-caked pubic hair. His arms have been cut off, a digital trick. Along with the angles of his head and torso, it forms a clear nod. Anyone could see it. Venus de Milo.

His caption beneath it:

Venus as a boy.

The image has thousands of likes, as it should. I've found it on another account, via the hashtag gayhot. I'm instantly drawn to his profile. The gallery is an Alexander's tomb of riches. . Here is a living god with the soul of a muse.

My comment on his post:

'Your wicked sense of humour suggests exciting sex.'

Without a moment's pause I follow him. Pixmalion, he calls himself. I laugh, sipping my neat coffee and flicking the ash of my cigarette over the railing.

Moments later, he likes my comment and follows back. A gesture he's returned to under a quarter of his fans. I limit myself to liking only three more of his previous hundred posts.

My first uploaded pic:

A photo of me with my daughter, taken by her mother. On the veranda at the old house, it was Green Monday. You can see my Yamaha in the background, under the grapevines. I could do with a ride on it now. My girl is on my lap, wearing my sunglasses, which are far too big for her. Her leggings came off at some point during the meal. She has a Master's now, from LSE. There's a bowl of octopus on the table, which she wouldn't touch these days. I'm smoking and squinting at the camera, smile caught between discomfort and joy.

The caption beneath it:

'My pride and joy.'

I used the hashtags FathersDay, love, dad, gaydaddy.

A smattering of likes and heart emojis.

I wonder how she's doing in England.

Pixmalion's stories:

Behind-the-scenes videos. Unknown hands massaging paint onto his pecs. His perfect teeth, smile nearing innocent. The fabric of his briefs turns see-through in the shower. A grin as the camera turns away.

Outtakes. Alternative versions of his pictures. Hand up instead of down, head turned left instead of right. Eyes to the lens, eyes to the side.

Endless reposts of him shared by other accounts, each of those filled with semi-clad demigods. That familiar picture of his, again and again: Venus as a boy. His most popular, it would seem. People are simple that way, proud of their limited knowledge. They fail to detect his layered nods to other myths. The beauty of his mind and eye.

One story photo leaps out:

The view from his flat. I recognise the neighbourhood.

So he lives in Athens.

I ignore the preset reaction emojis, opting for the simple word 'perfect'.

Then I add:

'Pygmalion himself would have admired Pixmalion.'

A few minutes later, my comment had a little heart beneath it. He liked it.

My latest post:

A day at the beach. I'm standing in my Speedos, not bad for my age—a bit of a belly but I'm clean shaven and sport a healthy tan. You can't see my eyes because I'm wearing a hat and sunglasses, but I look friendly, as if I've been caught mid-laugh. I'd rested my phone against a eucalyptus and set a timer.

Some likes and comments. Mostly from middle-aged men, Greek, Cypriot, Lebanese, Iranian, Israeli. We all look alike, maybe that's why they want me.

A notification. I have a new follower:

A pale, skinny boy. 17yo, Detroit, MI. He tells me in a private message that he's thirsty for a daddy, and sends me a picture of his pink arse spread out on a bed. I don't reply. He's too young and doesn't interest me. What a crude and artless closeup.

Pixmalion's latest post:

The birth of Adonis, from Myrrha in the form of a tree. He mentions neither god nor cursed princess in the caption, but I deduce from his sprawled limbs at the foot of the myrrh tree, 'fallen' leaves obscuring his genitals, branch reaching down to his navel, that this is the story he's telling.

My private message to him:

'I love that myth. I think of it every time I see a myrrh tree.'

Again, he responds quickly. This time with text:

'It's a great story.'

I stop myself from saying more.

My hashtag search:

A river of studs, all of them baring their physiques to the phone's eye. I hate the ones in gyms; there's no stimulus there, besides a flexed bicep or patches of moisture. Sweatpants make for flattering but dull costumes. Protein shakes are soulless props.

There are handsome boys who trek across the world. Pensively shirtless against giant Buddha statues. Heroically broad on a cliff's edge. Humbly vested amongst gap-toothed farmers.

An ill-advised caption under one such image:

The greatest wealth is to live content with little.—Plato.

As if the poor choose to die hungry, and the ugly choose to die loveless. My cheeks burn as I type my comment:

The most virtuous are those who content themselves with being virtuous, without seeking to appear so.—Plato.

I smoke. After that, I return to that account. I want something crass to masturbate to. A brainless hunk. Instead I find I've been blocked.

My post, on a day of numerous London Pride selfies:

Me as my wife for the Limassol carnival. I'm standing on Makarios Avenue, a satirical float behind me; priests laundering money. Earlier, my wife had screeched with laughter as she corrected my make-up and fixed my wig. In turn she put on a pair of trousers and drew a moustache over her lips to play 'me'. Me as the macho brute I've never been. I didn't care for drag. I only wanted, for half a day, to allow my body a release from its 'masculine' trellises. To kick over the wooden jig that propped me up and decided my shape.

How different my life, had I been free at 25. Had I any queer friends, apart from that shy medical student who also frequented poetry evenings in Old Town. Apart from my intermittent conquests in that sad little bar we balked to call our own. Pride parades, for us? We would have struggled to fill a single float. All we had was the carnival, our annual chance to be lost amongst the other clowns.

Pixmalion's stories:

On holiday with friends, Mykonos. Tanned, toned torsos, Ray Bans, Aussiebum swimwear. Glasses of sparkling wine or beer or frappés. Inflatable unicorns in swimming pools. Snapshots of bodies in mid-air, leaping into the water.

And here is Pixmalion—whose real name remains a mystery—posing on the sand in his water-taut briefs. By anyone's measure, a true man.

There's a 'sticker' on the photo, with a flame emoji to slide up so as to express your lust for him. It takes Herculean effort, but I only slide the flame to just over halfway. I'm sure I'm alone in doing so. Let his ego be starved a little; the doubt may even nourish him.

In my private messages:

A vet from Nicosia, 57, his gallery boasting low-angle shots of his chest. I'm turned off by his flab but he has startling grey eyes in a boyish face. Interspersed among the photos of shirts pulled open are the pugs and tabbies he treats at his practice.

'I saw Hadjis and Marinella at the Kourion. Best concert of my life.'

It's a response to my recent post, a picture of Hadjis. I'd had his melodies in my head all day.

I respond to the vet:

'I was there too. Unforgettable.'

'What do the youth have to reminisce about? Pokémon and Britney Spears.'

He couples his text with that laughing-crying emoji, far beneath a man of our age. But I sense that he's like this offline; a ball of youthful energy.

He suggests we meet. I ignore it.

In my feed:

A new upload by Pixmalion. He stares into a swimming pool. We see him from the back as he lies on his front. Buttocks to camera, right leg moved just enough to allow a glimpse of the shadowy pouch beneath his glutes. But in the background, peering over the white wall, is another version of him. Wounded, sad. The rejected Echo with her broken heart.

His caption:

Come to me.

The responses beneath the image:

Fire emoji.

Peach emoji.

'I'll come to you!'

Tongue emoji, splash emoji.

I choose to lift the tone. My own comment:

'Come to me, / To me, to me, to me.'

He liked my comment. I pop a cigarette in my mouth, and look out to the oil tankers on the horizon.

And then, a notification. Pixmalion has liked the photo of me with my daughter. Plus the one of me as my wife at the carnival.

I send him a private message:

'You are beautiful.'

He responds:

'Thanks x'

'So you live in Athens? I miss it.'

He doesn't respond.

In Pixmalion's stories:

His arm is around a beautiful blond friend. Their shirts hang open, almost without intent. I wonder if they have sex together, all these men sharing a holiday villa. A pack of wolfish hedonists. Swim together, dry off together, sink into a hot-tub together, sweat in a sauna together, drink together, get off together. I follow the link to the blond friend's profile. Boring selfie after boring selfie in the mirror. At home, at the gym, in a lift, in a public toilet. Each of them has hundreds of likes. The comments, the emojis, obscene as usual.

My latest story:

Videos, of my walk along the promenade. What else but a sequence of palm trees and lights on the pier? Joggers passing me in pairs. A photo of the ice-cream I bought, mastic and rose. I add a sticker to it: a slider with a tongue emoji. To my surprise, it gets a few responses. The grey-eyed vet, that pale American boy, the Israeli and the other tubby old men, all pushed the tongue up to the maximum.

Even more surprising, a response from Pixmalion. He's slid it halfway. Sly devil.

I respond with a message:

'What, you only like half of it?'

He must always be on his phone, for it takes him mere seconds to respond:

'That's right. The rose half.'

A winking emoji. I don't mind.

I respond:

'That's because you have no taste.'

I smile as I send my words to Mykonos, where he still appears to be with his hot friends.

His stories:

A picture of his head in three-quarter profile against the twilight. Breathtaking. I select one of those tacky set reactions: the emoji with hearts for eyes. Because he is beautiful, and his beauty does fill me with awe. Even if he knows it. Even if I'm only speaking to myself.

Next in the sequence:

A repost of another man's picture. That blond friend of his, the uninspired selfies in mirrors. Narcissus without Echo. He's put one of those sliders on it, so I move the flame to less than halfway. The pettiness gives me a childish thrill.

After my cigarette, I send him a message:

'You're better.'

He sees it, but doesn't respond.

In the morning, another new post from Pixmalion:

A recreation of the Bronze Boxer. Instead of boxing gloves, he's wearing marigolds.

His caption:

All lies and jest.

I don't recognise the reference so I look it up. What old music he likes for someone his age! I admire the image and give it a like, as always, though part of me longs to give it a miss.

Even on holiday, he makes an effort. That beautiful head in three-quarter profile, it buzzes with ideas. He must be electric in person.

Pixmalion's stories:

Final day in Mykonos. Volleyball on the beach. Lunch at a whitewashed café. Kalamari and cocktails. Pixmalion eats only a salad.

I respond to that picture:

'Don't tell me you're a vegan!'

If he asks why, I'll tell him my daughter is too.

I move along.

A group shot of his friends, all of them handsome and free. Inside me, a sad rage. I follow the link to every one of the other men's profiles. All of them dull, vapid, pointless. What is a man without talent, without thoughts, without wit? Yet they are happy, they are full. They are worshipped, they are loved. They speak and understand the language of others like them. They are out and proud, they are naked and desired.

I send Pixmalion a message, in response to the group shot:

'I told you, you have no taste.'

I picture him smiling.

My latest post:

The cat that comes to my flat. I don't know whose he is, but he looks well fed. He's orange and white, with a splotch across his mouth, and he looks much like a happy human as he rubs himself against the loquat tree.

Caption:

My boyfriend.

Every day I toss slices of ham to him, which he gobbles loudly. Then he leaps onto the balcony and purrs as I rub his back. In some ways I think I'd be more content with him than a lover. It's an easy existence. He'll allow me to watch porn and scroll through pictures of men in raunchy poses, and purr as I scratch his chin.

The vet from Nicosia has liked the picture, and left a comment:

'Leave him, he's mine!'

And that silly emoji, the cat face with hearts for eyes.

It makes me smile, but I don't respond to his comment.

I go to my own profile. My follower numbers are down. Some would be bots, swept away by the app; I'm savvy enough to know about that. I hate technophobes. Why be left behind as the world moves on? A thought strikes me and inside, a dim panic rises. I search my followers. No sooner have I typed *Pix* than I see:

He's left the list.

I toss my phone onto the table.

I smoke.

I pick up my phone again, and go to his profile. Snapshot after snapshot of youthful perfection. Teasing glimpses of a soul behind the marble. A waste. Another heartless young man, admiring only his own reflection.

In my private inbox, another message from the vet. I toss my phone away again.

There, against the loquat tree, my orange-white boyfriend rubs his head, his spine, his furry behind. I tap my fingers on the railing to summon him, and call:

'Come. Come here.'

I can't help but laugh, as I smoke, as I exhale my life to the air that will carry away and be gone to the past, as I say to the cat, to myself, to no one in particular:

'Come to me.'

And I tap on the railing:

'To me, to me, to me.'

THE DICK OF DEATH
Neil McKenna

I was blind and then I could see.

I can remember the hour, the day, the very moment of my conversion. It was not slow or measured or considered. No, it came upon me in a raging, angry torrent, more akin to a drowning than a baptism.

It was ten years ago and I was fifty. I was happy enough and content, more than content with my life and my lot. I'd been working for the same glossy interiors magazine I'd joined after university and I'd made it to deputy editor. My job was to source and oversee the photoshoots of the houses we featured. I loved my job. I liked travelling round the country, and sometimes round the world, seeing houses, meeting the owners. I thought of myself as a modern nomad with the added benefit of a flat in Hampstead to retreat to when I wasn't on the road.

One of the perks of working on a glossy interiors magazine with a small luxury travel section was the freebies. The magazine would be offered a free trip—a Mediterranean cruise, a skiing trip in the Rockies, a stay in a luxury vegan retreat in the Caribbean—in return for some modest editorial coverage. Generally speaking, I avoided these freebies like the plague. The transaction felt slightly grubby and the trips themselves tended to attract the type of journalists who liked nothing better than to moan and bitch and drink too much free champagne.

Beyond that, I had an aversion to anything that smacked of luxury or conspicuous consumption. It was the abiding legacy of my childhood. My father was a Methodist minister who brought me up to be thrifty and to eschew luxury in favour of authenticity.

So when the offer of a free, authentic, no-frills road trip from Jerusalem to Damascus came up, I jumped at it. I'd always wanted to visit the Holy Land, to see Jerusalem, Nazareth and the Sea of Galilee. I was still a Christian and, though my days of going to church every Sunday were long since gone, I was a reasonably regular worshipper.

The trip began well. I was met at Ben Gurion airport by our guide, Amira, a larger-than-life, extrovert Arab-Israeli woman in her late 40s with a dirty laugh. The others in the group had arrived on earlier flights. All women. Three Germans, two Italians and one Argentinian who could barely speak a word of English. But my Spanish was good so that wasn't a problem. They all seemed very pleasant. Middle-aged and rather serious. I suppose that summed me up too. I was middle-aged and rather serious.

The trip was to last a week, the first two days in Jerusalem, three days on the road, and then the last two days in Damascus. Amira had grown up in East Jerusalem and knew the city like the back of her hand. We went to places that tourists would never find. We ate in cafes and workers' canteens in backstreets and basements and we slept in a small convent guesthouse run by an order of elderly Ethiopian nuns, each in our own tiny whitewashed cell with just a small metal bedstead, a wooden table, a chair and a crucifix.

I found Jerusalem electrifying. There was an intensity, a vividity, about the city which made it like no other I'd visited. It was a city of contradictions and contrasts. Tense and yet relaxed. Noisy yet silent. Old beyond imagination yet contemporary. The colour of mud and dust and ancient stone but bright with flowers and bold colours. It was a city of smells too: spice and sweetness, must and age, drains and sewage— and sex. The city seemed suffused and saturated with sex, drenched in a powerful eroticism. Hardly any men wore deodorant: they radiated an animal musk smell which seemed to permeate my being and remind me of never-known and half-forgotten dreams and desires.

※

It was Thursday. Our last day on the road, and Ludwiga, the German lesbian librarian, was in tears again. We'd spent the night in a kind of hostel halfway up Mount Hermon, where David slew Goliath and where Jesus was transfigured from human to divine in front of three terrified apostles. The hostel was full of young people: Israeli, Lebanese and Syrian, one or two Iranians, a few hardy Scandiwegians and a dozen impossibly handsome young Mormons from Utah doing the sights of the Holy Land. It was noisy, none-too-clean and the food was terrible. Ludwiga had cried about the food, cried about the noise and cried about having to sleep in a dormitory.

We'd been woken up at 5am so we could see the spectacular sunrise over Mount Hermon, one of the highlights of the trip, or so we'd been told, but it was misty and damp and we saw nothing. We'd driven though the mist and the wet to the place where David supposedly slew Goliath but there was nothing to see, just a lay-by with a few dispirited traders selling plastic trinkets. Ludwiga was still complaining and tearful, and had put a damper on the already damp and miserable morning. Then, to cap it all, our ancient minibus got a flat tyre. There was no spare. Or rather, there was a spare but that was flat as well. We managed to limp along for a couple of miles to a small Druze village and parked up while Amira tried to sort something out on her mobile.

She came off the phone wreathed in smiles. Everything was fine. A replacement minibus was on its way. But it would be around two hours. There were one or two cafes in the village, she said. So why didn't we go off and explore the ninth-century mosque and meet again at 3pm? We would be in Damascus by early evening and we would be going out for a celebration dinner to put the travails of the day behind us.

I wandered off into the village heading in the direction of the mosque at the top of the low hill. I needed to get away and be on my own for a while. I wanted to avoid the chorus of moaning and recriminations that was bound to follow our disastrous morning. The village was larger than I first thought and, once away from the main road, it was pretty and unspoilt. I got myself lost in the warren of narrow lanes and passages and emerged in a charming tiny square. There was a cafe with a striped awning and chairs and tables outside shaded by an ancient olive tree. It would be a pleasant place to while away an hour or so.

The mist and rain of the morning had disappeared. It was now very hot and uncomfortably humid. I sat down and ordered a bottle of Almaza, a cold, light Lebanese beer which was very refreshing in the sticky heat.

As I sat in the square, the sky was getting darker and darker, and the humidity more and more oppressive. A storm was coming and I began to wonder how I'd make it back to the minibus without getting soaked. The phrase 'the calm before the storm' popped into my head for no reason. It had always struck me as wrong, meteorologically, and in every other sense. There is never a calm before a storm, I thought, only—like today—increasing pressure, growing tension, a palpable, physical sense of foreboding and a strange sense of rising excitement. I like the German phrase, *Sturm und Drang*, which speaks to the multiple possibilities of the storm. *Sturm* is obvious, but *Drang* is more interesting: it means pressure and stress, but it can also mean urges, impulses and longings.

It was time to go. I needed to pee. The cafe was deserted apart from the patron and a tall dark man with dense black stubble. He was dressed in a dusty, dirty uniform with a flag badge in each lapel. I recognised the red, white and black flag of Syria with its two green stars. I wondered if he was a border official on his lunch break as we were so close to the Syrian border. He smiled at me revealing a mouthful of gold teeth. I smiled back. There was something about him that attracted me, and those more ambiguous meanings of *drang* flashed though my consciousness. It must be the beer, I thought to myself.

From almost the first moment I arrived in Israel. I had been taken aback by the frank and intense sexual interest that Arab and Israeli men had shown in me. Not just a sly look, a passing glance, or a nervous smile, or even the discreet *Anblick*, the secret, special eye contact made by men looking for men. No, their gaze was explicit, their desire palpable.

The toilets were filthy, with open squat-down cubicles and a long zinc urinal half-full of stale urine. The stench was overpowering and I felt quite faint. After a minute, the Syrian man from the bar came in and smiled at me. He pointed to his chest and said 'Yusef'.

'Yusef,' I repeated and smiled.

He then unbuttoned his trousers and pulled out the most enormous cock I had ever seen. It must have been almost a foot long. I could not take my eyes off it.

Yusef beckoned me over. I wanted to resist, to leave and gulp down some fresh air but I couldn't. I was hypnotised by his cock, by the overwhelming stench of urine and faeces, and by the feelings of lust which made my head spin and my heart pound.

Yusef put his hand on the side of my face and caressed me like a lover. His eyes were brown and liquid and seemed to burn into me. I wanted him. I wanted him inside me more urgently and more powerfully than I had ever wanted anything before. I dropped to my knees, opened my mouth and devoured the head of his cock. He moaned and pushed it in further and further until I started to gag. Then he pulled me up, gently turned me around and bent me over a filthy sink. He spat on his fingers and smeared saliva over his cock and over my arse. And then he started to fuck me.

The pain was intense and agonising. I wanted to scream but I couldn't make a sound. It was torture—an exquisite, ecstatic torture. I could barely breathe. There was a bright white light in my eyes. It was not the sun. I felt I was suddenly no longer in my body. I was floating free, looking down as Yusef's Goliath of a cock pistoned in and out, out and in.

When I come to, Yusef is gone. I am slumped on the floor and my arse is wet with Yusef's roopy semen, with blood and with shit.

I have no strength. My legs are turned to jelly. I cannot control the wild erratic arrhythmia of my heartbeat. I wonder if I am having a heart attack, if this is the end, and I think how strange and how sad it would be to die in this stinking Lebanese toilet on the ancient road to Damascus.

I know one thing. I know that something—everything—has changed in an instant. I am no longer the person I have been.

I am transfigured.

Since Yusef, I no longer live in England. I've given up my job, rented out my flat for what seemed like a small fortune and bought a tiny house in East Jerusalem with a view and a wonderfully shady garden which Amira found for me.

Amira and I have become good friends. She has taught me *Madani*, the Palestinian dialect. After three years, I am more or less fluent, though people still laugh at my accent. I teach English now to handsome and serious Palestinian students and I write articles for British and US magazines.

I've never seen Yusef again, even though I return to the village regularly to see if I can find him. I don't know what happened to him and I don't think I will ever know. I fear he was caught up in the cataclysm of the Syrian civil war. Sometimes I dream about him and about that single encounter which so changed the course of my life.

Before Yusef, I used to think of my life in terms of happiness, of contentment, of feeling at one with my world. No more. Happiness and contentment are irrelevancies. I am a hunter now. I hunt for cocks. I live for cocks. I am alive when I'm fucked. I am a votary at the shrine of a savage priapic god. Like Heliogabalus, the boy Emperor of Rome who scoured the length and breadth of the Empire for men with enormous cocks to fuck him, I scour the world in my quest, my holy quest, my grail-quest to find men with bigger and bigger cocks to fuck me. None of the many men, the many hundreds of men, men of every nation, who have fucked me since then have ever matched Yusef for the length and girth, for the sheer beauty and power of his cock. A few have come close. Most are disappointing. Perfectly adequately, normally endowed, they leave me unsatisfied and unsatiated, though I take some pleasure, at least, in having given them pleasure, in having assuaged their hunger, even though I have merely piqued my own.

At the very heart of my new existence is a contradiction and a conundrum; a riddle without an answer; a journey without an end; a task that can never be completed. If I ever find a man with a cock bigger than Yusef, there will be no peace, no release, no resolution. For then I will simply be driven to find a bigger cock than the last bigger cock, and then a bigger cock after that, and so on and so forth.

I know, too, that I tread a desperate and dangerous path. After Yusef, I bled very badly. A bigger cock than his would rend and tear me like a wild animal, and perhaps result in my death.

I know this and yet I carry on. I have no choice: it is both my journey and my destination. I cannot deviate from the path that stretches before me, even if it leads to a bloody martyrdom. Like Mary, Queen of Scots, I am ready to meet my fate with head held high. And I carry in my heart the words she took with her to the grave: '*En ma fin gît mon commencement.*'

'In my end is my beginning.

THE FLOWER THIEF

Jonathan Kemp

It's not that warm here today, so there aren't that many cruisers around. Just one or two of the diehards, the regulars, prowling the cemetery's maze of insubordinate green pathways. When you spend as much time here as I do, you see that there are very definitely peak times for that kind of activity, especially in warm weather. They like the sunshine. Sunshine makes them horny.

I've been known to partake of the pleasures on offer, but not often. At sixty-six I've long since lost my appeal, except for the odd geron-tophile. And to be honest, I so infrequently feel the urge. Nowadays, I'd rather wrap my laughing gear around the firm shaft of a cheap red.

Today, as I was slaking the endless thirst of my demons, trying my best to blot out that great fugue of failure that is my life, quite by chance I solved the mystery of the stolen flowers.

Let me explain. About four months ago, a sign appeared on a tree next to two gravestones in the south-eastern corner of the cemetery, opposite a bench I've taken to calling mine.

The sign read:

TO WHOEVER KEEPS STEALING FLOWERS FROM THESE GRAVES, PLEASE DON'T. THESE ARE MY SONS, I AM THEIR MOTHER, AND YOU ARE CAUSING ME A GREAT DEAL OF UPSET. THANK YOU.

I looked at the two nondescript and flowerless stones, standing next to each other, each with its own small bed of turquoise gravel, newer than any others in their vicinity (all mould-streaked Victorian stone) and as a consequence drawing attention to themselves.

ALAN JENKINS 1963-1988
STEVEN JENKINS 1965-1989

Who would steal flowers from a grave, I wondered? Particularly after such a plea had been made. Who would continue to torture the dead boys' poor mother after reading that? I became increasingly angry at this flower thief, and grew curious to find out who it was, and so I've been planting myself on this bench day in, day out ever since, on the off-chance of catching the culprit red-handed. To be honest, I didn't apply myself too diligently to the task; you might say it's a fault of mine. I can't think of one thing I've ever truly applied myself to, except perhaps making my life increasingly unlivable. And certainly, over the past few weeks my curiosity has waned somewhat, though I've continued to spend a good deal of time at my bench. I'm nothing if not a creature of habit, these days. They keep me going. Though some of them are killing me, too, it has to be said.

Not once in the past four months have I seen the dead boys' mother depositing the flowers, nor the thief removing them. Once or twice, I've seen flowers there. I've even considered taking them myself, for no better reason than to see how it would feel thieving from the thief. But I never did. They were the bait, after all. To catch a thief, you need some bait.

One day it occurred to me that the culprit might be able to see me, which would no doubt put them off. Maybe they were spying on me and biding their time until I fucked off before snatching the bouquet. Once or twice, I secreted myself in the foliage behind the bench, crouched and alert as a soldier, eyes cocked. To no avail. But I haven't done that since the time a dog disturbed me, sniffing me out and barking till its owner came over and dragged it away, giving me the most unfriendly look. I think he thought I'd been having a shit.

So, today, I'd gone to my bench as usual, but hadn't really been paying attention to much. After the initial sentimental attachment to solving the crime for the poor mother's sake, and the intense curiosity over who might sink so low (though who am I to judge?), I'd kind of settled into a half-minded annoyance that I still didn't know the identity of the thief, and my interest was waning. Perhaps it is more than one person. After all, I considered taking them myself that one time. But what are the chances of that?

Today, it hadn't really been foremost on my mind. I can't remember exactly what daydream I was lost in at the time—probably the usual where did it all go wrong and why are you such an arsehole type of thing; some variation on the relentless twattery my life has become, and the tsunami of self-pity that's provoked. I can't seem to stop feeling sorry for myself. And the booze doesn't help; not anymore. It used to make the pain bearable but now it creates its own, and seems to magnify all the old griefs it used to hide. The loathing I feel at being a slave to it. As I was glugging away, a figure the size of a child appeared, wearing blue jeans and a red hooded top, hood up, face obscured. Snatching the bouquet from the grave, they broke into a run. Now, I'm not the most athletic of sixty-six year olds—I gave up running for the bus in my late forties when my midriff broadened irrevocably—but I immediately grabbed my bag of beer cans (you can't be too careful in here) and gave chase.

It suddenly became the most important thing to do, catch this thief, and I ran like my salvation depended on it. But still the figure ahead was younger, and slimmer, and darted with agility down the narrow sharp-cornered web of pathways that scar and grid the cemetery. I really had to go at full pelt to keep the quarry in sight, and pretty soon I was out of breath, with a stitch in my side, ready to give up the chase. But as luck would have it, the thief tripped, and fell, planting its face into the ground in a spectacular tumble which saw the bouquet somersault through the air, like a bride's on her wedding day. With no eager brides-maid to catch it, this one landed somewhere I didn't notice, too busy putting the thief's misfortune to my advantage, gaining ground and seizing them before they could rise and take off again.

The first thing I did was pull the hood down and turn the face towards me. To my surprise, a tumble of blonde hair soon revealed a young girl, her nose bleeding from the impact with the path.

'Get your fucking hands off me!' she said, struggling in my hold.

'I'm not going to hurt you', I said, 'I just want to talk to you.'

She must have been around eleven or twelve, maybe 5'2". At 6'4" and eighteen stone I had no trouble restraining her.

'If you don't let me go I'll scream', she said, and started screaming, so I had no choice but to place my hand across her mouth to silence her. She hummed a muffled scream or two until she was out of breath, and because I was suddenly aware of how it might seem to anyone who might come upon us—a large man overpowering a small female child—I dragged her off the path and through the grey-green stones, to a clearing in some trees, well-hidden from view. Twigs and small branches snapped above us, accompanied by the sounds of birds' wings and cries. I could feel her heart beating fast beneath my arm. I reassured her I had nothing untoward in mind, and merely wanted an explanation for the flower thefts. Once she'd stopped fighting and screaming, either through exhaustion or a desire to co-operate, I took my hand off her mouth.

'Why do you do it when you must know you're distressing their mother.'

'Whose mother?' she said.

'Can't you read? She left a note by the grave.'

She was all skin and bone, eyes full of panic and fury.

'So why'd you do it? Why do you take them?'

'What's it to you?'

I pondered whether to lie and say I was the boys' father. I said I thought it was cruel to keep robbing those graves when she knew it upset the boys' mother so.

'I didn't read the fucking sign.'

'Didn't or couldn't?' I said without thinking and immediately regretted it.

'Fuck off.'

'Well now you know you must find the flowers and return them to their rightful place. And never steal from there again.'

'Sez 'oo?'

'So it doesn't bother you that their mother is distressed by it?'

'What about my mum's distress?' she said, holding my gaze till I looked down, at the used condoms and empty wrappers by our feet.

'I don't just steal that lady's flowers, I take the first bunch I see. Not many people leave them here.'

'Why does your mother need them?'

'She's dying. I reckon the dying need flowers more than the dead.'

'I'm sorry', I said, for want of anything better.

'She's not got long, anyway, mum—so I won't be needing them soon. Doctor says any day now. I'm sorry to have caused that lady distress. I won't take them again, sir.'

She was suddenly meek, all aggression gone, and I took my weight off her and sat apart. She didn't move. I handed her my handkerchief to wipe the blood off her face.

'What's wrong with her?'

'Cancer.'

'What will you do, when's she's gone? Is your father around?'

'He's in prison. I'll go to live with my auntie in Stratford. Not that it's any of your business.'

I looked at her, at her hard, terrified face, and said, 'Come on, let's find that bouquet.'

It proved impossible to find the flowers so I gave her all the cash I had, which didn't amount to much more than a tenner. Afterwards, I walked around until I spotted a grave with fresh flowers on, and I removed them and took them over to the Jenkins boys. Alan and Steven. Their mother will no doubt notice they aren't the flowers she left; and it will no doubt puzzle her. But that can't be helped. At least there are flowers, I suppose. At least there are flowers.

I sat there speculating about those two young men, of whom all that remained lay in the ground before me, and in their mother's heart; their poor mother, losing both within a year of each other. I thought about who they were and how their young lives had been ended. Of course, I'll never know; and it isn't important. I imagine them tall and good-looking and in the prime of their manhood, of course. Twenty-five and twenty-four. Handsome as gold, shaped like gods. And as I was thinking all this, as luck would have it a beautiful young man walked by and gave me the glad eye. I followed him into a secluded place by the wall, behind bushes and trees and rows of gravestones, and as I fellated him I started to fantasise it was one of them; one of the dead sons. I don't know why, but once the thought took hold it I couldn't shake it off; it turned me on. It comforted me, somehow.

NOTES FROM A COMPOSER

Chris Simpson

conversations

To be lonely was to be an open mouth that did not know when to close. In caffs where the congregants of loneliness took their chance to sing hymns of alienation, Williams felt this most acutely.

While they waited for their coffee, they'd say to the owner how they always liked whatever brand of coffee the caff was selling: stating to the owner they came because of 'your' coffee. Others of their ilk would sit at an angle, their stomachs grazing against the bolted-down formica tables, their countenance a canvas for conversation.

As much as he refused to be like them, Williams started to understand the necessity of connection. It was terrifying. He'd got *too* close. Not vaguely. Not faintly. *Close*. Knowing a descent to their level could occur—frightened him. A burgeoning descent where no speech from another would break through the concrete of his id, caused him to pause when the waitress asked what he wanted. He knew he must, from now on, consider every word that left his mouth. He had to question whether what he had to say was needed, warranted, beloved—or not.

It was best to be as silent as possible. Regardless of where he was.

jogging

When he walked and saw someone jogging, Williams would look over and, if they didn't see him, smile. It was best to engage with life, at a distance.

bus rides

Williams recoiled and raised a hand up in apology. The person next to him, their attention on a film playing from their mobile, didn't notice either the apology or transgression.

Williams wanted it to happen again. He wet his lips before looking out of the window. Observing the blur of life, he spent the rest of the journey, millimetre by millimetre, bringing his leg back to the stranger's until they touched again.

He took the bus to work every day after that event.

It didn't matter who the leg belonged to. The touch became vital. A touch that confirmed he existed; a pressure on the outside of his thigh, gentle like the vibration of a Mozart concerto from a speaker onto the hand of someone deaf.

mu·sic | \ 'myü–zik: the science or art of ordering ...

He worked as a street sweeper. Menial work, while necessary for keeping him homed and fed, had also been a strategy to keep his free time uncomplicated for the pursuit of making music.

He no longer made music.

He no longer wished to be defined by it.

But music kept entering his head, an estranged sibling who always knew where he lived.

knock, knock

In a restaurant for a meeting with Sally, an old friend and film director who had made a short film he composed a score for, Williams walked up to her. He waited as she sat reading a menu. Turning to him, Sally stared. Long hair, beard, thick-framed spectacles. He was no longer himself: more Methuselah than his usual appearance of Michael Moore, sans baseball cap.

'Are you still creating?'

Williams had tucked a napkin into the collar of his work polo shirt.

'No.'

Sally was puzzled. 'Don't you want to keep making music?'

'Why?'

'Don't you miss it?'

Williams dipped a finger into his glass of water before circling the rim with the pad. 'Not particularly.'

'Are you sure?'

'I'm not a man who believes in certainty.'

Sally leaned forward. 'The music still comes, right?'

'Now and again.'

Sally sat back. 'Then you need to commit. Like Sigizmund, you need to commit.'

'Do I?'

'People need to hear your work.'

'I'm not Philip Glass.'

'You're missing the point, Williams.'

Williams made himself sit up. 'Knock, knock.'

'What?'

'Knock, knock.'

Sally sighed. 'Who's there?'

'Knock, knock.'

'Who's there?'

'Knock, knock.'

'Who's there?'

'Knock, knock.'

'Who's there?!'

'Philip Glass.'

take this rubbish away

Williams witnessed a man open his front door and tip his bin out onto the street. Williams said nothing before sweeping up the rubbish.

a pound for every fifteen minutes

The washing machine in the house, where he rented a box room, cost four pounds for a single wash. Each pound equated to fifteen minutes. If he overloaded the machine, his wash would cost six pounds. To try and circumnavigate this need, Williams would hang his clothes out on the washing line after his shift in an attempt to let Mother Nature take away with her breeze the smell of his work.

Not even a hurricane could carry away the stench.

By Friday evening he'd relent, dropping the pound coins into the meter once more. Sometimes, Williams would place a chair in front of the machine and watch it in action, trying to get his money's worth.

Sometimes, he'd bring popcorn.

alone

For years he lived alone and dined alone and walked alone and slept alone. When he met someone and started to see them, he had to relearn everything. He wanted to stop learning. He wanted to stop the desire for learning.

ache

He longed for his thoughts to have as much pull on his decisions as his shadow had in holding him down.

musical skull

A tune—it arrived like lightning on a calm summer's day. For weeks the tune, which sounded like a repetitive strain to something that could not end, refused to cease.

In morning briefings at the depot where he picked up his cart, he would see the mouths of his colleagues moaning and griping around him while he heard music.

Early afternoons in the library, the music compressed itself on his skull like one of the many hemmed-in books squished onto the shelves.

Evenings would come and Williams would have his sleep interrupted at odd hours with the doors of his housemates thumping shut. When waking—the music was there.

Before dreams, after dreams, during dreams. Music, music, music.

To exorcise the music, Williams left home with a small notebook and pen. The music kept coming as he turned the blank pages into shakily drawn musical sheets while on the top deck of the bus.

Later, as he pushed around his cart, he'd stop at every other lamppost and scribble down the notes of the piece.

As he took his cart back and started the long walk to the bus stop, Williams looked at his notebook and listened to the music. Closing the notebook, the music stopped. Opening, the music played from where he had left off. He snapped shut the notebook, pocketed it and continued his walk in silence.

Blessed silence.

At home, Williams placed the notebook in the drawer of his small desk. It sat with several others. They all contained music that would not leave his head until he went through the process of notation.

He could listen to any of the scores of his many yesterdays, whenever he felt like it.

All he had to do was open a notebook.

side a: monogamy

First problem: at one time, he couldn't find anyone who wanted monogamy. Second problem: he was unsure he wanted exclusivity.

worse

Williams wondered what he would do if he finally never had someone he could laugh with. How could he keep looking at the other side of the bed and not see someone there? How could he not see a naked form? How could he continue to not share the news of his day? How would it be possible to not have a fish supper with someone, or point at the news, or look in a mirror and be doomed to only ever see himself alone? What did monks do with their erections?

side b: multiple problems

Third problem: one year he found someone who wanted polygamy, but he wasn't interested. Fourth problem: the next year he found someone who wanted monogamy, but they weren't interested in him.

the man who died without a word published in his life

Sally called him one day as he was scraping bird shit off a bin. 'You sitting down?'

He looked at his scraper. 'No.'

'Okay, no time to find a seat—just listen. I've got funding to do that film I always talked about!'

'What film?'

'The one about Sigizmund Krzhizhanovsky.'

'Who?'

'The Russian writer I'm always telling you about.'

'Russian writer?'

'Yes!'

'Well, this is news to me. Who are they?'

'The man was a surrealist writer. The man wrote a screenplay of an escaped convict stealing from a church but he never got any credit for writing it. The man who nobody knows where he's buried. The man who wrote a story about a goblet which never ran out of wine. The man who died without a word published in his lifetime.'

'None of this is ringing any bells.'

'Listen—the man was amazing and his work is amazing and I'm going to make a film from one of his stories. And you're going to score it. You're going to give me notes and beauty for this long-dead man who was never known. You're going to get paid and we're going to make this a success.'

'I can't do that.'

'What?'

'I can't do that.'

'Why?'

'I already have a job,' Williams said.

He hung up and continued to scrape.

And …

he had wanted someone, anyone, to love him. And he had created. And he had wished for both to linger and be true and exquisite. And he knew love and creation *must* be on his terms or not at all. And if it was to be not at all, he didn't know what he'd do. And he didn't know what his own terms were anyway. And he felt that he'd *feel* his way into his own terms. And he knew these terms were a result of creating magnificence: music to start a heart beating again. And he knew he'd say 'no' until that day. And …

snap!

Williams knew of another failure who had a failed vocation. Geoff's failed vocation was of being a dad—a dad alone with no pretension of anything else. Geoff had confessed about his failing after a few pints and a couple of spliffs, saying that being a dad was the only pursuit he ever thought he'd be good at. He thought this because he was good with dogs. But he was not good with opening the post, or feeding himself, or bathing, or holding down a job, or vacuuming his rented room, or washing his bedsheets, or dressing appropriately for his job as a copy-writer, or driving a car, or making spaghetti bolognese, or filling a kettle with water, or dusting, or putting on deodorant, or making a cup of tea that wasn't too weak, or losing a pound of fat a week so he could eventually wear his dead dad's coat, or riding a bicycle, or organising a barbecue, or getting dried runny egg stains off a fork, or of sitting still at the barbers, or using chopsticks, or remaining calm in a shopping centre, or buying a well-fitting suit, and so he couldn't genuflect to the vocation and drank more as a result before he'd let his chin fall to his cupped hands and repeated his mantra to Williams:

'A brush of the teeth and a whiskey and it'll all be better tomorrow. A brush of the teeth and a whiskey and it'll all be better tomorrow. A br—'

seedlings

Passing a school, Williams watched the mums and dads who entered the gates to pick up their children. Watching normality, he vaguely wanted a child of his own to run up to him, arms out wide and a smile from proverbial ear to ear. As he continued walking and felt the thin soles of his boots giving way, Williams thought it a blessing that his seed, on rare occasions, as frequent as those of man landing on the moon, penetrated no further than the shield of a condom—to lie still and die.

financial metaphors that hit back like a dead cat bounce

Sometimes his failure was on him like debt and his role was both as debtor and creditor. To get himself back in the black, he knew what he had to do.

Thinking back to the drawer of notebooks he assumed there was one he could give to Sally for the film she was making about the Serbian writer. Or had he been Czech? Was it a he? Was she Hungarian? Were they even a writer? Wasn't it a Bulgarian photographer? He couldn't even remember Sally speaking about the project before. If she had, he would've remembered. He remembered everything: both the real and the false.

He remembered he had wanted two daughters. Five years apart. One would be called Sophie and the other Emily. He'd picture the older one, Sophie, walking Emily to school with the care of a jeweller carrying a rare find. She kept her safe from a world that was not indifferent when it came to harming. Williams had also pictured his eldest dream-daughter reading to his youngest dream-daughter. There were cuddles when it rained outside and giggles as they ate ice-cream.

He pictured Sophie's friends picking on Emily. Sophie, in an effort to keep her friends, would not do anything to stop their attack.

Then the day came where she pushed Emily down to make her friends laugh. Sophie walked off with them while her sister cried. Both grew up from that moment on—separately.

The girls graduated from university and neither showed up for the other's big day.

He continued to imagine. He'd gone on to imagine his two dream-daughters nursing a bitterness that stretched over the years. He imagined one daughter dying and the other regretting, many years later, never attending the funeral. He swapped the daughters round each time he thought of this part, never wanting either of these sprites to ever truly perish.

Williams was very good at spending time imagining all the worst things that could happen, before they did, before they had a chance, even when the conditions were not there for any of it to happen; an imagined atom containing more reality in his mind than the litter he swept up.

And so he opened the drawer and ran his hands over the notebooks, trying to divine which notebook would help him pay the debt of failure. He held them. He opened a couple and heard the music when he did.

But he didn't *feel* it. He only felt that to continue with music was to remain someone who should've given up. Someone who would stop picking up rubbish. Someone who would have to worry about real children as opposed to troublesome phantoms.

Williams walked out of his room, down the stairs and slammed the front door as he entered his 05:00 world: rain and tyres over wet roads obstructing his ears from what was no longer necessary.

There was a world he now needed to talk to.

His mouth was open.

ALIGNMENT
Elizabeth Baines

You've been sent for a brain scan. *In an MRI scan, a very strong magnet briefly aligns the hydrogen protons of the body along the axis of the scanner. As they relax they do so at different rates in different tissues, sending out different signals, and thus abnormalities can be detected.*

You make your way along the hospital corridor with the ringing in your ear, your one ear rather than both, which could be sinister, the consultant said, or maybe not; one chance in a hundred, he said, comfortable and urbane, intending to reassure you, but sending you for a scan nevertheless. One chance in a hundred that your brain is being sent lopsided, your wits, by which you live, upended by an aberrant growth. You follow the arrows, along a floor designed not to cause slips, to hush the footsteps and calm the nerves of those whose lives could be about to veer out of control.

You find the door: *Radiography.*

There's some kind of disruption going on inside.

A waiting room with three big leather easy chairs and a coffee-type table, designed to put nervous patients at their ease. One of the chairs is being pulled apart by a man and a woman. They have the seat cushion off, and the woman is pushing her hands down the back and the sides. They murmur quietly to each other, sounding troubled. They are a small couple, they look in their sixties, and they're dressed alike in boxy leather jackets and loose-fitting jeans. Both have long grey hair right down their backs, his in a ponytail, hers in a plait.

The man drops the cushion on the floor in a gesture of giving up.

In the opposite chair a woman in a business suit is looking down at her papers as if to dissociate herself. She catches your eye briefly as you sit in the empty chair and then looks away quickly.

The woman with the plait straightens up and sighs. The man stands back, his hands falling helplessly by his sides.

And here you are, you can't help it, your brain, diseased or no, is doing its usual thing, getting involved. 'What have you lost?'

The man says nothing. His partner seems reluctant to speak, but then says in a tight voice: 'His ring. We can't find it. He had it on before the scan.'

You jump up and begin looking in your own seat. She shakes her head. 'He was sitting here before his scan.' She bends and puts the dropped seat cushion back.

You are still putting your own cushion back when the door to the scanning area opens, and a tall young man in a pale blue tunic appears and calls the businesswoman through for her scan. When she's through he comes back. 'How are we doing?' he asks the couple.

Again, the woman with the plait seems reluctant to answer. 'We haven't found it.'

He turns to the man. 'Are you absolutely *sure* you wore it?'

The man speaks for the first time. 'I never take it off.'

The woman nods and confirms, 'No he never takes it off.' Her voice is weary. She seems strained.

'But you read the instructions?'

Due to the strong magnetic field produced by the MRI scanner, it is important to remove any metal objects from your body. You are therefore advised not to wear jewellery to your appointment.

'Yes, but I didn't think of the ring because I never take it off.'

His accent is strange. Something regional, yet also somehow non-British, as if English, though long ago embedded, is still not entirely easy on his tongue. The woman's accent, you noted, is upper-class. And there you go, your brain, threatened or no, is conjuring up a vision of the pair forty-odd years before, meeting at a sun-drenched festival, a hippy-clad upper-class girl in rebellion and a tanned itinerant worker from overseas.

'But where's your ring then?' asks the assistant rhetorically, spreading his hands to indicate the ringless room.

The man is quietly despairing. 'I told you, when I went through there for my scan the other man told me to take it off. And I didn't get it back.'

The assistant tells him: 'But we wouldn't do that.'

He turns to the woman. 'Why don't you go back to your car and check that he didn't take it off there?'

She opens her mouth and then shuts it again. Without a word she makes for the exit.

The ponytailed man sits in the chair with a sigh and says again, 'I never take it off!'

The assistant sits himself down on the low table in front of the man, bending towards him in an attitude that strikes you as patronising. It comes to you that because of the couple's unconventional appearance he doesn't respect them. You feel the beginnings of anger. You know what it's like to be disrespected, even despised, for your external trappings, and consequently deprived of power ...

'But you *must* have taken it off before you got here,' the assistant is saying.

'No, no, I told you. I didn't think of it. And the man through there noticed, and told me to take it off, and I didn't get it back.' The patient wipes his hand across his face.

The assistant shakes his head. 'We wouldn't do that.'

The man looks up in appeal. 'It's not the value. It's sentimental. That ring belonged to her mother. She'll be so upset.' He seems near to tears himself.

And here's another scenario opening up before you: a stately home, a daughter disowned for her rebellion, a ring on the big hand of a dying mother, passed on with a legacy of regret ...

The conversation is stuck. The long-haired man keeps recounting what he says happened, and all the assistant will say in response is: *We wouldn't do that.*

You think: He's just blocking him. He is refusing, in fact, to acknowledge what he's saying. It isn't professional. And: *We wouldn't do that ... Do* what? As far as you can see, they've not actually accused him or his colleague of *doing* anything. It's over-defensive. In fact, you think, he's making himself look guilty ...

You speak up. You say carefully to him: 'That's not the point, is it? The point is that a ring has gone missing.'

He half turns to you, a kind of flinch, then turns back, ignoring you, and says it again: 'We just wouldn't do that.'

Well, that's it, your mad is up now, your brain cells with their randomly-lying protons are fizzing and giving the muscle in your chest the thump. 'Look, you can't go on saying that. You need to acknowledge what he's saying and institute an investigation.'

He turns on you, his pointed face hostile beneath his bristling blond hair. 'What are *you* doing here?' His tone is angry, rough.

You're so shocked your heart stumbles. He's lost it, you think. It seems to you possible that he really is guilty ...

'Don't get cross with me,' you say, making a point of keeping your voice even.

'I'm here for a scan,' you add, in answer to his question.

He double-takes. 'Oh ...!' And you understand: he thought that you were with the couple—arty type as you are in your sweatshirt and leggings, someone else on the fringes of society—that you came in to join them and look for the ring.

He has coloured. He's understood your implication: that you could make an official complaint.

He stands and goes into the scanning area. The man sits with his head bowed. The woman with the plait returns just as the assistant brings back the businesswoman, who looks askance at the scene as she passes to the exit.

'Any luck?' the assistant asks the long-haired woman, carefully more caring.

She shakes her head.

He says to the man: 'Perhaps you should go to the car yourself. Maybe when you get there you'll remember where you put it.'

The man sighs and stands. Silent and resigned, the two make for the door.

The assistant takes your name. His manner towards you now is respectful and subdued. 'We'll be with you in a minute.'

He goes through to the scanning suite. It's a little while before he comes back with your papers to usher you through.

Just inside the door, a white-clad radiographer, an older man, is standing waiting for you, alert and ready and smiling. The man who, according to the other patient, asked him to take his ring off. The first thing he says after greeting you, nodding in the direction of the other patient and leaning towards you conspiratorially, is this: 'He's confused. That's why he had to have the scan.'

Again you are shocked and suspicious. Surely it's unprofessional to discuss one patient with another. He obviously knows you've got involved and was waiting ready to calm you down ...

He's asking you now to confirm that you're wearing nothing metal, no earrings or rings or fasteners, just as the other patient indicated he did with him.

You are more and more inclined to believe that the patient wasn't mistaken.

And then he says: 'You can put your bag and phone in here,' and points to a locker and gives you a key.

But of course! If the long-haired man had had a ring he would likewise have had the chance to lock it away and retrieve it himself ...

He's confused, that's why he had to have the scan.

Everything realigns. You see the man as simply lost inside a warped, alternative reality, and the woman, with her air of resignation and lack of conviction, accustomed to accommodating that; you see the assistant as understandably upset and knocked off his professional guard by the way the situation brings him and his colleague under suspicion.

You feel bad for having suspected him.

The assistant, who disappeared into a side room, reappears, and you make a point of smiling. He smiles back, looking relieved.

You are ready to be led off to the scanner when the radiographer says, 'Your key.'

You stare at it in your hand. It's made of metal.

You stand confounded. 'What shall I do with it?'

'Put it here.' The radiographer indicates a ledge right beside the locker.

You lie in the tube of the scanner, surrounded by loud hammering sounds. *The hammering sounds are caused by an electrical current being turned on and off and causing the hydrogen protons to align and then relax.* You lie there, and your brain, assaulted by the hammering, its protons aligning and realigning, plays the image of a ring lying in the darkness of the locker. Plays an image of the assistant in the room with the locker, the radiographer shut away in the computer room and the key beside the locker, out in the open and to hand. *As the protons relax, they send out differing signals which are translated by the computer into a visual image, creating a clear picture of any disease.*

The assistant helps you out of the scanner. The radiographer is still in the computer room. It is the assistant who leads you back towards the locker. It is the assistant who is responsible for making sure that anything left in the locker is returned.

You go to the waiting room. The couple are back, listlessly probing the chair again.

'Put it in writing,' you say to the woman as you pass.

☙

Months later your results come back. You don't have a brain tumour after all.

But you still find it difficult to know what happened that day.

Was the assistant guilty, or was the patient simply confused? Was his sheer conviction that the radiographer had taken away his ring conjured by a growth of alien cells in his brain?

Your own reasoning brain, given the all-clear now, tells you: just because the assistant could have taken the ring while the patient was in the scanner and the radiographer in the computer room, or appropriated it once the confused patient failed to retrieve it, doesn't mean he did either of these things. But your brain also keeps pulling up the image of his hostile, guilty look when you challenged him and the memory of his blocking behaviour. You keep remembering the couple's quiet distress and the woman's helpless, suppressed anger. You sense that because of how they looked, until you intervened, the assistant didn't think it mattered how he treated them.

You talk about it to a friend, a woman you've known since you were children, who lived in the same council block and went to the same school and ran the same gauntlet of the sneering posh kids.

You describe the incident exactly as it happened, and the way you still wonder about it now.

'Hm,' she says, looking cynical.

She offers a third explanation. 'They were probably scamming. People like that ...'

You drive away from her house, your tumour-free brain feeling constricted in your skull.

You remember the look on the woman's face when you suggested she make a written complaint: cynical and sad, as if to say, *What's the point?*

SUNDAY
Philip Ridley

I walk across the shingle to the scene of the crime—No, *not* across 'shingle'. *Gravel!* I'm on a side street in East London, not a beach in Brighton. I wish I *was* on a beach in Brighton. The weather's so hot, iguanas are falling from the trees. Not that East London *has* iguanas. Or *has* it? Everything changes so fast these days. You go to sleep in one world and wake up in—

'You can't go beyond this point, sir!'

I've been stopped by a policeman.

I can see tape stretched across the street, and further on—under a railway bridge—figures are clustered around (what must be) the corpse.

'I'm a private investigator, officer.'

'I'm sorry, sir, but—'

'IT'S ALRIGHT! LET HIM THROUGH!'

I recognise that shrapnel-in-a-cement-mixer voice. It belongs to someone I've met before. Someone I know well. Perhaps a friend? Jesus, this *heat*!

I duck under the tape and head for the underpass.

The bricks are covered with graffiti, torn posters, moss and bird shit. There's a dead crow dangling from some dodgy wiring—Wait! It's not *quite* dead. Its wings are trembling. Poor thing. If I had a gun I'd shoot it. Actually, I *have* got a gun ...No! I *haven't!* Where the fuck *is* it? ... *Shit!* I must've left it in the car. I've never done *that* before. Again, the heat!

'The paparazzi are on their way!' The man with the shrapnel-in-a-cement-mixer voice is walking towards me. 'And this one will *defi*-

236

nitely make the front page!'

I can't quite make out his face yet. But, with vocal chords like that, I'm expecting something beaten and wrinkled with years of—Nope! He's barely out of his teens, has a complexion that would shame silk, and the wounded eyes of a recently whipped whippersnapper. I should know; I've whipped a few.

He holds out his hand. 'Good to see you, bud.'

Bud? That's not my name *surely*. What *is* my name? I wish I could remember. I wish I could remember *his* name.

I shake his hand. 'It's good to see you too.'

He leads me over to the body. It's covered with a bloodstained sheet. There's blood splattered over the tarmac and pavement too.

I say, 'Forensics not here yet?' I've no idea where that question came from, but it felt the right thing to say.

'On another case,' he says. 'But it doesn't take a genius to work out the basics—YOU!' He points at a constable hovering nearby. 'PULL BACK THE SHEET!'

'Yes, Detective.'

He's a *detective*!

The sheet's pulled back.

The detective says, 'No weapon used. This was all done with bare hands. Victim's throat ripped out. Victim's head cracked open. Victim's brains scooped out and ...eaten!'

'*Eaten?*'

'According to the witness. A boy. Nine years old. Reddest hair I've ever seen. He said there were three of them. And—wait for this—he says they were all ...zombies.'

'*Zombies?!*'

'There's more. He said they all looked like old Hollywood movie stars.' The detective checks his notes. 'James Dean. Rock Hudson. And ...Farley Granger? Heard of him?'

'He was in Hitchcock's *Strangers on a Train*.'

'Never seen it.'

'Oh, you should. It's a masterpiece. The sequence in the fairground is utterly breath-taking. And, like many of Hitchcock's films, there's a distinct homosexual—in not homo*erotic*—subtext that—'

'You here to talk about movies or murder?'

'Oh ... sorry ... This hot weather is melting my—'

'Where's your partner? I thought you guys did *everything* together.'

'He's ... he's got another—'

'COVER THE BODY BACK UP!'

'Yes, Detective Highsmith.'

Detective *Highsmith*!

I say, 'How I can I help with your investigation, Detective High-smith?'

He says, 'Well, there'll be *plenty* to do once we've got the forensic report. Meanwhile—and I hate to ask you this—but could you possibly inform the victim's mother. I *would* do it myself but—'

'It would be my pleasure, Detective Highsmith. What's her address?'

'She's in Bethnal Green somewhere.' He reaches for his notes. 'That's *your* old stomping ground, isn't it?'

I'm not sure if it is or isn't, but I say, 'That's right,' anyway.

He gives me the rest of the mother's details (and everything he's been able to glean about her dead son), and I head back to my car.

I flinch at the heat of the upholstery and steering wheel.

I'm sure I had a bottle of Evian somewhere, but I can't find it now. Perhaps my partner took it. Whoever *he* might be.

I check the mother's address: 27, Corman Street. Yes, I know where that is. *And* I know it's best to park a couple of streets away: Corman Street is notoriously chock-a-block at this time of day. *How* do I know all this? And how do I know that number twenty-seven will have window boxes full of geraniums, and a brass knocker in the shape of a crane (that's the bird, not the machine).

I'm knocking with that crane now.

The door's opened by a man in his twenties, wearing a floral blouse and stonewashed jeans. He says, 'Hello. You must be her son. I'm Dario, one of her care workers. We spoke on the phone this morning.'

I step into the house. 'Nice to meet you, Dario. But I'm *not*—'

'I hope you're still taking her over the common to see the parakeets? She'll *love* that. She's in the living room. I'll be back this evening to put her to bed. But leave when you want. It's one of your mum's good days.'

'I'm not—'

'Bye!' He rushes out before I have a chance to tell him who I'm not

Not that, if he asked, I'd be able to tell him who I *am*.

I go to into the living room. An eighty-three-year-old woman is sitting on the sofa. How do I *know* she's eighty-three? Perhaps that detective—oh, what *was* his name?—told me.

She says, 'Hello. Is it Sunday today?'

'No, it's Wednesday. I'm afraid I've got some bad news regarding your—'

'Is it snowing?'

'No, it's a heatwave.'

'Oh, don't be ridiculous. I'm freezing. You've come to take me somewhere, haven't you? To *show* me something?'

'I ... well, yes, we can go to the common and look at parakeets, if you'd like? I'll tell you the bad news there.'

'I'll get my coat. I'm not wearing that beige thing. It's got a cigarette burn on the back.'

'The blue one's nice.' Why on earth did I say that?

'*What* blue one?'

'With the collar. Brass buttons.'

'Oh, that's not *blue*, it's *navy*.' She walks out of the living room and heads upstairs. She calls back, 'You do confuse me sometimes!'

There's a photograph on the mantelpiece. It's of the eighty-three-year-old woman but taken when she was thirty-eight. Her hair's bright red. She's standing next to her nine-year-old son. He's got bright red hair too. He's looking up at her and he's smiling—

'How do I look?' She's come back, wearing the beige coat. 'Tell me the truth.'

I tell her, 'You look great.'

And she does. Her hair still has a stain of red ('I'm a strawberry blonde now!' How do I know she says that?), and her face is less lined than mine. And when she smiles—oh, a glimpse of that old grit and glamour, faded now, but still eye-catching, like a matador in the fog.

'Can you see the cigarette burn?' She turns to show me the back of her coat.

I tell her, 'If you didn't know it was there, you wouldn't know it was there.'

'What's *that* supposed to mean? Just tell me if you can see it or not. Why's everything always like a bloody crossword puzzle with you?'

'No. I *can't* see it.'

'Thank you ... Where we going?'

'The common.'

'I know, I know.'

I open the front door and step outside. She hesitates on the doorstep. She looks so anxious I expect her to dash back inside. I hold her hand. 'It's okay ...' What do I call her? Perhaps 'Mum' is the simplest option. 'We'll take it slow, Mum.'

'I've got *you* with me, haven't I.'

'Yes, Mum. You've got me with you.'

She clutches my arm as we walk—slowly, so slowly—down the street.

'It is Sunday?'

'No, Mum, it's Wednesday.'

'I'm *sure* it's Sunday. It'll be snowing soon.'

'It's a heatwave!'

'Well, *I'm* freezing. I need to sit down.'

'There's a bench over there.'

We're on the common now.

I help her sit down, then look round for the parakeets. There's no sign.

A man wearing a green jacket is approaching us, smiling.

He stands in front of Mum and says, 'Hello, you.'

She says, 'Hello, you. This is my son. Philip.'

Do I tell her that's not my name? Do I tell her my name's something else entirely? Though *what* it is, I'm not entirely sure. Perhaps it's something like ... Bud. Someone *called* me that once. Who *was* it? Was it *today*?

The man says, 'My mother died recently. You know what plays on my mind? I never told her about the first boy I had a crush on. He lived in the flats opposite. I was eleven years old, and he was twelve. I followed him everywhere and feigned an interest in tractors for a whole summer. Bye!'

Mum says, 'Bye.'

I say, 'Bye.'

Mum looks at me. 'You're shivering. I *told* you it was cold.'

Am I shivering? I ... I think I am.

I look round for the parakeets. Still no sign.

The man wearing a green jacket's approaching us again.

He says to Mum. 'Hello, you.'

'Hello, you. This is my son. Philip.'

'Hello, Philip.'

'Hello.'

'I never told Mum about the first guy I fell in love with either. I met him at university. I was eighteen and he was twenty-one. He was the first person that I told I was gay. It happened during a heatwave. We'd bunked off a seminar and gone to Victoria Park. My feelings for him had, thus far, not been reciprocated. Not because he had shunned them, but because I hadn't told him. Afraid of rejection? You *bet* I was. But, then, as I sat with him on the grass, he took his shirt off and a surge of lust jolted me into blurting out, 'I'm gay! I love you!' He said, 'I know! And I feel the same about you.' He reached out and touched my little finger. And, suddenly, there was so much sky, and skin, and space, and time, and ... oh, I felt as if the whole world wanted to know me. Bye!'

Mum says, 'Bye.'

I say to Mum, 'I can't see *any* parakeets.'

Mum says, 'Perhaps they're all dead.'

'They're not *dead*, Mum.'

'How d'you know? Birds are falling from the skies all the time. Or is it iguanas? It's a sign of the end of the world apparently—Oh, that nuisance of a man is coming back. He's always telling me things I don't want to know. Take me home.'

I do as I'm told. Like when Mum bought me a bow-tie, and told me to wear it for school. The kids made fun of me all day. When Mum found out, she said, 'They're only jealous.'

Where's *that* memory come from? It's not one of mine. It *can't* be. Perhaps I saw it in a film. Yes! I remember the film now. It's about a boy with red hair who wants to be a writer. What's it called? ... I can't ...I can't remember—

'Make me a cuppa.'

'Yes, Mum.'

We're back in her house now.

I make a pot of tea while she watches the television.

I know Mum's favourite cup. I know where she keeps the teabags. I know where the biscuits are. In fact, I think I bought these biscuits. No, that can't be right? ... *Can* it?

I take a packet of digestives—along with the teas—to the living room.

Mum says, 'Oh, I've gone right off digestives.'

'It's the only biscuits you've got!'

'No, there's custard creams.'

'There's not, Mum.'

'Alright, alright, don't shout.'

'I'm *not* shouting.'

'You've got no patience with me.'

'Okay, okay, I'm sorry.'

A film's on the telly. It's in black and white. Two men are in a train, talking about murder. I've seen it before. Lots of times. It's called ... it's called ...Jesus! What's *wrong* with me today?

Mum says, 'Look at Farley Granger. Wasn't he handsome? He's dead now.'

I say, 'I can't remember the name of—'

'*Strangers on a Train*.'

'*That's* it!'

'The other actor must be dead too. We're watching zombies. Is it Sunday?'

'No, it's Wednesday.'

'I'm sure it's Sunday.'

'Well, it's not.'

'It must be.'

'It's not!'

'Don't shout at me!'

'I'm not shout—!'

'You *are*. You've got no patience with me. I don't *ask* you to come round and see me. I wish you *wouldn't* come if all you're going to do is cause an argument!'

'I've ... I've got to go. Mum. I'm sorry but ... I'm going through a lot of stress at the moment and I ... I can't ... I can't *do* it today.'

'Do *what*?'

I kiss her. 'I'll phone you when I get home. Love you. Bye.' I rush out of the house. I pull my collar up against the cold. I head for the car. It's getting dark now. So early? I thought it was summer. But ... perhaps it's not. Perhaps it's—

Where's my car? I thought I parked it *here*! This is where I *always* park it. Perhaps it's in the next street ...

No, not here. Next street ...

No, not here. Next street ...

No, not—How am I going to get home? Where *is* home? I search my pockets for a clue. I find a message on a Post It Note:

To get home from your Mum's:

take the 26 bus from Hackney Road.

Get off at Kenton Road.

You live at number 27.

Love you

Bud

XXX

Bud!? If *my* name's Bud (like someone once told me it was) why am I writing a note to myself? *And* putting three big smackeroos at the bottom. I'll tell you why. Bud's *not* my name. It *can't* be. Perhaps ...

perhaps it's my *partner's* name. Yes! That *must* be it! Bud, my partner, has written this note to help me. But how did Bud know I was going to forget where I parked the car. *And* forget where I lived.

No time to ponder all that now. I need to catch the 26 bus—There it is! I must be on Hackney Road. What luck!

I say to the bus driver, 'Can you tell me when we get to ...' I check Bud's note ' ... Kenton Road, please?'

The bus driver nods.

I sit down.

I take a mobile phone from my pocket. Has that been there all the time? It must have been. Is it mine? It *must* be.

I scroll through the list of contacts.

BUD!

I phone him.

He answers. 'What d'you want?'

'Well, *that* doesn't sound very friendly, Bud.'

'It's not *meant* to sound very friendly. What do you—?'

'I've just been to see my Mum. I lost my temper with her a little bit. I'm feeling so bad about it now. I feel like crying, Bud.'

'Why're you telling *me* this?'

'Because ... you're my ... my *partner*—'

'I'm not. It's over. I told you.'

'But ... but *why*?'

'You *know* why? All I ever got from you was, 'Oh, my Mum this, my Mum that'. And all you wanted to do every evening and was flop on the fucking sofa and watch those *trashy* movies.'

'*What* 'trashy' movies?'

'The splatter horrors. The clichéd murder mysteries. The end of the world sci-fi with tacky special effects—'

'I thought *you* liked those movies too!'

'Well, I didn't. Goodbye.'

He hangs up.

'KENTON ROAD!'

'Thank you, driver.' I get off the bus.

A street light is flickering on a nearby corner.

It strobes on the name of my street.

I have the fanciful notion it's guiding me home.

I start walking down Kenton Road. What's number do I need?

I check the note written by ... who? I forget now.

27.

What number am I at now?

3.

I keep on walking.

Hang on! Is that *snow* falling?

No, it *can't* be? It's green.

Feathers!

Green feathers are falling from the—

Thump!

Something lands on the pavement in front of me.

It's a parakeet!

A dead parakeet!

Thump! Thump! Thump!

More and more parakeets are falling.

I need to get home! Quick!

I start running.

I check the house numbers.

5, 7, 9, 11, 13—

Thump! Run! Thump! Run!

15, 17, 19—

A parakeet hits my shoulder. It doesn't hurt, but it's hard enough to throw me off balance. I tread on a parakeet. Its body bursts open. I hear and feel it more than I see it.

Run! Thump! Run! Thump!

21, 23, 25,

Thump! Run!

27—

Home!

Parakeets are piled so higher they're covering my doorstep.

And they're still falling and falling and—

I unlock the door and rush inside.

I lock the door. I bolt it.

I can hear parakeets thud-thud-thudding on the roof.

For a moment I just stand there, gasping for breath, too fazed to function.

Thud, thud, thud, thud.

Thud-thud-thud-thud.

Thudthudthudthud.

I go to the living room. Dead parakeets are flat against the window now, like a tapestry of feathers and claws.

I pull the curtains.

I wait ...

I wait ...

Thud ... thud ... thud ...

Less and less parakeets are falling.

Thud ...

Thud ...

...

...Thud ...

...

...

Silence.

Well, thank goodness that's over.

I phone Mum to make sure she's okay.

She says, 'Hello?'

'It's me, Mum.'

'Oh, I'm glad you phoned. I've got a question for you. Is it Sunday?'

'Er ... yes. I believe it is, Mum.'

'I thought so, dear. What's wrong? You don't sound yourself.'

'Mum ... have dead birds been falling where you are?'

'No, dear. Have they been falling where *you* are?'

'They have. Lots. They're at least seven-foot deep.'

'I *knew* something like this was going to happen. It's been *so* cold. But don't worry, dear. It won't settle for long. A heatwave's on the way. It'll soon melt.'

'You think so, Mum?'

'Of *course* I do. Why don't you flop on the sofa and watch a film on the telly. It's what *I'm* doing.'

'I will, Mum. Thank you. What would I do without you, eh?'

'Ooo, that's a bit if a cliché, isn't it? Even for you.'

'Ha, ha. It is a bit. Speak to you in the morning. Night, Mum.'

'Night, dear.'

What's on the telly tonight?

Oh! A murder mystery! A body's been found under a bridge. The detective in charge has asked a private investigator to help him. They're old friends. *More* than friends. They once made love on a beach in Brighton.

I watch the story unfold while, all around me, the parakeets melt.

BIOGRAPHIES

ELIZABETH BAINES' latest novel is *Astral Travel*. She is also the author of the novels *Too Many Magpies* and *The Birth Machine,* and two collections of short stories, *Balancing on the Edge of the World* and *Used to Be* (all available from Salt). She has written prizewinning plays for Radio 4 and for theatre, and has been an actor and teacher. She lives in Manchester.

NEIL BARTLETT is an acclaimed author of plays, adaptations, translations and novels. His first novel, *Ready To Catch Him Should He Fall*, was recently republished by Profile as a Serpent's Tail Classic, his second, *Mr. Clive and Mr. Page,* was nominated for the Whitbread Prize in 1996, his third, *Skin Lane,* was shortlisted for the Costa Award in 2007, his fourth, *The Disappearance Boy*, earnt him a nomination for Stonewall Author of the Year 2014. Neil is also a maker of theatre, and was awarded an OBE in 2000 in recognition of his work as Artistic Director of the Lyric Hammersmith. He has created work for the National Theatre, RSC, Manchester Royal Exchange, Bristol Old Vic, Edinburgh International Festival, Manchester International Festival, Aldeburgh and Brighton Festivals, Wellcome Foundation, Artangel, Tate Britain—and the Royal Vauxhall Tavern. An expanded version of *Twickenham* appears in Neil's new story collection *Address Book*, published by Inkandescent in 2021.

JULIA BELL is a writer and Reader in Creative Writing at Birkbeck where she is the Course Director of the MA Creative Writing. Her work includes poetry, essays and short stories published in the *Paris Review, Times Literary Supplement, The White Review, Mal Journal, Comma Press* and recorded for the BBC. Her most recent book-length essay *Radical Attention* was published by Peninsula Press.

BIDISHA is a broadcaster, writer and film-maker. She writes extensively for *The Observer* and *The Guardian* and broadcasts for the BBC, Channel 5 and Sky News—where she has been a regular since 2016. Her fifth book is *Asylum and Exile: Hidden Voices* (Seagull Books, 2015) and her sixth is the essay *The Future of Serious Art* (Tortoise Media, 2020). Her first film, *An Impossible Poison* (2017), was selected for numerous film festivals and her latest film series, *Aurora* (2020), is out now. Bidisha is a longtime trustee of the Booker Prize Foundation.

OLLIE CHARLES is a London born queer writer of prose & poetry. He enjoys exploring gender, identity, celebrity and pop culture within his work. His poem, *How to Fall in Love,* was a placed winner in the Streetcake Experimental Writing Prize (2020). His poetry has also featured in *Lucky Pierre Zine, Queerlings, Poem Atlas* and *The Babel Tower Notice Board.* Ollie is co-founder of Untitled, a literary salon founded to amplify the work of underrepresented writers, and co-editor of Untitled: Voices, a global online journal.

DJ CONNELL was born in New Zealand and has lived and worked in various countries including Australia, Japan, France and the UK. She began her writing career as a newspaper journalist, and also wrote for the international non-profit field and advertising before becoming a novelist. Her first novel *Julian Corkle is a Filthy Liar* was shortlisted for the Polari First Book Prize and optioned by Sarah Radclyffe Productions and Macgowan Films. Her latest novel will be published by Simon and Schuster in 2022. DJ Connell recently moved from London to Sydney.

JUSTIN DAVID is a child of Wolverhampton who has lived and worked in East London for most of his adult life. He graduated from the MA Creative and Life Writing at Goldsmiths, University of London and is a founder member of *Leather Lane Writers*. His writing has appeared in many print and online anthologies and his debut novella, *The Pharmacist*, was published by Salt as part of their Modern Dreams series. He is also a well-known photographer. His images of artists, writers, performers and musicians have appeared on the pages of numerous newspapers and magazines including: *The Times, The Guardian, Attitude, Beige, Classical Music Magazine, Gay Times, Out There, Pink Paper, QX and Time Out*. Justin is one half of Inkandescent with his partner, Nathan Evans. Their first offering, *Threads*, featuring Nathan's poetry and Justin's photography, was long-listed for the Polari First Book Prize. It was supported using public funding by Arts Council England.

KIT DE WAAL's debut novel, *My Name is Leon* was the winner of the Kerry Group Irish Novel of the Year 2017 and is being adapted for the BBC. In 2016 she founded the Kit de Waal scholarship at Birkbeck, providing a fully-funded place for the MA Creative Writing to a talented student who otherwise would not be able to afford to participate. It is now in its fifth year. Kit's second novel, *The Trick to Time*, was longlisted for The Women's Prize. Her first YA novel, *Becoming Dinah* was shortlisted for the Carnegie Medal Award. In 2019 she crowd-funded *Common People* an anthology of working class memoir by new and established writers. She co-founded the Primadonna Festival in 2019 and, in response to the Covid-19 crisis, she founded the Big Book Weekend, a free virtual literary festival which had an audience of 24,000. She has won numerous awards for her short stories and flash fiction and has written for performance for BBC Radio 4, The Old Vic, The Abbey Theatre, and co-wrote *The Third Day* for SKY/HBO. Her latest book, a collection of short stories called *Supporting Cast* was published in 2020.

NATHAN EVANS is a writer, director and performer whose work in film and theatre has been funded by the Arts Council, toured by the British Council, broadcast on Channel 4 and archived in the BFI Mediatheque. He's worked at venues including Royal Court, Royal Festival Hall and the Royal Vauxhall Tavern. His films have won awards at the London Short Film Festival and screened at festivals across the world. His poems have been published by Manchester Metropolitan University and longlisted for the Live Canon International Poetry Prize; his first collection, *Threads,* was shortlisted for the Polari First Book Prize, his second *CNUT,* is published by Inkandescent. His short stories have appeared in *Untitled: Voices* and *Queerlings*; his first collection, *All The Young Queers,* will be published by Inkandescent in 2022. Nathan is one half of Inkandescent and studied fine art at Oxford University.

LISA GOLDMAN is a writer, dramaturg, director and social tech entrepreneur. Plays include immersive, site specific *Hoxton Story* (2005), *Cable Street* (National Theatre Connections 2022 and screenplay) and *Remedy* (Writer's Attachment, National Theatre Studio 2021). Lisa is author of T*he No Rules Handbook for Writers* (Bloomsbury/Oberon 2012) and is a busy script consultant. As Artistic Director and Joint Chief Executive of the Red Room (1995-2006) and Soho Theatre (2006-10), she developed, directed and produced numerous award-winning new plays. This is her first published fiction.

GAYLENE GOULD is a creative director, cultural broadcaster and award-winning writer. Her short stories have been published in *Mechanics Institute Review, Closure: Contemporary Black British Short Stories* and *X-24 Unclassified*. She won the Commonword Penguin Young Adult Fiction Prize. She also creates interactive art projects and events through her company The Space To Come, is a regular contributor to BBC Radio 4 arts programmes, and writes for *Sight & Sound* and other culture publications.

ALEX HOPKINS is a journalist of many years standing. He has worked as an editor of several print and online magazines, including Beige magazine, a high-end quarterly publication and digital platform which provided a fresh approach to LGBT culture and heritage. Most recently, he was research manager for a leading NGO investigating civilian harm on the battlefield. He is currently working on his first novel.

KATHY HOYLE is a working-class writer, born and raised in a North-East fishing town. She came to writing late in life, after spending twenty years as Cabin Crew. She completed her BA (Hons) in Creative Writing from The Open University by writing essays in hotel rooms around the world. She has since completed an MA at The University of Leicester. Her work has been published in litmags including *Spelk, Ellipsizine, Lunate, Virtualzine* and *Reflex Fiction,* and her stories have been shortlisted in competitions such as The Exeter Short Story Prize, The Fish Memoir Prize and Spread the Word's Life Writing Prize.

KERRY HUDSON was born in Aberdeen. Her first novel, *Tony Hogan Bought Me an Ice-Cream Float Before he Stole my Ma* was the winner of the Scottish First Book Award while also being shortlisted for the Southbank Sky Arts Literature Award, Guardian First Book Award, Green Carnation Prize, Author's Club First Novel Prize and the Polari First Book Award. Kerry's second novel, *Thirst,* won France's prestigious award for foreign fiction the Prix Femina Étranger and was shortlisted for the European Premio Strega in Italy. Her latest book and memoir, *Lowborn,* takes her back to the towns of her childhood as she investigates her own past. It was a Radio 4 Book of the Week, a Guardian and Independent Book of the Year. It was longlisted for the Gordon Burn Prize and Portico Prize and shortlisted in the National Book Token, Books Are My Bag Reader's Awards and the Saltire Scottish Non-Fiction Book of the Year. She was elected as a Fellow of the Royal Society of Literature in 2020.

HEDY HUME was born in 1996, on the Isle of Man. They studied Drama & English Literature at Aberystwyth University, graduating in 2018. They are currently living and working in Cumbria, close to the Lake District. Their prose writing is inspired by Franz Kafka and Ursula K. Le Guin. They enjoy reading and writing poetry, and are obsessed with cats, frogs, and other uncanny creatures.

IQBAL HUSSAIN studied Mathematics at a small Welsh university, but later chose to earn a living with words. He worked as a journalist for many years, for publications ranging from *The Guardian*'s Education Supplement to *The Young Telegraph*. He was shortlisted for the Penguin Random House WriteNow 2017 programme and is an alumni of the inaugural London Writers Awards 2018. He won Gold for his short story *Home from Home* for the Creative Future Writers' Award 2019. Iqbal is working on his first novel, *Northern Boy*, a coming-of-age story about what it feels like to be a 'butterfly among the bricks'.

JULIET JACQUES (b. Redhill, 1981) is a writer and filmmaker, based in London. She has published two books, *Rayner Heppenstall: A Critical Study* (Dalkey Archive, 2007) *Trans: A Memoir* (Verso, 2015), with a collection of short stories about the history of trans and non-binary in the UK, *Variations*, due out on Influx Press in June 2021. Her essays, criticism and journalism have appeared in numerous publications, and her short films have screened at galleries and festivals worldwide. She also hosts the arts podcast *Suite (212)*.

KEITH JARRETT is a writer, educator and international poetry slam champion. His poem, *From the Log Book*, was projected onto St. Paul's Cathedral as an installation. His play, *Safest Spot in Town*, was performed at the Old Vic and aired on BBC Four. His collection, *Selah*, was published in 2017. Keith was selected for the International Literary Showcase as one of 10 outstanding LGBT writers in the UK. He has judged the Polari Prize, the Foyle Young Poets Award, and the Commonwealth Short Story Prize 2021. Keith is now teaching at Birkbeck University and completing his debut novel.

JONATHAN KEMP's debut novel *London Triptych* won the Authors' Club Best First Novel Award. *The Guardian* called it 'an ambitious, fast-moving, and sharply written work' and *Time Out* called it 'a thoroughly absorbing and pacy read'. His next book, *Twentysix* (2011), was a collection of queer erotic prose poems. A second novel, *Ghosting*, appeared in March 2015. His non-fiction includes *The Penetrated Male* (Punctum Books 2012) and, *Homotopia? Gay Identity, Sameness & the Politics of Desire* in 2016. He teaches creative writing at Middlesex University and London Lit Lab.

NEIL LAWRENCE grew up in Liverpool then moved to London where he taught Wellbeing Education in secondary schools for 25 years. He is now a life coach and organisational consultant. His short story *Diaspora* was chosen to be included in the Arachne Press anthology Solstice Shorts 2019: *Time and Tide*. He is currently redrafting a novella of short stories, *Absurdity of Truth: 11 Tales of the Fantastic and The Mundane* and an experimental novel *Sometimes Lies*. He is a member of writing groups WOOA (Writers of Our Age) and Leather Lane Writers, and lives with his partner in South East London.

GISELLE LEEB grew up in South Africa and lives in Nottingham. Her short stories have appeared in over thirty publications including *Best British Short Stories 2017* (Salt), *Ambit, Mslexia, Lady Churchill's Rosebud Wristlet, The Lonely Crowd, Black Static, Litro*. She has placed and been shortlisted in competitions including the Ambit, Bridport and Mslexia. She is a Word Factory Apprentice Award winner 2019/2020 and an assistant editor at *Reckoning Journal*.

POLIS LOIZOU is a multidisciplinary storyteller who draws on history, social politics, folklore and 'queerness' in all its forms. His debut novel, *Disbanded Kingdom*, was published in 2018 and was longlisted for the Polari First Book Prize. His second novel, *The Way It Breaks*, is set in his motherland of Cyprus and will be published in 2021. He lives in Nottingham with his husband.

NEIL MCKENNA is an award-winning journalist and writer. After a successful career writing about gay issues in the gay press and in the wider national press, Neil turned to gay history. He is the author of the acclaimed biography *The Secret Life of Oscar Wilde* and the best-selling *Fanny and Stella: The Young Men Who Shocked Victorian England.* Neil is now writing fiction and completing a novel. He lives in London and Norfolk with his partner, Robert, and their cat, Lupin.

PAUL MCVEIGH's debut novel, *The Good Son*, won The Polari First Book Prize and The McCrea Literary Award, and was shortlisted for many others including the Prix du Roman Cezam. Paul's plays and comedy shows toured the UK and Ireland including the Edinburgh Festival and London's West End. His short stories have appeared in anthologies, journals, newspapers, on BBC Radio 3, 4 & 5 and Sky Arts. He co-founded the London Short Story Festival. He co-edited the *Belfast Stories* anthology, and edited *Queer Love* and *The 32: An Anthology of Irish Working Class Writers* which included new work by Kevin Barry and Roddy Doyle.

GOLNOOSH NOUR studied English Literature at Shahid Beheshti University and completed a PhD in Literature and Creative Writing at Birkbeck. Her short story collection *The Ministry of Guidance* was recently published by Muswell Press. Her debut poetry collection *Sorrows of the Sun* was published in 2017. She has been widely published and platformed both in the UK and internationally, including on the BBC and Granta. Golnoosh teaches Creative Writing at the University of Bedfordshire and hosts a monthly radio show called *Queer Lit* on Soho Radio Culture.

AISHA PHOENIX is completing a speculative fiction novel. Her collection, *Bat Monkey and Other Stories*, was shortlisted for the SI

Leeds Literary Prize and she has been longlisted for the Guardian/4th Estate BAME Short Story Prize, the Bath Short Story Award and the Fish Flash Fiction Prize. Her work has appeared in: Peepal Tree Press's *Filigree*, *the National Flash Fiction Day* anthology, *the Bath Flash Fiction* anthology, *Strange Horizons* and *Litro USA Online*. She has an MA in Creative Writing (Birkbeck) and a PhD in Sociology (Goldsmiths). She tweets as @FirebirdN4.

PHILIP RIDLEY was born and grew up in the East End of London. He studied painting at St Martin's School of Art. He makes images and tells stories in various media. His first two novels, *Crocodilia* (1988) and *In the Eyes of Mr Fury* (1989), and his short story collection, *Flamingoes in Orbit* (1990), are now regarded as LGBTQ classics. In 2012 *What's On Stage* named him one of the most influential British writers to have emerged in the past six decades. He has won both the *Evening Standard*'s Most Promising Newcomer to British Film and Most Promising Playwright Awards—the only person ever to receive both prizes.

CHRIS SIMPSON grew up in Bracknell and Slough. He has worked as a waiter, a cinema projectionist, a shoe salesman, an attendant in an amusement arcade, hiring out construction and demolition tools, a pasty seller, a caretaker for a primary school, a teaching assistant, a tutor and a facilities manager. He has also performed as a stand-up comedian. In 2020 he had a special mention for the Spread The Word 2020 Life Writing Prize. In 2019 he was nominated for the inaugural Agora and PFD Lost The Plot Prize. In 2018 he was an awardee of the inaugural Spread The Word's London Writers Award. He received a First in Creative Writing at BA level from Birkbeck University. In 2016 he was nominated for the Royal Academy and Pin Drop Short Story Award 2016. He lives in London.

LUI SIT was born in Hong Kong, raised in Australia and now lives in London. She is currently completing her first middle grade children's book. She was longlisted in Spread the Word Life Writing Prize 2018 and shortlisted in the Penguin WriteNow 2018 Memoir category.

She is an alumnus of the Spread the Word 2018-19 London Writers Award. She has a Bachelor of Arts in English Literature from Murdoch University and a Graduate Certificate in Creative Writing from Birkbeck University. She won the 2020 Superlative Short Story Competition and is a recipient on the, A Brief Pause development scheme.

PADRIKA TARRANT was born in 1974. Her teenage years were complicated; she has had about ten psychiatric holidays in her time, and lived a few dull years in residential care. Much later, emerging blinking from an honours degree in sculpture, Padrika found herself unhealthily fixated with scissors and surrealism. She won an Arts Council Escalator prize in 2005. Her books include *Broken Things* (Salt 2007), long listed for the Frank O'Connor Prize and *The Knife Drawer* (Salt, 2011), shortlisted for the Authors' Club first Novel Prize. These days she lives in Norwich in a little council flat with her beautiful daughter and some lovely stuffed animals.

SUPPORTERS

Support comes in many forms and we really don't take for granted the army of allies who talked and tweeted and retweeted to spread news of this anthology far and wide. To everyone who lent a hand, no matter what form that took, THANK YOU. We couldn't have done it without you.

We make the books, but that's only part of the process. Each and every one of you who pledged to support this collection via our partner, Unbound, has made an important contribution: you have helped shine a light on talented writers who might ordinarily be overlooked. Diversity in publishing should be the norm. But it's not. You are helping to change that. THANK YOU. This book is real because of you:

Abi Fellows	Andrew Kaye	Ben Townley
Adam Wilkinson	Andrew Wille	Ben Walters
Adele Ward	Andy Brereton	Ben Whitehouse
Ailsa Power	Ann Phoenix	Benedicta Norell
Aisha Phoenix	Ann-Sofie Pokrant	Beric Livingstone
Aisha Phoenix	Anna Sutton	Brian Robinson
Alex Falase-Koya	Anna-Marie Crowhurst	Briony Newbold
Alexis Rigg	Anne Maguire	Carlo Navato
Alice Cox	Annette Routledge	Carlo Navato
Alice Krelle	Annie Murray	Caspar Aremi
Alison Coleman	Anwar Akbur	Cassie Moss
Alison Martin	Arden Fitzroy	Catherine McLoughlin
Alison Veal	Ashley Cabreza McGrath	Charles Waterhouse
Amanda Lorens	Audrey Anand	Charles Waterhouse
Anastasia Loizou	Autumn Haworth	Charlie Beaumont
Andi Wingate	Bea Symes	Cheyenne Thornton
Andrew Cabreza McGrath	Ben Thomas	Chris Arnephie

Chris Hulbert
Chris Penney
Claire Plant
D J Connell
Dan Oakey
Daniel Evans
Daniel Garlick
Daniel Ramsden
Daren Kay
Darius Amini
Darren Evans
Dave Wakely
David Cabreza
David Clegg
David Plans
David Ward
Decorah Flett
Dennis Da Silva
Diane Samuels
Donna Westall
Doug Laver
Drew Gummerson
Eamon Somers
Edward Chapman
Edward Doherty
Emma Rowson
Emma Rye
Emma Warnock
Esme Pears
Essie Fox
Felicity Browne
Franca Tranza
Gabriel Vogt
Gabriele Esser-Hall
Gary Cheetham
Gary Davy
Gary Kerridge
Gary Riley

Gavin Butt
Gaynor Jones
Georgina Hume
Gijs Boonzaaijer
Gillian OShaughnessy
Giselle Leeb
Glenda Evans
Greg Barnes
Greg Wetherall
Gustav Geldenhuys
Helen Eastman
Helen Evans
Helen Warrick
Holly Revell
Hugo Rocha
Iain Clarke
Ian Romanis
Iqbal Hussain
Ivan Tennant
James Adutt
James Kirkpatrick
Jamie Griffiths
Jan Goldman
Jane Richardson
Jane Roberts
Jason Dowler
Jennifer Block
Jenny O'Gorman
Jett Nyx
Jo W
Joane Griggs
John Evans
João Florêncio
Jocelyn Watson
Joe Storey-Scott
John Atterbury Davies
John Mercer
Jonathan Blake

Jonathan Holt
Jose Arroyo
Joshua Davis
Joy Ward
Jude Cook
Judith Mawby
Julie Radford
Juliet Shalam
Karen Rust
Karin Mochan
Katy Whitehead
Keith McDonnell
Keith Savage
Keith Worrall
Ken Wykoff,
Joe Davis
Kerrin Leeb
Kerry-Jo Reilly
Klaus Bruecker
Kristin Collins
Lachlan Smith
Laura Flemings
Layla Wolfson
Lezanne Clannachan
Lighthouse Booksellers
Linda Marlowe
Lisa Goldman
Louise Brown
Lowri Williams
Lucie McKnight Hardy
Lui Sit
Luke Buckingham
Lynn Wiseman
Lynne Armstrong
Lynne Trenery
Marcella Puppini
Marian Keyes
Marie Jarvie

Mark McLaughlin
Mary Senier
Mason Ball
Matthew Bates
Matthew Bright
Matthew Stradling
Megan Taylor
Melissa Fu
Michael Jury
Michael Langan
Mustafa Baygun
Mx D V E Higginbottom
N Rumball
Nada Savitch
Natasha Arnfield
Natasha Vassiliou
Nathan Shipley
Neil Alexander
Nicholas Alexander
Nicholas Daniel
Nick Coveney
Nick Hubble
Nicola May
Nikki S Dudley
Nina Goldman
Noemi Scheiring-Olah
Oliver Coleman
Paul Brown
Paul Crick
Paul Darling
Paul Handley
Paul Harfleet
Paul Oxley
Paula Dougherty
Paula Goodwin
Pauline Davis
Peter Milne
Petronella Carter

Philippa Griffin
Piero Toto
Piers Torday
Polis Loizou-Denyer
Polly Wiseman
Rachel Dixon
Rachel Worrall
Radclyffe Hermes Baker
Radu Stoica
Randolph Wilcox
Rebecca Carter
Rebecca Lyons
Rebecca Moses
Rebekah Drury
Reuben Roy Smith
Rhoslyn Norgate
Richard Taylor
Richard Ware
Richard Woffenden
Robert Hughes
Rosaleen Lynch
Rosalind Porter Tibbey
Rosemary Luz
Ross Williams
Rukhsana Yasmin
Rupert Dastur
Ruth Harrison
Sam Kenyon
Sam Missingham
Samuel Ludford
Sarah Blair
Sarah Franklin
Sarah Garnham
Sarah Greenwood
Sarah Tarbit
Sarah-Louise Young
Sasha Dovzhyk
Sean Myatt

Serena Falzon
Shaun Dellenty
Simon Casson
Simon McCallum
Sin Bozkurt
Smita Dave
Sonya Moor
Sophie Archer
Stefan Kumpfmüller
Stephen Haskins
Stephen Pelton
Steve Platt
Steven Moe
Susan Smith
T.B. Tayo
Tessa Garland
Thea Buen
Theodore Loucks
Toby Rye
Tom Powell
Tony Aitman
Torsten Højer
Trevor Norris
Vik Kelly-Teare
Vincent Borg
Wanda McGreegs
Winifred Baker
Yin Lim

ACKNOWLEDGEMENTS

Bringing this book into being has been no easy feat. We could not have done it without the enormous amount of goodwill that has been shown to us. For their support, advice and friendship, we are deeply grateful to the following, who have kept us both going:

Joy and Dave Ward, Kit de Waal, Sophia Blackwell, David Cabreza, Liz George, Rebecca Carter, Petronella Carter, Amy Redmond, Gareth Johnson, Trevor Norris, Sunny Singh, Tessa Garland, Emma Bourgeois, Toby Rye, Katie Vermont, Simon Reeves, Bryanne McIntosh-Melville, Christopher and Jen Hamilton-Emery, Tom Tivnan, Anna-Marie Crowhurst, Damian Barr, Drew Gummerson, Nikola Škundrić and Paul Darling.

And to: National Centre for Writing, Untitled, Creative Future, Clavmag, Canal Street, The Bookseller, Fruit Journal, The Publishing Post, Out on the Page, London Metropolitan University, Fireraisers, Queer Guru and Bluemoose Books.

To Joe Mateo, for his beautiful design.
To Daren Kay, for his beautiful words.
To Andrew M Pisanu, for his beautiful music.

To Aliya Gulamani, Keith McDonnell, Angelica Curzi and Alex Hopkins, for reading so many submissions and helping us select these beautiful stories. And to Lisa Goodrum for proofing the pudding.

Thanks as ever to Uli, Jimmy and Erica at Gay's the Word bookshop.

Special thanks to Kathy Burke, Cash Carraway, Ashley Hickson-Lovence, Ruth Harrison at Spread the Word and everyone at Unbound

Very special thanks to our digital marketing guru, Sam Missingham.

Bucketfuls of love to our feline interns, Jeanette and Genet, without whom 2020 would have finished us off completely.

Lastly, thanks to everyone who keeps buying and reading our books.
We love you.

Also from Inkandescent

THE PALE ONES
by Bartholomew Bennett

Few books ever become loved. Most linger on undead, their sallow pages labyrinths of old, brittle stories and screeds of forgotten knowledge... And other things, besides: Paper-pale forms that rustle softly through their leaves. Ink-dark shapes swarming in shadow beneath faded type. And an invitation...

Harris delights in collecting the unloved. He wonders if you'd care to donate. A small something for the odd, pale children no-one has seen. An old book, perchance? Neat is sweet; battered is better. Broken spine or torn binding, stained or scarred - ugly doesn't matter. Not a jot. And if you've left a little of yourself between the pages – a receipt or ticket, a mislaid letter, a scrawled note or number – that's just perfect. He might call on you again.

Hangover Square meets Naked Lunch through the lens of a classic M. R. James ghost story. To hell and back again (and again) through Whitby, Scarborough and the Yorkshire Moors. Enjoy your Mobius-trip.

'A real addition to the literature of the uncanny and an impressive debut for its uncompromising author.'
RAMSEY CAMPBELL

Also from Inkandescent

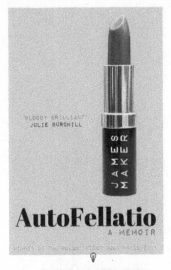

AutoFellatio
by James Maker

According to Wikipedia, only a few men can actually perform the act of auto-fellatio. We never discover whether James Maker—from rock bands Raymonde and RPLA—is one of them. But certainly, as a story-teller and raconteur, he is one in a million.

From Bermondsey enfant terrible to Valencian grande dame—a journey that variously stops off at Morrissey Confidant, Glam Rock Star, Dominatrix, Actor and Restoration Man—his long and winding tale is a compendium of memorable bons mots woven into a patchwork quilt of heart-warming anecdotes that make you feel like you've hit the wedding-reception jackpot by being unexpectedly seated next the groom's witty homosexual uncle.

More about the music industry than about coming out, this remix is a refreshing reminder that much of what we now think of as post-punk British rock and pop, owes much to the generation of musicians like James. The only criticism here is that – as in life – fellatio ultimately cums to an end.

'a glam-rock Naked Civil Servant in court shoes. But funnier. And tougher' MARK SIMPSON

Also from Inkandescent

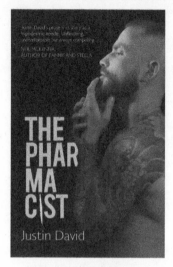

THE PHARMACIST

by Justin David

Twenty-four-year-old Billy is beautiful and sexy. Albert – The Pharmacist – is a compelling but damaged older man, and a veteran of London's late '90s club scene. After a chance meeting in the heart of the London's East End, Billy is seduced into the sphere of Albert. An unconventional friendship develops, fuelled by Albert's queer narratives and an endless supply of narcotics. Alive with the twilight times between day and night, consciousness and unconsciousness, the foundations of Billy's life begin to irrevocably shift and crack, as he fast-tracks toward manhood. This story of lust, love and loss is homoerotic bildungsroman at its finest.

'At the heart of David's The Pharmacist is an oddly touching and bizarre love story, a modern day Harold and Maude set in the drugged-up world of pre-gentrification Shoreditch. The dialogue, especially, bristles with glorious life.'
JONATHAN KEMP

'As lubricious as early Alan Hollinghurst, The Pharmacist is a welcome reissue from Inkandescent, and the perfect introduction to a singular voice in gay literature.'
THE TIMES LITERARY SUPPLEMENT

Also from Inkandescent

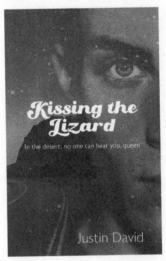

𝒦issing the 𝓛izard

by Justin David

Justin David's newly-released novella is part creepy coming-of-age story, part black-comedy, set partly in buzzing 1990s London and partly in barren New Mexico wildlands.

When Jamie meets Matthew in Soho, he's drawn to his new-age charms. But when he follows his new friend across the planet to a remote earth-ship in Taos, bizarre incidents begin unfolding and Matthew's real nature reveals itself: he's a manipulative monster at the centre of a strange cult. Jamie finds himself at the centre a disturbing psychological nightmare as they seize the opportunity to recruit a new member. Pushed to his limits, lost in a shifting sagebrush landscape, can Jamie trust anyone to help him? And will he ever see home again?

This evocatively set desert gothic expertly walks the line between macabre humour and terrifying tension.

'There's not much rarer than a working class voice in fiction, except maybe a gay working class voice. We need writers like Justin David.'
PAUL McVEIGH, author of *The Good Son*

Also from Inkandescent

THREADS
by Nathan Evans & Justin David

If Alice landed in London not Wonderland this book might be the result. Threads is the first collection from Nathan Evans, each poem complemented by a bespoke photograph from Justin David and, like Tenniel's illustrations for Carroll, picture and word weft and warp to create an alchemic (rabbit) whole.

On one page, the image of an alien costume, hanging surreally beside a school uniform on a washing line, accompanies a poem about fleeing suburbia. On another, a poem about seeking asylum accompanies the image of another displaced alien on an urban train. Spun from heartfelt emotion and embroidered with humour, Threads will leave you aching with longing and laughter.

'In this bright and beautiful collaboration, poetry and photography join hands, creating sharp new ways to picture our lives and loves.'
NEIL BARTLETT

'Two boldly transgressive poetic voices'
MARISA CARNESKY

Also from Inkandescent

CNUT

by Nathan Evans

'Poignant, humane and uncompromising'
STEPHEN MORRISON-BURKE

As King Cnut proved, tide and time wait for no man:
An AnthropoScene, the first part of this collection, dives into the
rising tides of geo-political change, the second, Our Future Is Now
Downloading, explores sea-changes of more personal natures.

Nathan's debut, Threads, was longlisted for the Polari First Book Prize.
His follow-up bears all the watermarks of someone who's swum life's
emotional spectrum. Short and (bitter)sweet, this is poetry for a mobile
generation, poetry for sharing – often humorous, always honest about
contemporary human experience, saying more in a few lines than
politicians say in volumes, it offers an antidote to modern living.

'a kaleidoscopic journey brimming with vivid imagery,
playfulness and warmth—a truly powerful work'
KEITH JARRETT

Also from Inkandescent

SWANSONG
by Nathan Evans

A gentleman called Joan lands in a subdued, suburban care home like a colourful, combustible cocktail. A veteran of Gay Lib, he dons battle dress and seeks an ally in the young, gay but disappointingly conventional care assistant Craig for his assault on the heteronormativity of the care system. Then, in this most unlikely of settings, Joan is offered love by a gentleman called Jim...

This bittersweet comedy explores issues surrounding care and LGBT elders. It premiered at the Royal Vauxhall Tavern, London on 17 October 2018, presented by 89th Productions as part of And What? Queer Arts Festival.

'Side-splittingly funny and achingly romantic.
A play about ageing disgracefully that's ferociously full of life.'
RIKKI BEADLE-BLAIR

Also from Inkandescent

FEMME FATALE
by Polly Wiseman

1968, New York. Nico, The Velvet Underground's glamorous front woman, is waiting to shoot Andy Warhol's latest movie when her room is invaded by Valerie Solanas, writer of the radical SCUM Manifesto. A battle to the death begins. Can these two iron-willed opponents become allies and change their futures?

With women's ownership of their stories and bodies still firmly on the news agenda, Femme Fatale draws parallels between 1960s feminism and today. It was first presented in Sussex and London in September and October 2019.

'Wiseman's writing sears and burns'
THE GUARDIAN

Also from Inkandescent

PERMISSION
BY MEMORY FLOWERS

PERMISSION by MEMORY FLOWERS was produced in association with www.inkandescent.co.uk to herald an exciting new publishing initiative, MAINSTREAM, which will brings together thirty authors from the margins to occupy centre-page. Queer storytellers. Working class wordsmiths. Chroniclers of colour. Writers whose life experiences give unique perspectives on universal challenges, whose voices must be heard. And read.

Composer Andrew M Pisanu, the mastermind behind MEMORY FLOWERS, weaves together an emotional call-to-action delivered in Depeche Mode baritone, an epic Hans Zimmer war drum and Scandi-Pop stylings, momentarily traveling to outer space before crashing to the disco dance-floor. The result? A thundering, transformative anthem urging the dispossessed to occupy spaces that have previously been prohibited to them.